CALY'S ISLAND

by

DICK HERMAN

Willowbank Books

Fifth Edition
June 1, 2022

This is a work of fiction and all characters, incidents, and dialogues are a product of the author's imagination and are used fictitiously. Any resemblance to actual persons, living or dead, places, or events, is entirely coincidental.

© 2011 Dick Herman. All rights reserved.

All rights reserved. No part of this book may be reproduced, stored in a retrieval system, or transmitted by any means without the written permission of the author.

Library of Congress Control Number: 2011903614

Printed in the United States of America

Cover art: Maria O'Neil

Also by Dick Herman

The Price of Mercy

Writing as
Richard Herman

The China Sea
The Trash Haulers
The Peacemakers
A Far Justice
The Last Phoenix
The Trojan Sea
Edge of Honor
Against All Enemies
Power Curve
Iron Gate
Dark Wing
Call to Duty
Firebreak
Force of Eagles
The Warbirds

For
All The Usual Suspects
The smaller the boat, the bigger the adventure.

"There is nothing – absolutely nothing – half so much worth doing as simply messing about in boats."
Kenneth Grahame
The Wind in the Willows

ONE

Zack Hilber was lost. That, in itself, was not unusual as he was often confused as to his exact whereabouts, especially at night when he should be tucked safely in bed and snoring peacefully. Angela, his long-suffering wife, had learned early on that he was directionally impaired. It was on their honeymoon, to not put too fine a date on it, when she first suspected he couldn't tell north from south if his life depended on it. His easting and westing was a little better, probably because the sun moved in that plane, but nothing Angela wanted to pass on to their two kids and four grandchildren. As a matter of survival, she quickly learned to navigate and became an expert map reader. She could also ask for directions in three languages. Angela may not have been happy with this particular shortcoming, but Zack did have other very worthwhile long comings, and most importantly, she was never bored.

Zack's immediate problem was that it was past midnight, well beyond his normal bedtime, and Angela was eight hundred miles away in Dublin, California, while he was wandering around trying to find the marina at Squalicum Harbor. The Admiral's instructions were as opaque and confusing as always: go north on I-5 for 805 miles to Bellingham, Washington. Take Exit 256, turn left onto Meridian Street, go .4 miles, and turn right onto Squalicum Way. Of course, he was lost. Who could make sense of all that? He scratched his full head of gray hair and squinted into the night.

At sixty-three years of age, Zack's hazel eyes were still sharp and clear and his night vision excellent. His lanky five foot ten frame wiggled under the seatbelt. While his sense of direction was shaky at

Dick Herman

best, his urinary tract never failed and always told him when and where to go. His bladder was an unfailing compass card and his penis the needle.

Never being one to stand on formality, and believing that darkness is decency, he pulled over to the side of the road and climbed out of Old Blue, his trusty Ford pickup. He stood on the shoulder and stared into the heavens, taking in the starry wonder that peeked from behind the clouds scudding across the moonlit sky as he relieved himself. The Belt of Orion magically appeared. "Orion the Hunter," he said to himself. The three stars could be a belt, he decided, but where was the rest of the hunter? It didn't make sense to him.

He shook his head in disbelief. "Gods on Olympus, constellations, where did the Greeks come up with all that crap? I bet no one on Olympus had a small bladder. Homer never mentioned that in The Odyssey." He snorted in contempt. "The Greeks and Homer were full of it." A police cruiser flashing a blue light pulled to a stop behind his trailer, the little sailboat simply didn't provide the privacy required by the local constabulary, and Zack never saw the three stars in the Belt wink at him. The lone officer adjusted his nightstick as he walked up to Zack.

"Cute little boat you got there," he offered.

"Thank you, officer. It's a fifteen-foot sloop called a microcruiser or pocket cruiser. They're good little boats, pretty rugged and you can sail them most anywhere."

"I see it's got a cabin. You got a Porta-Potti in there?"

"Yes, sir, I do. But it's kind'a hard to get to with the mast tied down on top for trailering."

The patrolman unzipped his pants and joined Zack. "Use it next time."

"Thank you, I will."

"I see you got California plates. Where abouts are you from?"

"Dublin, near San Francisco."

"Going sailing in the San Juans?"

"Yep. With five of my buddies. We all sail microcruisers and call ourselves the FOGs, that's short for Freakin' Old Guys." The Freakin' part was really a euphemism for the actual word. The FOGs did travel in polite society. "We come up here every year in September and sail around the islands for a couple of weeks. We usually tie up at a marina at night, and hold a happy hour on the dock. We're not sure if we're a sailing club with a drinking problem or the other way 'round."

Caly's Island

The patrolman gazed wistfully at the small boat with its bright yellow hull and read the name on the side. "*Wild Turtle*." He stared at the boat, envying the older man. "Where do you sleep?"

"We sleep on the boats. It's kind'a cramped but you can get two in the cabin, if your partner has a sense of humor . . . and is a contortionist."

"I always wanted to do something like that, but my wife wouldn't hear of it." The admission hurt, but for some reason he felt better talking about it. Zack inspired that type of reaction.

"Take her along," Zack said.

"That will be one cold day in hell." The patrolman zipped up his pants. "Where you headed for now?"

"Squalicum Harbor in Bellingham."

The cop laughed. "Turn around and go back eight miles. Go under the freeway and take the second right. The road goes right past the harbor. You can't miss it. It's opposite the rail yard."

Zack almost said that he could miss the harbor and the rail yard in a heartbeat. He was a man who knew his limitations. Instead, "Thank you, officer."

The patrolman walked back to his cruiser. "*Wild Turtle*, I like it. What did you say your boat was?"

"It's a microcruiser," Zack called. "Like in mini." He watched the cop pull out and accelerate down the deserted road. "I ought'a get a commission for selling these puppies," he muttered to himself. Determined to find the harbor, he scooted behind Old Blue's steering wheel and noted the mileage on the odometer. He mentally added eight, and jotted the number down. He threw a U-turn and headed back for Bellingham. True to form, he passed under the freeway and turned left into the Bellingham Parks Department. Fortunately, it was a roundabout that pointed him back in the right direction. Two miles later, he breathed a sigh of relief when he saw the railroad yard in the moonlight and a forest of masts on the other side of the road. Zack Hilber, to his total amazement, had finally arrived and was only twelve hours late. Angela would be proud of him.

It was easy spotting the FOGs' cars and Rufus's big white utility van in the parking lot. The van was parked under a streetlight and the big golden anvil painted on the side was easily visible from the street. Zack pulled in and parked at the far end of the five vehicles with their empty trailers, well away from the streetlight and Rufus's van. The five other

FOGs had already launched their boats and were tied up at the guest dock, bedded down for a good night's sleep.

Zack checked his watch; it was just after one in the morning. The thought of crawling into the boat's small cabin for a few hours of welcome snoozing and snoring grew more appealing with each passing moment. First, he had to move the mast to get to the hatch. He untied the sixteen–foot aluminum tube and climbed onto the boat. It didn't take a genius to figure out that it would be easiest to step the mast and finish rigging in the morning. The mast was half way up when he caught movement in his peripheral vision. Someone was moving along the side of Rufus's van. He froze.

Unbidden, his training was back, undimmed by time and sharp as ever. He slowly lowered the mast, never taking his eyes off the shadowy figure, and not certain if it was a woman or a small man. With the mast down, he crouched in the cockpit. The shadow opened the van's waist-high side access panel to see what was inside. Zack's eyes narrowed as he tightened and double knotted his shoelaces. He emptied his pockets of anything that could rattle or clink at a critical moment, slipped over the side of the boat, and dropped to the ground in one fluid motion. He crouched and shed his jacket, now certain that a thief was pilfering Rufus's van. There was a treasure house of tools inside. Zack's muscles tensed and adrenaline shot through his body. You poor stupid bastard, he thought. His fangs were out, and for the first time since retiring from The Company eleven years ago, he was fully alive.

Did the thief have a buddy or was he alone? Zack played it by the book and scanned the parking lot, looking for telltale movement or a car with an occupant. Nothing. Certain that he was dealing with a loner, he moved, closing in on the unsuspecting thief. He ghosted to the next car, using it for concealment. Zack crouched behind the front wheel and looked underneath the cars. He could see the thief's legs, still standing beside the van. Like a cat stalking its prey, Zack moved again, reaching the next car. Again, he looked underneath. The thief had set a bag on the ground and was still rummaging inside the van. Zack heard a loud clink and froze. The thief had dropped something heavy into the bag. The figure came up on its tiptoes and reached further inside. Now his feet completely disappeared as he crawled inside the van, his belly scraping over the access panel's sill.

Caly's Island

Zack came to a running crouch and darted forward, a soundless shadow in the night. He rounded the car next to the van and leaned against the door, studying the figure half inside the open panel, feet dangling in the air, as he rummaged through Rufus's tools. "Find anything interesting in there?" He could have been talking about the weather. "I got'a speak to Rufe about locking his van up."

The thief jerked back and collapsed to the ground. He held one of Rufus's prized hammers in his right hand. He looked up at Zack, glaring with hatred. "Oh, Sweet Jesus," Zack moaned. "You're just a kid." The boy was raggedy thin and wore all the trappings of a gangbanger. He looked no more than fifteen, and judging by the droop of his pants, at least a lieutenant in the hierarchy of lowlifes. But the stylish cut of his blond hair suggested someone with good taste was working on the teenager's top end. "Interesting tattoos you got there, son," Zack said, intrigued with the skulls and bones intermixed with phallic symbols that marched up both his arms.

"I'm not your fuckin' son, Bud." The teenager came to his feet and waved the hammer menacingly at Zack.

"Bad move. That hammer is a weapon and it changes the ground rules." Zack deliberately let his voice trail off, not about to signal his intentions.

"You're damn right it does, Bud." He lunged at Zack. "You lose."

Zack easily sidestepped him. They were experiencing an obvious failure to communicate, and Zack went to Plan B. "I didn't know you were a Christian."

"Whaa?" The perplexed look on the boy's face matched his voice. He lowered the hammer.

"That tattoo." Zack pointed to the teenager's right arm. "The ancient Romans used it to identify the Christians before they fed them to the lions." The boy studied his artwork. It was the distraction Zack needed. He grabbed the boy's right wrist and twisted. At the same time, he drove the heel of his right hand into the boy's left shoulder, hard, spinning him around. Zack wrenched the boy's arm around to his back, and straightened it out. He held it in a firm grip as he pushed against the teenager's back with his free hand. "You might want to drop the hammer before I get mad." The boy bucked and Zack twisted his arm. "You are a slow learner. Drop the hammer. I don't want to hurt you." He twisted harder and applied pressure to his elbow.

The boy screamed in pain. "You're going to jail, Bud!"

"I'll be out of jail before you get out of the hospital." Zack didn't expect to ever see the inside of a police station, not after he pulled his ID and the investigating officer made the phone call. He twisted the boy's arm and applied more pressure. "I don't want to hurt you, son." The boy screamed louder and Zack twisted harder. The hammer fell to the ground. Zack stepped on it and released the boy. "That's better. By the way, don't ever call a geezer 'Bud.' It really pisses us off."

"So, what do I call you? 'Asshole?'"

Zack shook his head. "You can use my nickname. Just call me 'sir,' and we'll get along fine."

"Blow it out your ass." The boy spun around and ran into the night.

"Ah, don't do that." Zack counted to three to give him a head start. "You run pretty good with those pants down around your knees," he called. "But you might want to pull 'em up." The boy did, and Zack ran after him. It felt good as he warmed up, just like the state finals in the Senior Olympics when he had won a gold medal in the 5000-meter event. His fangs were out. He easily closed on his prey and could hear his labored breathing. "You got to run faster than that, son." He poked him in the back to urge him on to a better effort.

The teenager put on a burst of speed as he ran down Roeder Avenue beside the railroad tracks. A switch engine labored past, pulling a long line of freight cars as it made up a train. It clanked to a stop and the boy darted across the tracks. He cut between two railcars and climbed over the coupling. Zack never slowed as he jumped over the coupling. It was almost too easy. "You're starting to make me angry, son," he called. He was breathing easily as the boy turned left on F Street and puffed up the gentle slope leading into town. He turned left onto Holly Street and Zack was lost. "Now you've really pissed me off!" he shouted. He would never find his way back to the harbor on his own.

The pursuit continued in earnest as Zack chased the boy up Holly Street and onto Eldridge Avenue. Now they were on the bluffs overlooking the rail yard and harbor. Nice houses, Zack thought, admiring the restored Victorians. "What do they call this area?" he called. There was no answer as the boy gasped for breath. Zack closed the gap and was right behind him. "You are one unsociable twerp," he said. "Let's cut a deal. You stop, sit on the curb, don't move, and I won't plant your young ass in the gutter."

Caly's Island

"Fuck you, Bud," the teenager rasped, not able to turn and look at him.

Zack had enough of the juvenile and his limited vocabulary. His right hand flashed and he drove the heel of his hand into the base of the boy's skull in an upward motion, snapping his head forward and lifting him off his feet. The boy stumbled and skidded in the gutter on his stomach, kicking up a bow wave of muddy water and leaves. His head disappeared into an open drain on the side of the curb. His shoulders stopped his forward momentum and wedged his body tightly in the drain's opening. A strange echo reverberated from the drain. The gasping for air blended with a retching sound as the teenager puked what was left of his dinner. Zack bent over him, his hands on his knees. He was breathing a little hard and he made a mental promise to get back in shape. "Nice pickle you got yourself into, Oliver," he said to the lower half of the kid's body. The boy coughed and choked on the water flowing over him. "Too bad you fell like that. I was good for a few more miles." The choking sound grew louder.

"Ah, crap." Zack grabbed the boy's shirt and pulled his head out of the drain. The teenager tried to break free, but Zack grabbed his collar and forced him to sit on the curb. He didn't let go as the boy bent over and coughed up the water that had almost drowned him. "You wouldn't happen to have a cell phone on you?" He twisted the boy's collar to reinforce his request. No response. He twisted harder. The boy fumbled in a pocket and produced a cell phone. Still holding his collar, Zack punched in 9-1-1 and made the call.

The first police cruiser arrived eight minutes later. It was the same patrolman Zack had met earlier. He unlimbered his tall frame from the driver's seat and walked towards them, but this time he pulled out his handcuffs. "I see you've met Sean," he said.

"You know him?"

"We all know him. What was he doing this time? Graffiti? Breaking off sprinkler heads? Keying your car? Breaking and entering?"

"Ripping off tools out of a van," Zack said. The cop clamped the handcuffs on Sean and pulled him to his feet. The officer quickly searched him, emptying his pockets. "Good grief," Zack said. "No wonder he couldn't run with all that crap in his pockets." He examined a small micrometer. "That looks like Rufe's. It's pretty expensive."

"Rufe can make a statement in the morning," the patrolman replied. "At the police station."

Sean snarled at the cop. "Whatcha gonna do, Bob? Take me downtown and book me? I'll be out before Bud here gets back to the harbor."

"Sean, my name is Officer Roberts. You know that."

"You're not going to turn him loose, are you?" Zack asked.

"Unfortunately, we won't have a choice. His mother will sign him out within twenty minutes and blame us for harassing her son."

"Yeah, Officer Bob. Stop picking on me."

"Sooner or later, Sean," Roberts said, "you will be rendered. I hope I'm around to see it." Another patrol car with two cops drove up and slammed to a stop. The three officers briefly conferred. Roberts checked Zack's ID card, saw the telephone number, and pulled out his cell phone. He looked at Zack with definite worry as he made the call. It was answered on the first ring. Roberts identified himself and quickly answered a series of questions. He listened and answered with a respectful, "Yes, sir. That won't be a problem. Thank you, sir." He broke the connection and spoke quietly to the other two officers, explaining the situation. The three cops studied Zack for a moment, and, without a word, loaded Sean into the second cruiser. Roberts turned to Zack. "Sir, I'm very sorry you had to meet the village idiot this way. This is really a friendly town. We would be very appreciative if you could come down to the station in the morning and file a report."

"No problem. Any chance I might hook a lift back to the harbor?"

"My pleasure, sir." He opened the car door for Zack.

Angus licked at the ear of his master. Hornsby Blair, who fancied himself more stubborn than the Jack Russell terrier, ignored his pet's loving but wet ministrations. Refusing to be discouraged, Angus focused on his task and nuzzled Blair's ear with his black nose. Blair turned over in his sleeping bag and poked his head out like a mole emerging from his burrow. Angus immediately considered the possibilities, and had it been anyone other than Blair, would have immediately burrowed in. Fortunately, the terrier knew who the pack leader was. The dog barked, signaling his urgency.

"You got'a take a whiz, right?" Blair said.

Angus yapped in the affirmative.

Blair reached out of his sleeping bag and removed the top companionway board, letting the light into *Wee Dram*, his fifteen-foot sloop-rigged microcruiser. The white and brown terrier bounded out of the cabin and into the cockpit. His paws touched down briefly and the dog's short, but powerful legs, propelled him over five feet onto the dock. Angus disappeared down the dock, heading for the pet area. Blair pulled on his clothes and sniffed the morning air. Coffee. Most likely, Gib was up and brewing the potent brew that was rumored to grow hair on the proverbial billiard ball. Unfortunately, it failed to work on Blair's bald pate.

Blair emerged from *Wee Dram's* small cabin and stretched. He was sixty-two-years old, stood exactly five foot four, and his wiry frame was a perfect fit for the boat. Most people who knew the retired Air Force pilot agreed that *Wee Dram*, with its rounded stern, lapstrake hull and classic lines, and Blair were a match made in heaven. "You're up early, Gib."

"Good morning, H," Gibson Stanford called from *Habeas Corpus*, his cream colored, lapstrake-hulled, seventeen-foot sloop. He was the only FOG who didn't call Blair 'the Admiral.' However, out of sympathy, he never called him Hornsby and only used the initial 'H'. Gibson Stanford was a dignified sixty-eight-year-old widower who was invariably formal and polite, even to the mass murderers he had sentenced to death. At six foot three, he was the tallest of the FOGs, and with a mane of gray hair and piercing blue eyes that made Shakespearian actors instantly hate him, looked like a chief justice. "Zack arrived after midnight," the retired jurist said. "He's in the parking lot rigging *Wild Turtle* and should be launching shortly." He handed Blair a steaming cup of coffee.

Blair nodded. "Good. We can catch the morning tide out of here as planned." Blair planned the cruise and was anal about keeping to the sail plan, even though the FOGs took great delight in doing exactly what they pleased. The phrase 'herding cats' had meaning for him when the FOGs were on the water. He was fortunate to get them all going the same way the same day, but he held an inner vision of the six boats arriving at their destination under sail and with naval precision. He was an incurable optimist.

"Unfortunately, Zack apprehended a juvenile last night in the process of pilfering Rufus's van." Gibson Stanford had been retired four years,

9

and still spoke with a formality befitting his status as a former appellate court judge. The FOGs accepted it without question, never suspecting there was a far different side to the man. "Zack needs to file a report, and Rufus has to identify the stolen articles at the police department. I'm going with them."

"I'll tag along if you don't mind." Blair checked his watch. "We can still make the tide, but Rufe will need help." The fifty-nine-year-old Rufus Gunnermyer was considered the guru of blacksmiths in northern California, but Blair doubted that he could write a coherent sentence.

Gib sensed what Blair was thinking. "H, don't ever underestimate Rufus," the judge said. "He is full of surprises." He finished his coffee. "Pete and Steve are still asleep."

"Let 'em sleep in," Blair said. "The three of us should be able to keep Rufe out of trouble." He believed there was safety in numbers.

"Give me a moment to secure *Habeas Corpus*," Gib said. He carefully lifted the deeply varnished hatch boards into place, closing the companionway into the cabin, and snapped a stainless steel lock on the chrome hasp. Like everything on *Habeas Corpus*, the hatch boards, lock, and hasp reflected exquisite craftsmanship and care. The two men made the long walk to the parking lot and collected Angus along the way.

Rufus and Zack were waiting by Gib's Lincoln Town Car. "We won't get your leather seats dirty," Zack promised.

Gib laughed. "That is not a problem." It wasn't his car and he never worried about it getting dirty.

Twenty minutes later, the four men walked into the police department and spoke to the duty sergeant. Within moments, they were talking to the shift supervisor, a grizzled veteran who resembled a basset hound. He opened the evidence locker and they examined the items taken off Sean. "The micrometer is mine," Rufus said. He held the delicate instrument in his big rough hands and turned the dial. "It was used to make the prototype of the Rolls Royce Merlin engine that powered the Spitfire and Mustang in World War II. It's a tool that made history." Rufus Gunnermyer may have been a blacksmith of the old school, adept at forging wrought iron gates, fences, hinges, and even shoeing the occasional horse, but behind the weather-beaten face and stout body beat the heart of a romantic who collected rare tools.

"What's it worth?" the sergeant growled, his voice gravelly from years of smoking and hard drinking.

Caly's Island

"Maybe five thousand dollars, with its case and provenance," Rufus replied. "It belongs in a museum."

A very satisfied look spread across the sergeant's face. He finally had Sean on a charge of grand larceny. But before he could say more, a woman burst through the door and bore down on them. "Now there's a lady on a mission," Gib warned.

"Ah, shit," the sergeant moaned in a low voice. He replaced the micrometer in the box and braced himself.

The men sucked in their collective breath as they took the woman's measure. She was an African American, tall, big boned, husky with full hips, and her dark skin glowed with health. There was nothing small about her, and while she was full figured, no one would ever call her fat. Her mouth was full and sensual, and her dark eyes flashed with intelligence and fire. Her nostrils flared with anger as she tossed her long, straight black hair. A mental image of the woman carrying a spear and a shield as she chased a lion through an African Savannah flashed in Zack's mind. Zack felt sorry for the lion. She glared at Zack and jabbed a two-fingered V at him. "Look at my eyes, white boy. Not my boobs." Zack obediently raised his eyes. "Now which one of you idiots thought it was fun to harass Sean and wants to throw him in the slammer?"

"That would be me," Zack admitted.

The woman stared at him, her eyes hard and unblinking. She liked Zack's rugged good looks and wished they had met under more encouraging circumstances. "You're no Robert Redford, boy. So give up trying."

Gib retreated a few steps and flipped open his cell phone. He hit the speed dial. The woman turned on him. "Who are you?" Her eyes moved up and down, taking him in. "Damn, man. Were you Michelangelo's model for God in the Sistine Chapel? You're old enough."

Blair held his hand up, palm out, gaining her attention. "May I introduce The Honorable Gibson Stanford, associate justice of the California State Appeals Court, now retired?"

She eyed Blair with cold contempt. "My God, you're a pitiful excuse for a man. Did the best part of your daddy trickle down his left leg?"

Blair wasn't having any of it. "I'm the part of my father that never tolerated rude and uncivilized behavior." It was the wrong thing to say. Totally.

The sergeant threw himself between Blair and the woman, saving him from grievous bodily harm. "Both of you! Cool it."

Gib never raised his voice as he spoke into his cell phone. "Peter, Gibson Stanford here. Please come to the Bellingham Police station immediately. Your presence is required."

"Calling for help, Mr. God?" the woman asked.

"Absolutely," Gib replied. "Mr. Peter L. Lacy is our lawyer." She snorted in contempt.

"Gentlemen," the sergeant said, "may I introduce Mrs. Helena Homes? Sean's mother." The four FOGs stared at her.

"I'm Sean's stepmother," Helena said, clarifying her relationship to the blond-haired juvenile delinquent.

"Mrs. Homes was Sean's nanny," the sergeant explained. "Before she married his father."

"That's none of your business," Helena snapped.

"Would that be Senator Brian C. Homes?" Gib asked.

"You know Senator Homes?" the sergeant asked.

"I know of him," Gib replied. "I understand his family owns most of this part of Washington."

"They did," Helena said, "until Brian pissed it away. Someone had to take care of him. Now, which one of you is claiming my son stole his one and only tool?"

"Me," Rufus said, stepping forward. "Do you want to hear the whole story?"

Helena studied Rufus. "What do you do for a living? Kill people with your bare hands?"

"Actually, I'm a blacksmith." There was something in his voice that dampened Helena's anger. "Why don't you give us a chance to explain what happened?" Rufus gave her his shy grin. "We might be able to help." Rufus Gunnermyer spoke to difficult and high-spirited dogs and horses the same way.

Helena listened as Zack recounted his encounter with Sean. Her eyes flared when he described how he had chased the teenager through town. "You made a bad mistake when you pushed him into the gutter, boy."

"And what mistake was that?" a voice asked.

Helena whirled and looked directly into the eyes of Peter L. Lacy. They were both six feet tall, but Pete was more evenly proportioned and could have been an advertisement for a fitness center. He possessed broad shoulders, a narrow waist, flat stomach, and well-conditioned muscles. His square jaw was slightly misshapen and he walked with a limp from a football injury that ended a promising career in the pros. His dark brown hair hung over his green eyes, and Helena's right hand involuntarily moved to brush it into place. She judged Pete to be in his late forties although he claimed fifty-eight. "Ooh-ee," she breathed. "Fresh meat. Who are you?"

"Pete Lacy, Zack's lawyer."

"You gonna screw with me, Mr. Lawyer?"

Pete grinned at her. "Oh, I hope so."

For a moment, Helena's quick rejoinder and slashing verbal attacks were gone. She fixed Pete with a long look and tried to stare him down. It didn't work. Years of courtroom experience had given Peter Lacy an arsenal of weapons for taming the likes of Helena Homes. "You don't know who you're taking on," she finally said.

"Why don't we sit down over coffee and let me find out?"

"You like Starbucks?"

"I need two cups to jumpstart my heart in the morning."

"Well, why don't we go find out what else we can jumpstart?" She took his arm and they walked out.

"I'll be damned," the police sergeant said.

"The cavalry to the rescue," Rufus said.

"Can we finish the paperwork and get this show on the water?" Blair asked.

"What got into Pete?" Zack wondered. "You could smell the testosterone from ten feet away."

"That wasn't testosterone or Peter," Gib replied.

TWO

Steve Latrans savored the late-Friday afternoon. It was unusually warm for September on the water, and flags hung listlessly in the still air. He gazed at the small group of friends gathered on the dock for drinks and hors d'oeuvres beside their boats. It doesn't get much better, he thought, sinking deeper into his camp chair. He sipped Blair's Scotch and listened to the chatter. A very nice single malt, he thought. I wonder how Blair affords it?

For a moment, Steve considered adding his favorite Scotch to the collection, but Blair would know what it cost and that wouldn't be a good idea. At seventy years of age, Steven C. Latrans was the oldest of the FOGs. He was a quiet, pleasant, nondescript individual a person could pass everyday on the street and never notice. That was fine with Steve, and he was content to remain in the shadows and fade into the background. "What do you think happened to Pete?" he ventured. "He sure put a dent in the sail plan." That should get a rise out of Blair, he thought.

Surprisingly, Blair wasn't upset by Pete's disappearance and the resultant delay in their departure. "I have no idea," Blair said. "I just hope he survives that woman."

"She is something else," Zack said, conjuring up a mental image of Helena Homes doing pretzel-like things to Pete's body.

"If she wore horseshoes," Rufus said, "I'd need to use a tranquilizer." A little grin played at his lips. "For me, not her."

Gib spoke in his quiet, authoritative way. "Helena Homes is a force of nature. She is an Alpha, and not to be trifled with. Not only is she physically strong, she is pure sexuality questing to dominate the male. But at the same time, she is searching for a dominant male to mate with."

"Is that why you called Pete in?" Blair asked. "To distract her?"

Gib smiled. "Well, H, Peter does claim, shall we say, a certain expertise in these matters." The FOGs laughed. The often-married Pete Lacy was an accomplished raconteur, and if ten percent of his stories were true, no attractive woman's virtue was safe in his presence.

"Well, you did throw him to the wolves, or wolf, so to speak," Blair said. "I'd sure like to know what he's been doing all day."

"Perhaps you should ask him," Steve said from the back. "Here he is." As one, four heads turned to see Pete ambling down the dock.

"Pete," Blair called, "I hope you didn't take advantage of that poor woman."

Pete grinned. "I wish. She is something else." He climbed onto his wooden, home-built, sixteen-foot sloop *L'Amour*, and dug his camp chair out of the cabin. He shook it out and joined his friends on the dock. They all looked at him expectantly, eager to hear a good story. Without asking, Zack poured him a glass of red wine. He swirled the wine and held it up to the light. Among the FOGs, Pete was considered a wine snob. "Ah, a six-week old Two Buck Chuck from Trader Joe's."

"Taste it," Zack replied. "I think you'll be surprised."

Pete settled into his chair and sipped the wine. "This is very good," he allowed. The lawyer thought for a moment. "This reminds me of a 2005 Chateau Mouton Rothschild. Zack, did you spring for a ninety dollar bottle of wine?"

"Actually," Zack confessed, "it is a Two Buck Chuck."

Pete roared with laughter. "Touché! Well done, Zack."

"And it is a very fine wine, indeed," Gib added. He held out his glass for a refill. "May I enquire what transpired with the formidable Mrs. Homes?"

"Not what you dirty-minded geezers are thinking," Pete replied. He laughed at their disappointed looks.

"And here I thought you lawyers screwed everyone and anything," Rufus said.

Again, Pete laughed. "Rufe, my man, you've been watching too much TV. Not that it didn't cross my mind." He pulled into himself and composed his thoughts. His voice grew serious. "Helena is dealing with a series of problems involving Sean. She claims he's a good kid, but he's not coping well at all."

"That's an understatement," Zack said. "You didn't see the way he came at me with a hammer. He's a vicious thug."

"Teenagers of that age," Gib said, "are a cauldron of smoldering emotions. It is the age of storm and thunder. Luckily, most grow out of it before they do real harm – or garner a police record." He liked the word 'garner' and used it as much as possible.

"That kid ain't gonna make it," Zack predicted.

"Perhaps not," Pete said, "but that's their problem, and we're doing a legal whifferdill to sidestep the situation. It so happens, Zack, that you were the first person to ever manhandle Sean. It has upset his emotional balance, delicate creature that he is. On the upside, you've provided years of gainful employment for a team of shrinks to restore his fragile psyche. On the downside, Washington state law protects teenagers from physical abuse. Helena was going to prefer charges against you, but I talked her out of it and withdrew all charges against Sean." It was a classic legal quid pro quo. He pulled the micrometer out of a pocket and handed it to Rufus.

"So the little bastard walks," Zack said.

"And you escape all charges," Gib said. "Under the circumstances, a satisfactory compromise."

"I know surrender when I see it," Zack grumbled, doing a slow burn.

Steve sensed the tension simmering below Zack's normally calm exterior. Long experience had taught him there was more to the lanky sixty-three-year-old than they knew. It was time to cool things down. "Gentlemen," he said. "I heard of an excellent restaurant downtown. If Gib will drive us in the style we want to be accustomed to, I will treat." They all looked at him in disbelief. Steve did have a reputation for squeezing nickels until Jefferson's eyes popped in alarm. "We are celebrating Mr. Zack Hilber's deliverance from incarceration at the expense of the Washington taxpayer."

"Here's to a first," Zack said, "Steve paying." He smiled and offered his glass in a toast.

They all laughed as Gib reevaluated Steve, seeing his friend in a different light. "To the peacemaker," Gib said, lifting his glass.

* * * *

Dick Herman

Steve's mental alarm went off at exactly 02:06 in the morning and woke him from a light sleep. His eyes snapped open and he was fully alert, listening in the dark of his boat's snug cabin. Nothing. Without thinking, Steve started the ingrained routine that was part of his existence. He wiggled out of his sleeping bag, pulled on a pair of dark pants and a black sweatshirt, slipped into his deck shoes, and jammed a knitted black watch cap over his white hair. Next, he pulled a matte-black revolver from its hiding place. The Judge was a compact, heavy weapon that weighed almost two pounds. He pulled a pin key from another hiding place, inserted it in the base of the hammer to unlock the revolver, and laid it on the bunk.

Silently, Steve slid the top hatch slowly back and lowered the companionway board. He paused when he felt someone, or something, moving along the dock. Was it Angus doing a midnight duty? Too heavy for a Jack Russell, he reasoned. He picked up the revolver and climbed silently into the cockpit of *High Flyer*. Like all the FOGs, Steve had rigged a boom tent over the cockpit, creating a small room at the back of the boat. He cocked the hammer. The soft click echoed in the quiet but blended with the creaks and groans of the dock. He gently moved the boom tent's entrance flap to one side and raised the revolver. In one easy practiced motion, Steve swept the deck, sighting over the red bead sight on the muzzle. A slight hissing sound caught his attention.

The seventy-year-old exhaled in relief when he saw a boy spray painting graffiti on the boom tent covering Zack's boat, *Wild Turtle*. That explained the hissing sound. He pulled back into the boom tent and locked the revolver before slipping it back into its hiding place. He grabbed a handheld air horn and moved back into the cockpit. He pulled the entrance flap aside and stepped onto the dock, holding the canister in his left hand, his thumb poised over the button. The boy never saw Steve as he walked up behind him. Steve held the air horn a few inches behind the boy's head and depressed the button. A loud blast split the night air.

Sean Homes jerked and almost lost control of his bladder when Steve hit him with another blast from the airhorn. Sean spun to his left as Steve gave him a hard push, sending him over the edge of the dock and into the water. Sean sputtered as he surfaced and reached up, grabbing *Wild Turtle's* dock line. "Looks like you just failed Dockwalking 101," Steve said.

Caly's Island

Rufus was out of his boat, a seventeen-foot catboat, and ran up holding a flashlight. He directed the beam over the side of the dock. "Well, well. What do we have here? I bet you're freezing your cojones off." He reached down, grabbed Sean by the collar, and lifted him out of the water with one easy motion. He stood him up on the dock, not letting go of his collar. Sean shook uncontrollably from the cold. "Better get a blanket on him."

"Let me go, you fuckin' idiot!" Sean screamed. Rufus lifted him up and dropped him back into the water.

Blair joined them and looked over the side. "How's the water?" Blair asked. Sean sputtered an obscene answer. "Sorry, I didn't catch that."

Zack emerged from the boom tent over the back of his boat as Pete and Gib arrived on scene. "What the . . . " Zack muttered, still groggy. He held up his right hand that was wet with green paint. "Where did that come from?"

"Our little tagger here," Steve replied, pointing at the water.

"Ah, crap," Zack moaned. "That's Sean Homes."

"He was decorating your boom tent." Steve held up the spray can. The six FOGs huddled around the evidence.

"We could strip the little bugger naked and paint him with it," Zack suggested. "He likes tattoos."

"But would he look good in green?" Pete wondered.

"Gentlemen," Gib said. "We have a more pressing question. Can he swim?" They all looked over the side of the dock.

Steve was puzzled. "I don't recognize that stroke."

"That's the double-breasted wart-headed clam crawl," Pete told them.

"You ever eat one of those?" Rufus asked. "Double-breasted wart-headed clams."

"All the time," Pete replied. "Tastes just like chicken."

Blair took charge. "Get him out before he goes hypothermic."

Again, Rufus lifted Sean out of the water with an easy motion and stood him on the dock. Gib handed the teenager a blanket. "A thank you would be in order," the jurist said.

"Fuck you," Sean said, shrugging free of Rufus's grip. He wrapped the blanket around his shoulders and walked away.

Dick Herman

Rufus's left hand darted out, rattlesnake quick, and grabbed Sean by the arm. He jerked the teenager back like a rag doll, his arms and legs flailing. "That's a no-no," Rufus said in his quiet way. He held up his right forefinger as he squeezed. "My left is my weak hand." He squeezed harder. "Would you like to see what I can do with my strong hand?" He wagged a finger under Sean's nose. "Now be polite." Sean started to snarl an answer but Rufus bore down. Sean gasped for air.

"Mr. Gunnermyer," Gib said, "I suggest you let him go." Rufus did as the judge said. "Mr. Homes, I strongly urge you not to move and keep a civil tongue in your mouth, or I will allow our gentle friend here to use both hands." Sean got the message.

"We've got company," Steve said. A police officer was walking down the dock towards them.

"Good morning, Officer Roberts," Zack said. "Nice seeing you again."

"Good morning, Mr. Hilber." There was a cautious respect in his voice. "A horn was reported. Is there an emergency or problem here?"

"That was me, officer," Steve said. "Sean fell in the water and I needed help."

"You lying, fucker!" Sean screamed. "You pushed me in! Look what they did to my arm!" He held up his right arm for Roberts to see. The policeman directed his flashlight on to the swollen upper arm. It was red and bruised.

"That was where I grabbed him," Rufus admitted.

Roberts nodded. "To pull him out of the water and save him from drowning, no doubt. Most commendable. Sean, what were you doing here at two in the morning?" There was no answer.

"He's an artist," Blair said, shinning his light on Zack's boom tent. The bright green letters stood out under the light. A chuckle worked through the men. "Sean," Blair said, "you spelled 'shit' correctly, but 'head' has an 'a' in it."

"It was dark," the teenager muttered.

Zack snorted. "At last, a coherent sentence without an obscenity. I'm amazed. So what happens now?"

"The same as yesterday," Roberts said. "I take him downtown and book him. You know the rest of the drill."

"May I make a suggestion?" Gib asked. Without waiting for a reply, he continued. "We know arresting Sean will be an exercise in futility.

Caly's Island

Why don't we call his mother, apprise her of the current situation, and let her decide what to do."

Pete liked the idea. "What do you have in mind?"

"Perhaps we can have an informal talk," Gib replied.

Blair made the decision. "Call her." He gestured towards the picnic area on the breakwater. "We can build a bonfire over there and get warm. Gib, would you brew up some of your coffee?" He studied Sean for a moment. They were the same size. "I've got some dry clothes that will fit you."

"Officer Roberts," Gib said, "would you please stay. Your familiarity with the situation will be most helpful in any conversation."

"My pleasure," Roberts said. He wasn't going to miss this one.

"What the fuck you assholes gonna do?" Sean snarled. "Put me on trial?"

Without a word, Rufus picked Sean up by the arm, carried him to the edge of the dock, and tossed him kicking and screaming into the water. Roberts shined his flashlight on the boy. "He is rather clumsy."

"Just a slow learner," Rufus said.

Helena Homes wheeled her silver BMW to a stop. She clenched the steering wheel for a few moments, waiting for her frustration to subside. She walked towards the group of seven men standing around the small fire in a pit at the far end of the picnic area. The fire cast flickering shadows on the men as they stood around the glowing coals and clutched mugs of coffee. For a moment, she was caught in a time warp and was looking at a tribal council from the mists of antiquity. Pete turned to meet her and handed her a hot mug. "It's good stuff," he said.

She took it and sipped gratefully. "Where's Sean?" The men parted and she couldn't believe her eyes. Sean was wearing a dark warm up suit with white stripes down the side and white running shoes. For the first time in over a year, he looked his age and could have been any normal, healthy fifteen-year old. She liked what she saw and a tear streaked her cheek.

"Mom," he cried, "get me out'a here before I kick the living shit out'a these old farts."

Rufus reached out and clamped his shoulder with a firm grip. "For now, speak only when spoken to."

Helena sensed that something very different was happening, and a basic instinct warned her not to intervene. "Sean, do as you're told." Sean glared at her and fell silent. Rufus released him.

"May we start?" Gib asked. By the simple act of sitting down in a camp chair beside the dying fire, he claimed the heritage of his ancestors. He was a chieftain of an ancient clan bringing justice to his people. "Mrs. Homes, we are here for one reason, to help Sean. Mr. Peter Lacy will speak for your son."

Helena's anger flared. "I speak for Sean, not him."

Gib spoke with an authority she had never heard. "Mrs. Homes, look at your son. You will make the final decision here, but for now, hear us out." She looked at Sean and nodded. "Mr. Lacey," Gib said, "please proceed."

Pete stepped forward. "Mrs. Homes, please tell us about Sean."

Helena's eyes misted over as she told them of the boy she knew and how he had gone off the rails in the last year. "He was a good, lovin' boy. I don't know what went wrong."

Sean exploded. "It was you, bitch! Screwin' around with those shit heads."

Rufus's hand clamped his shoulder. "You'll have your chance to speak. For now, listen." Sean started to protest but Rufus pinched his collarbone and sent waves of pain down his arm. "That's my right hand," Rufus warned. Sean quieted and Rufus let up.

"Officer Roberts," Pete said, "will you please relate your experiences with Sean?"

Roberts cleared his throat. "It started small, you know, juvenile pranks. We see it all the time. But with Sean, it didn't stop. He just kept at it, all low level stuff." Helena flinched as the policeman detailed a long list of incidents, all ending with her at the police station, throwing her family's weight around, and never holding Sean to account. "But in Sean's defense, we have a saying in the department, 'Show me a problem kid, and I'll show you a problem parent.'"

Helena's head came up and her nostrils flared. She wasn't going to stand for that. But Gib cut her off by simply holding up his hand. "Is that true, Mrs. Homes?"

Helena gulped her coffee before answering. The warm brew did its magic and she calmed. "It's complicated." That was as far as she could

Caly's Island

go down that road. For a moment, only the soft lapping of water on the breakwater was heard.

Pete broke the silence. "Sean, why are you doing this?"

The teenager shifted from foot to foot. He eyed Rufus before answering. "I don't know. People hurt me and I get angry."

"Did we do anything to hurt you?" Pete asked.

"You sure the fu. . ." He strangled the last word as Rufus reached for him. "Yeah you did." Rufus dropped his hand. "I got chased and shoved down a drain. Then you guys pushed me in the water over and over." He gestured at Rufus. "And he grabs me every time I move or say anything. He's stronger than a gorilla."

"You're talking now and he's not grabbing you," Helena said. "And he's not a gorilla."

Gib gave the boy a gentle look. "Sean, could it be they were reacting to your actions?"

Sean shifted his weight from foot to foot and looked down. "I don't know. Maybe."

"Your Honor," Pete said, "for the record, Sean Homes has been subjected to physical handling that, according to Washington state law, constitutes physical abuse."

"Officer Roberts, is that true?" Gib asked.

"There is evidence to support that charge," Roberts replied.

"Sean, may I see your arm?" Gib asked. Sean shuffled over to the judge and rolled up his sleeve. His left bicep was red and slightly swollen were Rufus had held him. Gib gently prodded his arm. "Does that hurt?" Sean shook his head. "Is there anything else?" The teenager unzipped his jacket and pulled the collar aside to reveal his collarbone. There were bright fingerprints on his skin where Rufus had squeezed him. "That must have hurt," Gib conceded.

"Yes, sir," Sean said. Everyone stared at him, not crediting the words they had just heard escaping Sean's lips.

Gib turned to the policeman. "Officer Roberts, does Washington law allow the use of reasonable force to stop a crime or detain a suspect?"

"Yes, sir, it does."

"Mrs. Homes," Gib said, "we have reached an impasse. Sean was engaged in the destruction of private property. He was detained by the victim's friends in a physical manner that may, or may not, have been legal. Both are issues for a properly constituted court to decide. But the vital question before us is, what is best for Sean? To that end, what would you have us do?"

Tears flowed down Helena's cheeks. "Your Honor, I don't know. Please help us."

Gib leaned back in the chair and his finely manicured hands clasped the ends of the arms. He was ready to render justice. "Sean, what you did was morally wrong and illegal. But the way you were treated was also wrong, whether it was legal or not. But neither are issues for us to decide. We can place the matter before the courts, and perhaps we should, but I doubt that will solve the problem of your conduct. I believe the solution is to change your environment, to present you with new opportunities and new challenges. To that end, I am recommending that your mother allow you to sail with us on our upcoming cruise through the San Juan Islands for the next two weeks."

"Give me a break," Zack moaned.

"I don't know," Steve said.

"I'm not a babysitter," Pete groused. "What if something happens to the kid?" Pete was always the lawyer.

"I'd rather not," Rufus said. "But I can go with it."

They all looked at Blair. "He can sail with me and Angus."

Gib nodded at Blair. "Thank you, Mr. Blair." He turned to Helena. "It is your decision. Sean can go with us or we will defer to Officer Roberts and the law will again become involved."

Helena studied the six men. Could she trust them? But the more she looked at them, the more certain she became that they wanted to do the right thing. Gib's finely tuned sense of justice and common sense impressed her, and the one they called the Admiral seemed to like Sean. Were they of the same spirit? She simply liked the way Zack looked, and he seemed under a firm self-control. Rufus was a soft-spoken individual and not afraid to discipline Sean. Pete was a lady's man and a lawyer, two types she fully understood and could handle. As for Steve, he was a total unknown, and for a moment, she wondered if any of them really knew the man. She made the decision.

"We need to pack. Will someone help?"

"Ah, Mom," Sean protested.

"You were the one who started this," Helena told him.

Caly's Island

"I'll help," Pete said. "He doesn't need to take much, and he will need a sleeping bag." The three walked towards Helena's BMW. Sean followed the two adults, kicking and scuffing his feet.

"I wonder if she'll change her mind," Rufus said.

Steve shook his head. "You never know. But she is one strong-willed lady."

Blair poured the last of the coffee over the burning coals as he banked them. For a moment, he stood taking in the moonlit sky. "I can't believe I did that," he muttered to himself.

Gib overheard him. "H, you did good. Very good."

THREE

Together, Helena and Roberts wandered down the dock and watched the FOGs prepare to cast off. It was Saturday afternoon, and it had taken longer than expected to get Sean organized and ready to go. The teenager had insisted on packing for a permanent change in residence rather than a two-week voyage on a small sailboat, and that had led to a major dockside tantrum. While Helena and Sean had argued, Rufus had solved the problem by quietly sorting Sean's considerable possessions into two piles; one quite large that would be left behind and the other of a manageable amount that could be stowed on a small boat.

Finally, they were ready to launch. Blair handed Sean a personal flotation device, a fancy name for a life jacket, or PFD for short, and told him to put it on.

"I ain't wearing that. It's dorky."

"It won't be dorky if we capsize and you're in the water up to your neck," Blair told him. The other FOGs listened, very interested in how Blair would handle the kid.

"You mean these things turn over?"

"Happens all the time."

"Mom! I ain't going. You can't make me go."

"Sean, get in the damn boat," Helena ordered. Rufus moved Sean's way and the teenager scampered aboard.

Blair handed him a very small PFD. "Put this on Angus, okay?"

"Your dog wears one of these?" Sean asked.

"You bet he does. He's been in the water twice, and you know how cold it is." Sean mumbled under his breath as he fitted the PFD to the terrier. Angus didn't move and kept looking at him. After the third try, it was on and Angus licked his hand. "He's saying thank you," Blair said. "You can say 'you're welcome' back."

"You're welcome," Sean muttered. Angus yapped in answer and settled down in the forward left corner of the cockpit bench next to the cabin bulkhead. "Where do I sit?"

"On the other side. You'll have to move when I tell you and handle the jib sheets."

Rather than admit he didn't know what a jib sheet was, Sean plopped his wiry frame in the right forward corner of the cockpit. He looked around and saw that all the other FOGs were wearing PFDs. He picked his up and tried to sort out the straps. "What are these? Suspenders?"

Blair untangled the straps and showed him how to wear it. "It automatically inflates in the water. But if doesn't, pull the yellow tab." Satisfied the PFD was properly fitted, he raised his mainsail. The blue and white striped, ninety-square-foot sail flapped in the breeze. "We'll raise the jib when we're out of the harbor." He looked up and down the dock checking the FOGs. Their mainsails were all raised. Only Gib's sail was the traditional white. The others were different colors, a vibrant tribute to the sailmaker's art. But Steve was still pacing the dock, his cell phone to his ear. He broke the connection and punched in another number, a very worried look on his face. He spoke for a few minutes before hanging up. He stood there, not sure what to do.

"Hey," Blair called, "let's do it." Steve hesitated and then climbed onto his boat.

Roberts walked along the dock, casting off the dock lines and giving each boat a little push away from the dock. He reached *Wee Dram* and stared at Sean. "I wish I were going with you," he said. He pushed them away from the dock, and Blair hauled in the main sheet as he put the tiller over. They were sailing and he fell in behind Gib and Steve as the six boats paraded out of the marina in a neat line.

All semblance of order ended when they cleared the breakwater. Steve fell off to the right while Gib headed for their destination, Inati Bay on Lummi Island, eight miles across Bellingham Bay. "Where's Steve going?" Blair wondered. They pitched over the first swell and Sean grabbed the cockpit rail. "Keep an eye on Steve, okay? He's the red and white sail." He headed into the wind. "Take the tiller while I raise the jib." From the look on Sean's face an explanation was in order. He told him to move to the aft of the cockpit and hold the rudder's tiller. "Keep us pointed into the wind."

"Which way is that?" Sean asked, keeping a death grip on the tiller with one hand and the rail with the other.

"Straight ahead," Blair said. He moved forward and pulled the jib halyard just as they crested another swell. The boat broached sideways as Sean lost control. Blair was a blur of motion as he released the main sheet, depowering the sail, and grabbed the tiller. The boat was going over. Blair threw his weight against the windward rail, righting them as Angus barked.

"I did what you said!" Sean cried. "I tried to turn into the wind, but the dumb boat went the other way."

Blair hooted with laughter as he got the boat under control. "Indeed you did. Except on a sailboat, you have to push the tiller the opposite way you want to go."

"That's stupid," Sean said.

"Hey, if it's stupid but works, it ain't stupid. You'll get the hang of it." They practiced for a few minutes and Blair cocked an eyebrow. "Ready to try again?" Sean did not look happy. Again, Blair scooted forward, and the blue jib went up effortlessly. "Head to the right a little," he told Sean as he secured the jib sheet. He moved aft and took the tiller. "Now watch this." He fell off the wind a little more and adjusted the main sheet. Now they were moving along at a respectable three knots and punching into the swells as they headed for Inati Bay.

"Is it always this rough?" Sean asked.

"Nah," Blair replied. "Bellingham Bay is tough sailing in this direction because the wind and the swells are coming right at us. We call it the Bellingham Bash." Sean's face turned white and he leaned over the rail. "The other side!" Blair shouted. "Never puke into the wind." Sean retched loudly, too sick to listen. Blair headed up into the wind so Sean wouldn't get too much blow back. "Well, your mother does feed you well." He was rewarded with a whimper.

"Okay, where is everybody?" He looked around to count sails. Zack's red and yellow sail was right behind him, where it always was so he wouldn't get lost. He could easily make out Gib's white sail to his port. Pete's sail, a classic cream-colored Egyptian cotton and Rufus's dark red tanbark sail were harder to see. Unfortunately, Steve's red and white sail had disappeared. "Now where did he go?" He turned on his

29

radio to maintain a listening watch as Sean collapsed on the cockpit bench, still heaving from motion sickness. Angus jumped down onto the cockpit sole, and nuzzled the sick kid's ear with his nose.

"I'm gonna die," Sean moaned.

"Not today," Blair reassured him as he searched the horizon, looking for Steve's red and white sail.

As usual, Pete Lacy was the first to reach their destination, Inati Bay. His sixteen-foot home-built sloop was probably the most seaworthy of the group and there was no question that he was the fastest sailor, which the FOGs attributed to a deal cut with the wind gods that only a shyster lawyer could negotiate. But in reality, Pete was simply the most wind-aware of the six sailors, and he could read the wind and turn it into an extra knot of speed in his sleep. He coasted by the entrance marker of the pretty little cove as he furled his jib. He put the tiller over and glided along the shore, looking for a place to anchor. The water was unusually clear and he easily found a spot. Pete headed up, let the main sheet go, and threw out an anchor. Rather than strike his sail, he let it flap. He tidied up *L'Amour* and pulled out his log. He stretched out on the port bench in the cockpit with his back against the cabin and started to write, bringing the detailed journal up to date.

Helena was sending all the right signals yesterday. She's a player. Was Steve holding a gun last night? Couldn't be sure in the dark when I looked out. Sean is a pain in the ass, but Gib was right about changing his environment. The Admiral did the right thing, taking Sean on as a passenger. If Helena saw Sean's bruises, she would have gone ballistic. Rufe is unbelievably lucky and coasts through life on a charmed roller coaster. But I worry about Zack. He's wrapped tighter than an airport sandwich. And what was Steve's phone call all about? The sail across Bellingham Bay was a little sporting but fun. Now if we can just get rid of Sean.

He put the log back in its watertight case and drifted off to sleep.

* * * *

Caly's Island

A gentle nudge against *L'Amour* woke Pete as *Wee Dram* came alongside to raft up. "Hold on," Blair warned as *Wild Turtle* slammed into the other side of Pete's boat.

"Sorry," Zack said, truly contrite. He appreciated *L'Amour's* pristine condition and the pride Pete took in his small craft.

Pete couldn't help himself and smiled. That was Zack; always lost and always sorry. "The fenders were out. No harm, no foul." He helped the two boats tie up alongside. Now they had to wait. "There's Rufe," he said, pointing to *Nailing On's* tanbark sail. The white sail of *Habeas Corpus* was hiding in Rufus's lee when the two entered the bay. "Where's Steve?" Pete asked.

"Haven't got a clue," Blair replied. He unfolded a waterproof chart and spread it out. He pointed to a spot in Bellingham Bay. "The last I saw him was here."

Pete looked over his shoulder. "He might have gone around Portage Island." The lawyer tapped the big island on the western side of Bellingham Bay.

"I don't think so," Blair replied. "It's all mud flats on the northern side at low tide."

Sean's head appeared over *Wee Dram's* gunwale. He looked like death warmed over but was feeling much better. Angus's head bobbed up beside Sean's. "Maybe he capsized," the teenager smirked.

Blair considered it. "Possible, but I don't think so. Steve's a damn good sailor and he'd have signaled – a radio call, flare, horn, whistle." Rufus guided *Nailing On* alongside Zack's boat and tied up. "Rufe," Blair called. "You see where Steve went?"

"He was headed for Portage Island the last I saw," Rufus replied.

Gib was the last to raft up next to Blair. "He was going around Portage."

"Then he's aground," Blair said. "Pete, Rufe, would you two go check on him before it gets dark? Try to stay in radio contact."

"Will do," Pete said. "Can you get an anchor out?" The men worked quickly to re-anchor and separate the boats. Within minutes, Pete and Rufus were motorsailing out of the bay.

"Why didn't you go?" Sean asked. "Aren't you the leader?"

Blair snorted. "Lead this group? You got'a be kidding. I asked them to go because Pete's the best sailor of the group and Rufe is the youngest and strongest." Sean fell silent. With Rufus the enforcer out of the picture, he could take off. "Don't even think about it," Blair warned him. Sean glared at him. Angus growled. It was low and primeval, a clear warning. Sean's face paled and he pulled back. "Angus is a Jack Russell terrier," Blair explained. "They're devoted, loyal, and even loving. But they're a hunter, totally fearless and with the heart of a lion. They'll take on just about any animal or person. He wants to be your friend, but don't rile him." Sean stared at the dog and suddenly understood – Blair and Angus were an extension of each other.

"Hey, how about some dinner?"

"I'm not hungry," Sean mumbled.

"No problem," Blair replied. "But the next meal is breakfast."

It was twilight when Pete and Rufus found Steve on the northern side of Portage Island. As expected, Steve's fifteen-foot sloop, *High Flyer*, was aground on the mud flats between the island and the mainland. Steve had furled his sails, rigged his boom tent, and anchored. Pete coasted up to Rufus and released his main sheet. They were in sheltered water, still a good mile from Steve. "I think he's there for the night. I'll see if I can raise him on channel 16." The lawyer keyed his handheld VHF radio. "*High Flyer, High Flyer. L'Amour* on channel sixteen. How copy?"

"Read you loud and clear," Steve replied.

"You okay?"

"I'm fine, no problems. I tried to raise someone on the radio, but I think the island is in the way." Their VHF radios were line-of-sight with a very limited range.

"The tide is still going out," Pete transmitted. "You're stuck until high tide tomorrow morning. I'll let the Admiral know."

"Roger," Steve replied. "Standing by on channel sixteen."

"Rufe, you stay here and keep in contact with Steve. I'll sail into open water and radio the Admiral."

"Sounds like a plan," Rufus replied. "This looks like a good place to anchor."

Pete gave Rufus a thumbs-up and cranked his four-horsepower outboard motor. He set off into the growing dark as Rufus set his anchor. Satisfied he was secure, Rufus crawled into the cabin and rummaged around until he found his electric lantern and butane stove. He switched on the lantern and hoisted it to the top of the mast. Certain that Pete

Caly's Island

could find him in the dark and other boats see him, he quickly rigged his boom tent and settled in for the evening.

It was dark when Pete returned. Rufus helped him tie up along side. He invited Pete aboard to share a beer, chili, and the fresh cornbread he had steam baked in a pot. "I raised the Admiral on the radio," Pete said. "He said to stay with Steve, and we'll rendezvous in the morning when they head out."

"What time?" Rufus asked between mouthfuls.

"Around eight." Pete tasted the chili and reached for his beer. "Damn, this is hot!" His eyes were watering. "Talk about burnout. I won't need to use toilet paper for a week."

"It ain't that hot," Rufus replied. "Except for a few peppers."

Pete poked at his chili and found a red and green bit with a touch of bright orange. "Like this one?" He threw it on the cockpit sole.

"Careful," Rufus said. "You'll burn a hole in the bottom."

Pete tried the chili again, this time without a pepper. "Much better. Your recipe?"

"Nope. I got it from a lady I do odd jobs for. Good-looking old gal. A widow. I work for free, she feeds me. I think she's trying to seduce me."

"Strange courtship rituals you blacksmiths have."

Rufus stirred his chili and finished it off. "Was I in trouble last night?"

Pete was brutally honest. "You could have been. You can't treat a kid like that, not in this day and age."

"If it works, why not?" Rufus subscribed to the theory that humans were pack animal like dogs and horses. "You have to get their attention first and establish who's the boss."

Pete shook his head. "Too many bleeding hearts think differently. But Gib had your back. Luckily, Roberts went along with it. He's had a bellyful of Sean. Fuckin' little creep."

"He's not that bad," Rufus said. "He just needs taming a bit."

"Not our job," Pete replied. "Any more cornbread?"

* * * *

Dick Herman

Sean's stomach started to growl from hunger just after eight o'clock that evening. "I'm hungry," he announced. He was sitting in *Wee Dram* while Blair, Zack, and Gib huddled on board *Habeas Corpus* and planned the next day's sail.

"Breakfast is in the morning," Blair replied.

Zack threw him an apple. "Munch on that."

"I don't like apples," Sean said.

"Tough tacos," Zack said. "Go hungry."

"Assholes," Sean mumbled under his breath. The men didn't hear him but Angus did. The terrier growled and eyed him with canine interest. Acutley aware that Angus had a healthy set of fangs, Sean decided silence was better than a bite in the butt. He sat with his back against the cabin bulkhead and pulled his knees up. "I'm cold."

"Then put a jacket on," Blair said.

"Where is it?"

The three men looked at each other and grinned. Zack threw him a jacket. Sean fingered the dark red material and sensed it was very expensive. His finger moved down the right sleeve, tracing the big gold lettering that announced *L'Amour*. Pete's name was embroidered on the left breast. "Pete really likes that jacket," Zack explained. "Take good care of it." The men laughed. Pete had designed a team jacket, but that was far too much togetherness for the FOGs, and the jacket had become a standing joke. Pete enjoyed the game and went to great lengths to leave it on other boats to annoy them. Sean pulled it on.

"Where do I sleep?" Sean demanded.

"In the cabin," Blair told him.

"With you? I ain't sleepin' in there with some old prevert."

"Sleep wherever you want," Blair replied. "And it's 'pervert'." He spelled it out.

Sean humphed and decided he would sleep on a cockpit bench under the boom tent. "I'm bored. What do I do now?"

"Did you bring any school assignments?" Gib asked.

"I don't do no fuckin' homework."

"Sean, keep a civil tongue in your mouth," Blair warned him. There was steel in his voice and Angus growled in punctuation. "Reach around inside the cabin and there's a book in the rack on the aft bulkhead. Get it. Now." Sean did as he was told and pulled out Reed's Nautical Companion. "Read the section on 'Safety at Sea in Small Craft.' It just might save your young body if something happens to me." Blair grinned wickedly. "I've got a bad heart, you know."

"And I'm senile," Gib said.

"And I get lost in a flash," Zack added. "There's a headband in the jacket's pocket with a light. Great for reading at night."

Sean gave them the disgusted look teenagers specialize in and pulled the headlamp over his head. He thumbed through the book. "Where's the crap on safety?"

"Use the index," Blair answered.

"Dumb," Sean said in a low voice. Angus curled up beside him. Sean started to read and took a bite of the apple.

Rufus was up at first light and poked his head out of his boom tent. A thick fog drifted over the two boats and he could barely see ten feet. Pete was gently snoring in his cabin. Rufus pulled the flap closed and lit the stove to make coffee. He settled back to wait for the water to boil and thought about Cheryl, his ex-wife. Her image was crystal clear and he didn't need a photograph to remember every detail of her face. The memories of their divorce were still painful, but he wanted her back. That's what I get for marrying a woman eighteen years younger, he thought. He loved her unreservedly and didn't care that she was living with a toy boy, a considerably younger stud in his early twenties. Was it a pre-menopausal thing? He felt the boats rock when Pete came to life. "Coffee's almost ready," he called. A grunt answered him. Pete was not at his best in the morning.

Rufus poured the boiling water into a coffee press as Pete unzipped his boom tent. "Where did that come from?" Pete asked. Rufus stuck his head out to see what had gotten Pete's attention. The fog had lifted a little and a long, sleek, white-hulled offshore racer was anchored twenty yards away.

Rufus shook his head. He hadn't heard it arrive or anchor during the night, but he was a sound sleeper. "Now that's a go-faster boat."

"It's a Cigarette. I'd say 46 feet long, twin engines, a thousand horsepower, good for eighty knots, half a million bucks." From the look on Rufus's face, an explanation was in order. "One of my clients, a Mafia type, had one. He wanted to pay his legal bill with it."

"You took it?"

"Sure. I sold it and returned what money was left over."

"Why did you do that? I'd have kept it. The money, not the boat."

"He was Russian Mafia, Rufe. You don't mess with them."

Rufus pointed at the Cigarette. "Check 'em out. I don't think they're Mafia." Two young women had emerged from the long forward cabin. They were bundled up against the cold but even from a distance it was easy to see they were blonde and beautiful. "They named that boat right," Rufus observed. The boat's name, The Sirens, was emblazoned on the bow in big gold and blue-shadowed lettering.

"Oh, Lordy," Pete said. The old familiar rush was back and it wasn't his brain doing his thinking. "We got'a say hello." He cupped his hands around his mouth and shouted. "Ahoy, The Sirens. Care for some coffee?" He held up a mug. One of the girls waved and shook her head, her blonde hair flipping from side to side. "Not a coffee lover," Pete groused.

"Too young, anyway," Rufus said. "I feel a breeze. We need to get moving and get Steve off the mud." The two men quickly struck their boom tents and were soon ready to go. Now they could just make out Steve's boat in the fog, still a mile away. His red and white sail was up and he was sailing away from them, to the west, and into Hale Passage. Rufus weighed anchor as the breeze freshened.

Pete keyed his VHF radio. "*High Flyer*, *L'Amour*. Where you headed?" The radio transmission echoed from the nearby Cigarette, which was monitoring the same frequency.

"I'm making for the main channel," Steve answered. Again, they heard an echo from the Cigarette.

"My chart shows a bar between you and the channel," Pete radioed. "Can you clear it?" The most their boats drew was four feet with the centerboard down, and less than a foot with it up. The centerboard acted like a depth sounder and dragged noisily when they got into shallow water.

High Flyer sailed resolutely over the bar, which was now underwater. "Not a problem," Steve transmitted. "My depth sounder is showing six feet. It looks like we got a very high tide."

The roar of two big marine V-8 engines crackling to life split the air. Pete and Rufus stared at the Cigarette as it accelerated straight ahead, kicking up a high rooster-tail. Its bow wave washed over the two boats as it sped past. The two women wore crash helmets and were strapped into

Caly's Island

the Cigarette's heavily padded seats. The boat cut a graceful arc as it headed for the bar. "I guess they were listening and are going for it," Pete called to Rufus. They followed at a much more reasonable pace of three knots, while *High Flyer* cleared the bar and disappeared around Portage Island, heading south to rendezvous with Blair, Zack, and Gib.

"Jesus H. Christ!" Pete shouted. The Cigarette had run aground and broached sideways, listing at a dangerous angle. Black smoke poured from the aft engine compartment. Pete reached back and pulled the recoil starter handle on his outboard. The small motor coughed to life on the first pull, and he gave it full throttle, making for the bar at five knots.

Rufus was right behind him.

FOUR

Pete approached the Cigarette from the stern. He eased his main sheet and idled back on the outboard. His centerboard clunked, warning him he was in 'skinny' water. He raised the board before he grounded. Must be something wrong with Steve's depth sounder, he thought. Steve had definitely said he was reading six feet. Pete filed it away and would ask about it later. The Cigarette was listing fifteen degrees to port. The big engine access hatch was open and black smoke poured from the port engine. The smell of burnt oil and fire retardant scorched the air. "Scratch twenty-five grand," Pete said to himself. His little outboard cost a thousand dollars.

"Rufe," he called, "stay back in case I run aground."

"Will do," Rufus answered. "Hold on." He threw a line at Pete. "Just in case." The line plopped across *L'Amour's* cockpit.

Pete was impressed with the throw. "How do you do that?"

"Practice," Rufus replied.

Pete cut his outboard and bumped up against the port side of the Cigarette. He stood and looked into the big open cockpit. "Nice," he said. The seats were upholstered in white leather and the control console sported every conceivable gauge and electronic device known to nautical man. "Ahoy," he called.

A woman's head appeared in the companionway in front of the seats. "Hello," she said.

For the first time in his life, Pete suffered a complete and total brain seizure. The woman was beautiful beyond words. She was a natural blonde with magnificent blue eyes, high cheekbones, perfectly shaped lips, a nose plastic surgeons dreamed about and a killer smile. She had shed her heavy jacket and was wearing a halter-top and hip-hugger jeans that accentuated her flawless skin, flat tummy, and magnificent breasts. Pete recognized perfection when he saw it. His knees almost gave out when her twin joined her. The two women stood in the companionway and took his measure. "Yes?" the first asked. The other smiled at him.

"Ah," was the best he could manage.

"Are you alright?"

Pete didn't recognize her accent, but it was definitely not American or Canadian. "Ah, I was until a moment ago," he finally said. "Are you okay?"

"Oh, yes. We were shaken up a little but help is on the way. There it is." She pointed behind him. Pete turned and saw a shallow-draft RIB, a rigid inflatable boat, speeding across Portage Bay towards them.

"Did you call the Coast Guard?" he asked.

"There was no need," the woman said. She gave him a little smile.

"Well," Pete said, "they're on the way." He pointed to the north. A Coast Guard cutter was coming down Hale Passage at flank speed. The woman spoke in a low voice to her sister. Pete strained to understand what she was saying, but he didn't recognize the language. The two women disappeared into the cabin and quickly reappeared wearing their coats. Each carried a duffel bag, a PFD, and helmet. They climbed into the cockpit and waited as the RIB pulled alongside, tying up immediately behind *L'Amour*. The two burly, dark-haired men in the RIB helped the women climb aboard and stowed their duffle bags. The helmsman shoved the throttles in reverse and backed away from the Cigarette. He spun the wheel and gunned the two big outboards. The RIB leaped forward and came on step as it sped away, retreating across Portage Bay and away from the Coast Guard cutter, which was still over a mile away.

Pete smelled smoke and pushed off from the Cigarette as flames shot up from the engine compartment. He gunned his outboard and sped across the bar, reaching deep water in Hale Passage. Rufus was right behind him. "What's going on?" Rufus shouted.

"Beats me," Pete shouted back. "Did you hear any radio calls for help?"

"Nothing," Rufus replied.

Pete's VHF radio squawked. "This is the U.S. Coast Guard cutter Stockdale hailing the two small sailing craft in Hale Passage opposite the

Caly's Island

burning boat. Heave-to and standby for boarding. Repeat, heave-to and standby for boarding."

"Now that's a first," Pete groused. "Two microcruisers boarded on the high seas by the Coast Guard."

"We ain't on the high seas," Rufus observed.

"The weight of a boarding party will sink us," Pete replied. The heavy staccato of a .50 caliber machine gun cut the air and a line of splashes walked across their bows. Pete grabbed his handheld radio and mashed the transmit button. "We surrender!" he screamed.

Pete and Rufus craned their necks back and looked up nervously as the Coast Guard cutter came alongside. The rail was lined with armed men and their weapons were all pointed at them, insuring their undivided attention. An officer with a bullhorn stepped onto the flying bridge. "Cute little boats you got there," he called. The men lining the rail didn't smile. "Stand down," the officer ordered. The men stepped back as a rope ladder dropped over the side. "Please come aboard and bring identification." The two FOGs didn't need any further encouragement. They tied their boats to the ladder and scampered up the side. The officer was waiting for them by the rail. "Commander John Charles. Welcome aboard the Stockdale."

"Are we under arrest?" Pete asked, coming right to the point.

"Probably not," Charles replied. "But you do keep some interesting company." He gestured at the burning Cigarette. A fire control team was directing a stream of water onto the flames from the cutter's fantail. He spoke to a petty officer and two men went over the side and dropped onto the two boats. "They're searching your boats."

"What for?" Rufus asked.

"Drugs." Rufus started to protest, but Charles stopped him. "We don't need a reason."

"The Cigarette ran aground and we were responding to the emergency," Pete explained.

"No doubt," Charles said. "But we didn't monitor any radio calls."

"Neither did we," Pete said.

A loud explosion echoed over them as the Cigarette fireballed. "Damn," Charles muttered.

41

"Sir," the petty officer said, pointing to the south and four small sailboats. Blair was leading the rest of the FOGs as they approached the Stockdale.

"They're with us," Pete explained.

The two-man boarding party climbed back on board and reported that *L'Amour* and *Nailing On* were clean. "Thank you for your cooperation," Charles told Pete and Rufus. "We're going to be here awhile to see what we can recover from the wreckage. Can I interest you and your companions in coffee?"

Pete considered it. "Are you going to search their boats?"

Charles smiled. "Not at all. But Senator Homes did ask if we would check on Sean, if we ran into you."

"Coffee sounds great," Pete answered. This was a chance to get rid of the kid and he didn't want to pass it up. He and Rufus stood by the rail while a detail was organized to search the wreckage floating in the water. They watched as the other four FOGs came aboard. Gib was the first up the ladder closely followed by Steve, Zack, Blair, and finally Sean. Pete made the introductions. It was obvious Charles knew who they were. Someone had done their homework and checked them out.

"This way," Charles said, leading them to the wardroom. He turned to Sean. "Ever been on a cutter?" he asked. Sean muttered an answer that was a cross between a simian grunt and a pig moaning from an overdose of Viagra. "Would you like to go on a tour and fire a machine gun?" Charles asked. Suddenly, Sean was very interested. Charles spoke to the petty officer and sent Sean on his way. "Boys like that," the Commander said. "Gentlemen, we do need to talk."

"Why did I know that?" Pete muttered to himself.

Charles was a gracious host and they were soon comfortably ensconced in the wardroom and nursing hot mugs of fresh coffee. "I take it you met the Sirens," Charles said to Pete and Rufus. "They are beautiful women."

Blair shook his head. "That figures."

Charles ignored him. "They're sisters and older than they look. They, along with their two cousins, run a most interesting business called 'The Family.' They specialize in providing services of all types, all illegal, to the highest bidder. You name it, they do it; drug running, arms dealing, smuggling illegal aliens, laundering money, bribery. All for a price. I suspect there was something, shall we say, of interest on the Cigarette."

"They did take two duffel bags with them," Rufus said. "They didn't seem too heavy. The duffel bags, not the ladies."

"I assure you, they are not ladies. One is rumored to be a very accomplished assassin."

"If she screws her victims to death, I'll volunteer," Pete said.

"I wouldn't joke about them," Charles said. "They don't have a sense of humor."

"I have heard of them," Gib said. "Were they on a delivery run?"

"Given the duffle bags," Charles said, "I expect so." He changed the subject. "Judge Stanford, are you experiencing any problems on this trip?" As one, five heads swiveled around to the jurist.

"Not at all," Gib, replied.

Blair and Pete exchanged glances. "What type of problems are you talking about?" Blair asked.

Gib set his mug down and folded his hands. "The good commander has let the cat out of the bag. As a retired judge, I am in the judicial protection program."

"Why?" Rufus asked.

"Please remember I have sentenced individuals to death and long prison terms. I have rendered verdicts and upheld appeals that have had broad ranging financial implications."

"Are you in any danger?" Blair asked.

"I seriously doubt it," Gib replied. "Never during my tenure on the bench, nor during the four years that I have been retired, have I ever experienced, or received, a threat of any kind." He took a deep breath. "And I would never put my friends at risk. I hope you know that."

"You might have told us," Blair said.

"It is a highly confidential program," Charles explained.

"So that explains the bullet-proof windows in your car," Rufus said.

Gib nodded. "You don't miss much." He looked at his friends and stood. "If you will excuse me."

"Where are you going?" Zack asked.

"Leaving. I assume you would feel safer without my presence."

"Sit down," Zack said.

"You're proof I've got a friend," Steve added.

Pete laughed. "Hey, I'm a lawyer. I get threats all the time."

Rufus chimed in. "Who's gonna keep me out of trouble?"

"Well," Blair said, "you do make life more interesting." The loud retort of a machine gun echoed in the wardroom. "Commander, I can't believe you're letting Sean fire live rounds."

"Training rounds only," Charles said. "Wad cutters."

"Were those wad cutters you fired at us?" Rufus asked.

Charles shook his head. "Target piercing ammo. You didn't heave-to. Besides, we save the HE for the heavies." HE was short for 'high explosive,' and the 'heavies' were drug runners.

"Crap," Pete breathed. "You didn't give us much time. What if you had hit Sean?"

"We had you on our high-definition optics and infrared. We knew he wasn't with you."

"You can tell at that distance?" Rufus asked.

Charles didn't answer. The cutter's detection and weapons systems were a close hold secret. He sipped his coffee. "His parents are concerned about his well-being. I can take him off your hands, if you want."

"Yes!" Pete said.

"He is a sullen little bastard," Zack added.

They fell silent when the door opened and Sean shuffled in. He fell into an armchair and stared at his running shoes. "How did it go?" Blair asked.

"Okay, I guess," Sean said.

"Was there a problem?" Charles asked.

At first, Sean didn't answer. "One of those dorks said I'd make a great lampshade."

Charles waited for an explanation but Sean just stared at his shoes. "I assume," Gib said, "that one of your men was commenting on Mr. Homes' tattoos. I believe it was a reference to Nazi atrocities in World War II."

"Sean," Blair said, "please show Commander Charles." Sean stood and held out his arms.

The Commander examined Sean's tattoos. "I'll take care of it," he promised.

Blair shook his head. "I'd prefer you drop it. You can tell Sean's parents that he's doing fine, and we'd like for him to stay with us."

"I will," Charles said. "But please call Mrs. Homes when you can."

Caly's Island

"We will," Blair promised.

Pete was the first to round Point Migley at the northern end of Lummi Island and clear Hale Passage as the sailboats turned to the west, heading for Fossil Bay on Sucia Island. The other five boats were less than a mile behind with Steve bringing up the rear. As usual, Zack was happily wallowing in Blair's wake. "What's the matter with him?" Sean asked.

"Zack?" Blair answered. Sean grunted, which Blair took to be an affirmative. "He's directionally impaired. He gets lost at the drop of a hat. He's a nice guy, but that really pisses him off. I think he gets more mad at himself than anyone else."

"Was he lost when he chased me?"

Blair sensed Sean wanted to talk. "If you took more than two turns, guaranteed."

"Is that why he got mad and took it out on me?"

"How do you feel when you get mad at people?"

"I wanna hit 'em."

"Zack is different. He's a watchdog and stands guard."

"You mean like a German shepherd?"

"More like a bull mastiff. He's friendly, but when something goes wrong he's genetically wired to correct it. Why don't you ask him? He's a good guy. He'll talk about it."

Sean extended a raised rigid middle finger at Rufus's tanbark sail in the traditional gesture of contempt. "What about him?"

Blair laughed. "Digitus impudicus. Giving someone the finger has been around since ancient Rome. But in those days, you could lose a finger if you flipped off the wrong person." Sean recalled his recent encounters with the blacksmith and looked worried. Again, Blair laughed. "You don't have to worry about Rufe. He's the most gentle of people. He just won't put up with any nonsense. If you act like an animal, he'll treat you like one."

"I don't act like no animal."

"Ask him about it." Sean grunted in disgust, but Blair knew he was listening. And thinking. Automatically, Blair counted sails, keeping track of his flock. Behind him, Steve's red and white sail had disappeared into a fog bank that was forming in Rosario Strait. "Where did that come from?" he wondered. "Sean, please take the tiller." The teenager traded places and took over steering while Blair cycled the VHF radio to channel one for the latest weather report. There was no mention of fog but the dew point was two degrees below the reported temperature. He checked the temperature gauge on the barometer in the cabin. The temperature read the same as the dew point and the hygrometer dial read 100% humidity. He estimated the wind was less than three knots. "Ideal conditions for fog," he told Sean. He cycled to the hailing channel and hit transmit. "*Wee Dram* transmitting in the blind. It looks like fog is forming and I've lost *High Flyer*. I'm going back to get him. Meet you at the dock at Fossil Bay on Sucia Island." Pete and Gib acknowledged and said they would press ahead for Fossil Bay.

"Let's come about and go back," Blair told Sean. A worried look shot across the boy's face. "I'll walk you through it," Blair said. He quickly explained the procedure. "When you're ready to turn, say 'ready about.' When I reply 'ready,' you say 'hard a-lee,' and push the tiller the opposite way you want to turn. Got it?"

Sean nodded very tentatively, looked around and said, "Ready about." Blair grabbed the jib sheet and responded with a "Ready." More assured, Sean said, "Hard a-lee." He put the tiller over and they tacked smartly through the wind. Now they were headed back the way they had come.

"Well done," Blair told him. This time there was no grunt in answer. As expected, Zack in *Wild Turtle* followed them. "Okay, what's Rufe doing?"

"He turned around with us," Sean said.

"Now you got your head up," Blair said, "as opposed to up and locked."

"Up and locked? What's that mean?"

"You got your head stuck up your ass and can't get it out," Blair replied. "You can't see a thing in that position." A flicker of a grin shot across Sean's mouth. But just as quickly, it was gone. That's a beginning, Blair thought.

Rufus fell in behind Zack as they headed for the fog. Blair checked his GPS. "Heads up. We're in the northbound traffic lane."

"What's that?" Sean asked.

"The channel where the big ships go." The wind slackened as they approached the fog.

Caly's Island

They were barely moving when Sean said, "I think I see something." Blair stared straight ahead, trying to pierce the fog, which was getting heavier by the moment. Suddenly, a dark mass loomed in the mist. A huge container ship punched out of the fog, headed straight for them.

"Turn right!" Blair shouted. But Sean had never seen a mountain of steel moving at twenty knots and bearing down on him. Deep down inside, he was a normal fifteen-year-old kid and he panicked. He put the tiller over to the right.

Blair was pure motion as he reached for the tiller. But the wind had totally died and they were drifting. He jerked the starter cord on the outboard. For once, the motor started when it was truly needed. The motor coughed to life just as a puff of wind caught the sail and jibed *Wee Dram* into the ship. The container ship closed to twenty yards before Blair gunned the engine and spun the boat around. The massive bow wave pushed the fifteen-foot boat aside as the motor raced. *Wee Dram* rocked violently as the container ship shot past. For a moment, Blair was sure they were going over, but the small craft was all cork and bobbed up, rocking the other way as the wake hit them.

Angus fell overboard and disappeared into the whirling mass of water. The terrier's empty PFD bobbed to the surface.

FIVE

Sean dove over the side and swam for the floating PFD as Blair put the helm over to come about. Sean reached Angus's PFD and tried to dive, but his own PFD had inflated, keeping him afloat. The teenager unsnapped it and shook it off. He took a deep breath and kicked, his legs in the air. He went down.

Blair idled the engine and let the sheets go to depower *Wee Dram*. He quickly hit the Man Over Board button on his GPS and reached for his VHF radio. "Mayday, Mayday, Mayday," he transmitted on channel sixteen. "Man overboard two miles west of Migley Point, northern end of Lummi Island. Dog also overboard."

"Copy all," Rufus replied. "On my way."

A woman's voice came over the radio. "Boat saying 'Mayday,' this is Coast Guard. What is emergency?"

Before Blair could reply, Sean's head broke the surface ten yards away. He held up Angus by a back leg. Zack coasted *Wild Turtle* to a stop beside him and grabbed Angus by the scruff of his neck. He lifted the dog aboard while Blair threw Sean a line. The teenager held on as Blair pulled him to the boarding ladder at the stern of his boat. Blair held onto Sean's shirt and pulled as the boy tried to climb the ladder, but his foot slipped off the ladder rung and he fell backwards, breaking Blair's grip. Blair snagged a handful of Sean's shirt, heaved, and pulled him over the transom backwards. "Get in the cabin and strip off," Blair ordered.

"Angus isn't breathing!" Zack called from his boat, a few yards away from *Wee Dram*.

"Do something!" Sean cried.

Dick Herman

Blair reached for his radio. "Rufe, we got Angus on board. He isn't breathing."

"Give him CPR," the blacksmith calmly answered. Blair turned up the volume so Zack could hear. "Check his mouth and throat to make sure it's clear." Zack opened the dog's mouth, inserted two fingers, and pulled out Angus's tongue as Rufus continued to give instructions. Zack laid Angus on his right side and lifted his left forepaw. He placed his ear against the dog's chest and shook his head. There wasn't any heartbeat. The two boats bumped together as Blair shouted the news to Rufus over the radio.

"Be calm," Rufus answered. "Start chest compressions. Not too hard. At the same time, extend Angus's neck as if he were stretching his jaw forward. That will free his airway. If that doesn't work, try mouth to snout."

A stricken look shot across Sean's face when he realized what that meant. He looked pleadingly at Zack, knowing he couldn't do it and hoping the older man would.

"How do I do it?" Zack asked.

"Rufe," Blair transmitted, "please explain."

"Piece of cake," Rufus radioed. "Close his mouth and place your mouth over Angus's nose. Blow through his nose. You should be able to see his chest expand. Do it easy, not too hard."

Zack blew in the dog's nose, but there was no response. Sean scrambled over the rail and onto *Wild Turtle*. He knelt beside Zack as he continued to blow rhythmically into Angus's nose. The dog coughed and opened his eyes. His tongue flicked out, licking the boy's face. "He's okay!" Sean shouted. He gathered Angus into his arms and cradled him.

"Well done, Zack," Blair said. He keyed the radio. "Thanks, Rufe. Angus is breathing. Do you have Pete and Gib in sight?"

"They're about a mile to the west," Rufus answered. "We'll meet you at the dock at Fossil Bay. *Nailing On* standing by channel sixteen."

"Sean," Blair said, "you've to get out of those wet clothes." Sean handed Angus to Blair and scampered back on board *Wee Dram*. He was shaking from the cold as he disappeared into the cabin. Angus was right behind him. "Crawl into your sleeping bag and get warm," Blair ordered. He closed the hatch and inserted the companionway board to give him warmth and privacy.

"Zack," he called, "have you seen Steve?"

"I caught a glimpse of him."

"Which way was he headed?" Blair asked. Given Zack's directional abilities, he knew it was a stupid question. "Into the fog or away from it?"

"Away from the fog," Zack replied.

"He was headed west," Blair reasoned. With his flock accounted for, he keyed his radio. "Coast Guard, *Wee Dram*. Cancel my Mayday call."

A man's voice came over the radio. "*Wee Dram*, this is U.S. Coast Guard cutter Stockdale. Say reason for declaring Mayday."

"I declared a Mayday for a man overboard on my first call. He's safely recovered. The emergency is terminated."

Commander Charles answered. "*Wee Dram*, be advised this is the first we've heard of your emergency. Do you require assistance?"

"Negative, Stockdale. We're proceeding to Fossil Bay. Roche Harbor next."

"Copy all," Charles replied. "Stockdale standing by on channel sixteen."

Zack had monitored the exchange. "It sounds like the Coast Guard needs to get its act together." He sheeted in his main and pulled away from *Wee Dram*. "Which way to Fossil Bay?"

"Follow me," Blair replied.

The FOGs clustered around the picnic table on the dock at Fossil Bay and finished the last of their dinner. Rufus poked at the lone bratwurst still sizzling on the barbecue. "There's one more brat if anyone is still hungry." No one took him up, and after a decent pause, he offered it to Sean who was sitting on the stairs leading to the island.

"Admiral," Zack said, "that was a one close call today. I thought you were going over."

"We were lucky," Blair conceded.

Rufus slapped the bratwurst onto a bun and carried it over to Sean. "You did good today," he told the teenager. Sean didn't reply and took the brat. He wolfed it down. "Hungry, I take it."

Sean looked up, aware that the men were looking at him. "Ah, thanks." Then, "Where did you learn that about dogs? Breathing in their nose."

51

"I worked for a vet when I was your age," Rufus replied. "But it was Zack who actually did it."

"It's all about team work," Blair said. "Sean, that took guts, going into the water like that. I wouldn't have done it."

Sean looked at him in disbelief. "You'd have let Angus drown?"

Blair told him the hard truth. "I'd never risk a life to save an animal or a boat."

"So I screwed up," Sean muttered under his breath. "Again."

"Not at all," Gib said. "What you did was very courageous. You put your life at risk. It was your decision and only yours. It was something I couldn't have done."

"Nor me," Steve said.

"Ditto," Pete added.

"I'm not a very good swimmer," Rufus said. "You would've had to rescue me."

Zack chimed in. "I'm not a dog lover."

"But you saved him," Sean said.

Zack shrugged. "Not really. I just blew in his nose. No big deal. Rufe knew what to do. You did the hard part."

Sean looked at the men. "I did?" Nods all around answered him. He stood and walked into the night, a very confused teenager. Angus bounded after him.

"I think Angus bonded with him," Rufus said.

"When did that happen?" Blair asked.

"Who was the first person Angus saw when he regained consciousness?" Rufus asked.

"Sean," Blair replied.

The blacksmith smiled. "There you are."

Pete stood up and stretched. "Well, folks. It's been a long day. I'm hitting the sack. See you in the morning." The lawyer made his way to *L'Amour* and climbed aboard. He settled in and pulled out his journal.

What a day! Met the Sirens on their Cigarette. Talk about good-looking femmes!!! But after talking to Charles on the Stockdale, they sound like the sexiest bad news known to man. They were probably on a drug run and were caught by the fog and low tide. Losing half a million bucks worth of boat like that must be the cost of doing business. I checked out Steve's depth sounder and it was way out of calibration. I actually felt

Caly's Island

sorry for Sean on the Stockdale, but he would make a nice lampshade with those tattoos. The Admiral was lucky today, very lucky, when that ship came out of the fog. It had to be going fifteen knots, and I don't think it even saw us. Zack said fiberglass boats are invisible to radar. I didn't know that. I've got to give Sean credit for saving Angus when he fell overboard. And what's with Steve? He hasn't been the same since getting that phone call just before we cast off at Squalicum.

Pete closed the log, sealed it in its waterproof case, and crawled into his sleeping bag.

Thirty feet down the dock, Blair sat in the cockpit of *Wee Dram*, listening to the weather forecast. He didn't like what he heard. Sean was snuggled down in his sleeping bag with Angus, both sound asleep. Zack was still at the picnic table, talking to his wife, Angela, on his cell phone. At the end of the dock, Rufus sat in his cabin, wondering if his ex-wife was still with her toy boy. Aboard *Habeas Corpus*, Gib worked on his manuscript, 'Legalizing Prostitution, a Contemporary Solution,' while Steve sat in his cabin cleaning his revolver.

It was still dark the next morning when Blair woke and clicked on the radio. He sat up, fully awake when he heard the latest weather report. A fast moving cold front had overrun a slower moving front over northern Vancouver Island and a doozie of a storm was bearing down on them. He quickly dressed and climbed into the cockpit. Sean was curled up in his sleeping bag with Angus. "Rise and shine," he said. "We have to get moving." Sean heard the urgency in his voice and sat up. Blair climbed onto the dock and looked at the sky. It was dark and overcast, and the wind was freshening. Steve's boat, *High Flyer* was gone. "What now?" he wondered. He hurried from boat to boat, rousing the sleeping FOGs. Then he saw *High Flyer* anchored well away from the dock in the middle of the bay. He shook his head.

The FOGs gathered around *L'Amour* as Blair explained the situation. "The weather prophets blew it big time. The mother of all storms is headed our way, and it should hit late this evening. We either ride it out here, and maybe get caught for a couple of days, or make a break for Roche Harbor. Roche offers the best protection, and they've got docks with electrical hookups, hot showers, a store, a first-class restaurant, a

53

great hotel, all the goodies. It's sixteen nautical miles to Roche, five to six hours sailing time. We can crank the outboards if we have to. If we leave now, we can make it by noon with plenty of time to spare."

"If it's gonna rain like a cow pissing on a flat rock," Rufus said, "I want a nice room with a fireplace. Let's do it." The decision made, Rufus cast off and motored over to wake Steve while the FOGs ate a hasty breakfast, struck their boom tents, and hurried to get under way. The sun was just breaking the horizon when they sailed down Fossil Bay and turned south to enter President's Channel for the run past Orcas Island.

Within twenty minutes, the six boats had shortened sail and were sailing under a single reef as the winds kicked up. Blair was worried and almost turned back for Fossil Bay, but that would have meant punching into the current and the wind, and he wasn't sure the small boats could make headway. Their southerly heading was much smoother sailing and they were moving at five knots. Fortunately, Blair had an extra set of foul weather gear and both suited up. Sean dropped Angus into the cabin and closed the hatch and companionway. Finally, Blair snapped a lifeline onto Sean's PFD. "It's gonna get sporting," he warned the teenager.

For the first time in his life, Sean was truly frightened. "Are we gonna make it?"

Blair tried to make light of it. "No problem. Once buttoned up, our boats are like corks. They can take it."

"Yeah, but can we?" Sean asked.

Blair gave him the best grin he could muster. "You'll have a good war story to tell your buddies."

"I ain't got no buddies," Sean muttered.

Thirty minutes later, Blair was worried. The wind had backed and was threatening to push them onto the lee shore of Orcas Island. He keyed his radio and the FOGs checked in. "Listen up," he transmitted. "Crank up your outboards and power away from the shore."

"Piece of cake," Zack said.

"I'm making good headway," Steve said. "It's a bit rough, but not a problem."

"Just a typical summer afternoon in the Slot on San Francisco Bay," Pete radioed.

"We can head for Reid Harbor on Stuart Island," Rufus suggested.

Caly's Island

"I'm not sure," Blair replied. "There's a lot of rocks around Spieden Island that could be a problem. I'm about ready to send a Mayday."

"We've experienced worse conditions," Gib radioed. "A Mayday call at this time would be premature. Let's continue to make for Roche Harbor. Besides, I would rather die than sound bad on the radio."

The decision was made and the six captains continued to sail south. An hour later, they were hard pressed as the winds kicked up past thirty knots. Four of the boats struck their jibs and were sailing under a double reef with their outboards at full throttle. Rufus had double-reefed *Nailing On's* large single sail and the heavy catboat had the easiest time. Pete in *L'Amour* was still flying his main with a single reef and a storm jib as he pulled away from the five other boats. Blair keyed his radio. "Gib, stay with me and Zack. Pete, keep Steve and Rufe in sight."

"Will do," Pete said. He put the tiller over and jibed, coming about to join Rufus. For a shattering moment, he almost went over, but he quickly righted *L'Amour* and rocketed back to *Nailing On*. This time he tacked into the wind and came about into *Nailing On's* wind shadow to put another reef in his main.

"That was close," Rufus called. "I saw a lot of bottom when you jibed. I thought you were going over for sure."

"So did I," the lawyer admitted. "Where's Steve?"

"I lost him," Rufus replied.

Pete stood and held onto his boom as he scanned the area. "I got him. He's just off Spieden Island. Conditions should be a little calmer over there." But he was wrong and the wind gusted past forty knots.

On *Wee Dram*, Sean was terrified. "I got'a take a leak."

Blair opened a watertight hatch and pulled out a Little Johnny. He handed Sean the red plastic bottle. "Kneel on the sole with your back to me and pee in this. When you're done, dump it over that side." He pointed to the downwind side of the boat.

Sean nodded. Within moments, he had done the deed and emptied the bottle. Suddenly, he felt better. "I'm not seasick," he announced. "Can I steer?"

"You bet," Blair said. He moved aside and let Sean take the tiller. "Hold the main sheet in your left hand and let it go if you feel us tip too far. Steer up the swells at a thirty-degree angle, not straight into them. When you get to the top, turn back about sixty degrees, and go down the backside at a thirty-degree angle and up the next swell. On top, turn back about sixty degrees."

Within minutes, Sean was steering the boat safely through the mounting seas. "Yeah!" he shouted.

With Sean steering, Blair checked on Angus and the bilge. Both were dry. He buttoned up the cabin and swept the horizon. Zack and Gib were right behind him like ducks in trail. Zack pointed at *Wee Dram* and gave a thumbs up. A wave washed over *Wee Dram*, filling the bottom of the cockpit ankle deep, but thanks to their foul weather gear, they were still dry.

"Are we gonna sink?" Sean shouted.

"Nah," Blair replied. "It's just slow to drain. Be patient. If it's too deep, I'll use the bilge pump." Now the rain was driving hard and they had to look away. Blair clenched the side rail and checked on Pete and his group. He could see *L'Amour's* Egyptian cotton sail and *Nailing On's* tanbark sail. But there was no trace of *High Flyer's* red and white sail. He mashed the radio's transmit button. "*L'Amour, Wee Dram.* Do you have *High Flyer* in sight?" Nothing in Blair's voice betrayed his worry.

"Negative, Admiral," Pete answered.

Steve's voice came over the radio, weak but distinct. "I'm on the south side of Spieden Island and making for Reid Harbor on Stuart Island."

"Roger that," Blair replied, wondering why Steve had gone that way. "We're making for Roche." Another wave hit them, flooding the cockpit. "*Wee Dram* standing by on channel sixteen." He snapped the radio onto its holder and pulled out the bilge pump. He pumped hard and drained the cockpit. Again, he checked his GPS. He pointed to their eleven o'clock. "Roche is that way, two miles."

"Are we gonna make it?" Sean asked.

"Oh yeah." A wave crashed over them and flooded the cockpit, forcing Blair to pump hard as the boat started to wallow. Then they were moving and the cockpit drained on its own. Ahead, *L'Amour* and *Nailing On* turned south into the channel leading into Roche Harbor. "Follow them," Blair told Sean. He checked on Zack and Gib. Zack was sitting on the windward rail, keeping the boat upright. Zack Hilber may not have had a clue as to where he was, but he had no trouble handling heavy weather. Gib was sailing in Zack's shadow, using *Wild Turtle* as a windbreak. "Clever devil," Blair muttered, giving the judge high marks.

Caly's Island

"We're almost there," Blair told Sean. "I'll take it." They switched places just as a wave hit them, again flooding the cockpit. "Pump!" Blair shouted. He put the tiller over and turned into the channel. But the boat was wallowing and didn't respond. Blair gave the motor full throttle to give them the push they needed to maintain way. The engine coughed and died as yet another wave hit them, pushing them towards a big rock on their starboard side.

Sean dropped the bilge pump and crawled on top of the cabin. He held the braided wire stay with one hand and the teak handrail with the other as he pushed off the rock with his feet. Another wave hit them and pushed them into the calm waters of Roche Harbor. Zack and Gib rode the next swell to safety, surging through the channel. "Hee-yah!" Zack shouted.

Blair unlashed a gas can and bent over the outboard. "Wouldn't you know it," he groused. "Ran out of gas at the wrong time." He refilled the gas tank and cranked the motor to life. He looked at Sean. "Why don't you check on Angus?" Sean quickly removed the companionway boards and Angus bounced into his arms. Blair pulled out his cell phone and hit the speed dial. Steve answered on the first ring. "Where are you?" Blair asked.

"Stuart Island," Steve answered. "I'm all alone at the dock at Reid Harbor. A bit wet, but no problems."

Blair suspected that was a huge understatement if not a downright lie. Steve had to round Spieden Island and punch into a heavy current to make Reid Harbor. "We'll talk in the morning." He broke the connection and headed for the guest dock to join the other four boats. "There's your mother," he told Sean. Helena Homes was pacing the dock, waiting for them. Pete caught *Wee Dram* as it coasted into the dock. Without a word, Blair and Pete tied the boat up. Helena marched towards them.

Pete gave her his best lopsided grin. "Hello there. What brings you to Roche?"

Helena answered with an angry look. "Commander Charles said you were coming here and I'm checking on my son. What in God's name were you idiots doing?"

"Sailing," Pete replied. "That's why we're here."

Helena glared at him. "Sean," she said, "get your things. We're going home."

"Ah, Mom. I don't wanna go."

Helena whirled on him. "You what?"

"I'm okay. It was fun out there."

For a moment, Helena was at a loss for words. "Sean," Blair whispered, "ask nicely and say please."

"Mom," Sean said, "may I please stay? You said I could go for two weeks."

Gib decided it was time to get involved. "Mrs. Homes, may we speak for a moment? In private." He took her arm and guided her gently down the dock. Once out of earshot, he said, "This is a new experience for Sean and he is truly being challenged. I also suspect that this is the first time he has ever been in the company of adult males for any length of time. Look at him." Helena turned around. Her stepson was standing next to Blair with Angus at his feet, his shoulders back, his head erect. "You are beginning to see the man emerge. Give us a chance and let it happen." She didn't answer. "Please think about it," Gib counseled. He gave her a nod. "There's something we have to attend to." He walked back to the men.

The five FOGs gathered at the edge of the dock and grinned like idiots. Without bidding, they chorused, "Cheated death again!"

Helena shook her head. "Men!"

SIX

The FOGs were gathering for dinner at McMillin's when the storm rolled over Roche Harbor. The wind and rain hit hard, rattling the windows. "There's your cow pissing on a flat rock," Zack told Rufus. They all stood by the windows and peered into the night, trying to penetrate the curtain of rain obscuring the view. "I hope Steve is okay over at Reid Harbor," Rufus said.

"He'll be fine unless the wind veers around to the east," Blair said. "Then it could get sporting."

Pete humphed. "It's rough enough here. Anyone gonna sleep on the boats tonight?" Everyone admitted they had checked into the hotel and planned on enjoying the creature comforts of Roche Harbor until the storm blew through. "What about Angus?" Pete asked Blair. The hotel had a no pets policy.

"He's stayed on the boat alone before," Blair replied.

"I'll stay with him," Sean offered.

"Angus would appreciate that," Blair said, "but your mother hasn't decided if you're staying. Besides, I've got a two-room suite with an extra bed that you can use."

"Angus doesn't snore," Sean said.

Pete laughed. "Gotcha, Admiral!"

"The Admiral is a world class honker," Zack allowed.

"Our own fog horn," Rufus added.

"Gentlemen," Gib said, "I believe dinner is served." They returned to the table and settled in as two waiters brought out trays laden with food. Gib came to his feet when Helena made an entrance worthy of a prima donna of the old school of grand opera. Every eye in the restaurant followed her progress across the floor. "Please join us," he said, holding a chair for her. She sat with a flourish between Gib and Pete.

"The ferry is not running because of the storm," she announced. "And there are no vacancies on the island."

"I'm not surprised," Blair said. "Everyone is running for safe harbor. I was fortunate to get the last room here."

"The Admiral has an extra bed if Sean sleeps on the boat," Pete said. "I can move in with him, and you can have my room." Always the considerate companion, Pete beckoned for the waiter to take her order.

Sean hunched over his fish and chips, his elbows on the table, and played with his dinner. He picked up a rhythm; finger a french fry, snap it up, glare at his mother, bite the fry in half, and drop the remains in his plate. Rufus gave him a gentle poke with his right forefinger, gaining his attention. "So what's your problem?"

"Her," Sean muttered, shooting Helena a look that registered on the Richter scale. He fingered another french fry.

Rufus reached over and held his wrist, breaking the routine. "It's okay to be angry or upset, but you're eating like a pig." He released Sean's wrist. "Gib and the Admiral are eating fish and chips. Watch how they do it." He wagged his forefinger as he talked, holding Sean's undivided attention.

"She's gonna make me go home."

"She might let you stay if you ask right," Rufus counseled. "You got her to reconsider when you asked if you could 'please stay.' It's worth a shot." Sean studied Gib and Blair for a moment. He sat up straight and pulled his elbows off the table as he imitated them. "She's watching you," Rufus said. "Wait for a break in the conversation and tell her what you've been reading."

Sean nodded and waited. When a lull presented itself, he was ready. "Hey, Mom, I've been reading about boat safety."

Helena's head came up. "Really." She sat her fork down, folded her hands in her lap, and leaned forward as Sean related what he had learned from Reed's Nautical Companion.

"It's working," Rufus whispered to Sean. "Now ask if you can please stay on the boat tonight to take care of Angus."

"Mom, can I stay on the boat tonight to take care of Angus? Please."

"Let me think about it," Helena answered. "It's raining very hard."

"Boats are meant to get wet," Pete told her.

Caly's Island

"And what do you know about getting wet?" she asked. Sean listened as Helena and Pete bantered back and forth, their words charged with a not so subtle message. At first, Sean didn't catch it. Finally, he understood and shot Pete a hard look.

Gib caught the look and sensed Sean's anger. It was time to intervene. "I think there's a lull in the rain. This might be a good time to check on the boats and insure they are all double tied." He stood to leave.

"I need to walk Angus," Blair said, joining Gib.

"Sean," Helena said, "go with them, if you still want to stay on the boat tonight." Sean bounced to his feet.

"Say thank you," Rufus murmured. Helena heard it and smiled.

"Thanks, Mom," Sean said.

"Now go kiss her on the cheek and say goodnight," Rufus whispered to him.

At first, Sean hesitated. Then he rushed over and gave her a quick peck on her right cheek. "Guh-night," he muttered. He almost ran from the dining room and didn't see the tears well up in her eyes.

"Rufus," Helena said, "Thank you. I'm sorry for what I said when we first met . . . about your hands."

Rufus blushed and made light of it. "That's okay. I only strangle people in my spare time. You know, Sean really is a good kid." He hurried after Blair and Gib.

"I better go with them," Zack said. He stood and left Pete and Helena alone.

"Well," Pete said, "care for some coffee?"

"Thank you," Helena said. She waited while he poured. "We need to talk." She lowered her voice. "My husband ran background checks on you. Did you know Zack worked for the CIA?"

"Sure did. He told us all about it. But he wasn't an agent or anything like that. He worked in a lab testing electronics. Pretty routine stuff."

"I don't think so," she replied. She sipped her coffee. "There's not much on Steve. We think he's in a witness protection program."

Pete laughed and shook his head. "Steve? No way." He reached out and touched her hand. "Steve is the last guy you need to worry about. He wouldn't harm a fly."

Their fingers intertwined. "I hope you're right." she murmured. "What about you?"

"The same. I'm harmless."

"Oh, I hope not."

Long experience had taught Pete were the conversation was going. A tingle of anticipation ran down his back. "Can I interest you in a drink?"

Helena smiled at him. "Oh, yes. But I'm paying."

Pete played the timing to perfection before returning her smile. "Did you say 'staying' or 'paying'?"

Sean followed the four men down the dock. His shoulders hunched over against the driving the wind. He hovered in the background as they retied *Wild Turtle* and put out another dock line. Satisfied that it was secure, the men moved onto *Habeas Corpus* to check its lines. Gib held back when they were finished and waited for the teenager. "Okay, what's bugging you now?"

For a moment, Sean stared at his feet. "Is Pete sleeping with my mom?"

"I have no way of knowing," Gib replied. "That's very private, but I don't think so."

"Yeah, sure."

Gib took a deep breath and exhaled. "Sean, your mother is a force of nature beyond the control of mere humans. She does what she wants to do, and God help the poor mortal who gets in her way."

From the look on Sean's face, there was no doubt he was a deeply confused teenager. "At school, they call her my big black-assed nanny."

The hurt in his voice tore a hole in Gib's humanity, and he wanted to crush the miserable cretins who could hurt another human that way. No wonder you have problems, Gib thought. "Sean, that's racist, and it was directed at you as well as your mother. Those idiots are incapable of understanding what they're seeing. Your mother is the most beautiful woman I've ever met. Period." He paused to let it sink in.

"She is?"

"Absolutely. Did you see the way everyone looked at her when she came in the restaurant? Half the men wanted to meet her and the other half were afraid to."

"What about the women?"

Caly's Island

"Sean, I'm sixty-eight-years old, and I haven't a clue what women think, especially about other women." The last was the total truth. "Come on, let's get you bedded down. If it gets too rough tonight, come on back to the hotel."

"I can take it," Sean said.

Blair was waiting for them at *Wee Dram*. "It's too windy to rig the boom tent," he told Sean. "But you should be okay. Call me on your cell phone if you have any problems." Sean climbed aboard, and Blair made sure the cabin was sealed tight. He checked the dock lines one last time before joining the other three men at the end of the dock. They were watching the crew of a recently arrived forty-six foot trawler set a second anchor. A burly, dark haired man moved aft to rig a second line to the RIB floating off the stern.

A woman with long blonde hair climbed onto the flying bridge and looked their way. She waved at them. "You know her?" Blair asked.

"Yep," Rufus answered. "She's one of the Sirens."

The storm went nuclear as the sun broke the eastern horizon. An airliner overhead at 38,000 feet witnessed a golden sunrise with a clear blue sky above and a tangled carpet of gray and black clouds below. But at Roche harbor, it was the perfect storm as sustained winds of fifty-eight knots pounded at the buildings and rocked the boats in the harbor. An occasional gust reached hurricane strength and blew shingles off roofs. The docks were awash and impossible to walk on, and the driving rain blinded anyone caught outside without goggles.

Blair was worried about Sean and called him on his cell phone. "How's it going?" he asked.

"S'okay," Sean answered. "I found some Spam and crackers to eat. There's lots of dog food for Angus."

"Stay off the dock until the wind dies down."

"Okay. But Angus has to take a leak."

"Lower the top hatch board and let him out. He knows what to do."

Sean broke the connection and talked to the Jack Russell. "Dude, I hope you know how to do this." He carefully lowered the companionway board and Angus bounced out. Sean struggled to keep it cracked open enough to watch the dog as the wind and rain lashed at him. Angus squatted on the cockpit sole in three inches of water and did his thing. He gave Sean a pathetic look and the teenager roared with laughter. Finished, Angus barked. Sean lowered the board and Angus jumped back inside.

Sean closed them in and rolled the dog up in a towel, rubbing him dry. "Dude, I know how you feel." Angus curled up in his space in the bow while Sean rummaged through the cabin, searching for something to read. He found a sealed plastic box under the V-berth. "What's this?" He pried the lid open and examined the three books inside. They were old, dog-eared, and judging by the Post-it notes stuck to the pages, well read. The books were obviously Blair's constant companions.

Intrigued by his discovery, the teenager picked one up. "Seven Pillars of Wisdom . . . what's that? . . . a religious book?" He laid it aside. "The Illiad." He flipped the pages. "It's a poem. Dumb." The next book was carefully wrapped in thin cardboard with a thick rubber band holding it together. "Dude, this one's falling apart." Sean carefully removed the rubber band and opened the book. He turned to the title page and read aloud. "The Odyssey – translated by Hornsby Bradford Blair." The teenager snorted. "No way the Admiral wrote this. It's got'a be a hundred years old." He started turning pages, continuing to read aloud. "'Dedicated to T. E. Lawrence, commander, mentor, and friend.' Never heard of him. How 'bout you?" Angus barked, alert and listening to every word. Sean was hooked and turned to the opening page. Again, he read aloud.

> "Sing in me, O, Muse, that I may tell
> Of that hero of twist and turns who roamed far and wide
> After he had conquered the sacred heights of Troy."

He rummaged in a box of crackers and pulled out a handful. He threw one at Angus. "What the fuck is a Muse?" Angus barked. "Okay, okay. I get the message." He settled in to read as *Wee Dram* rocked back and forth.

Blair couldn't help himself. Being a worrier by temperament and trade, he called Steve at Reid Harbor. The elder FOG reported that all was well and he had spent a fairly calm night. Blair relaxed a little. He surfed the TV until he found a news channel with on-going coverage of

Caly's Island

the storm. An hour later, he stood at the window until the wind and rain subsided enough to see the docks. Their boats were rocking wildly but still secure. Then the rain descended, howling in fury, and sealing them in a gray darkness.

Zack and Rufus decided to watch movies and settled down in front of the TV in Blair's sitting room. They laughed through a Jim Carrey comedy without too much brain damage, but then made the mistake of watching an Adam Sandler masterpiece cleverly designed to destroy all cognitive function. Fortunately, their loss was only temporary and both regained full use of their thought processes after imbibing half a bottle of Blair's Scotch. The Admiral chalked it up to the curative powers of a good single malt and helped them destroy the bottom half of the bottle.

Gib spent the day in more productive pursuits and worked on his great American legal tome, 'Legalizing Prostitution, a Contemporary Solution.' The legal arguments were straight forward enough, but finding a rationale that a politician could understand was another matter. Frustrated, he called one of his sources, a former call girl he had met in the course of his prosecutorial duties as a deputy district attorney years before. The image on the cell phone was sharp and clear. The woman was in her late forties and tall and slender. On second glance, most men found her regal; on the third, mesmerizing; and on the forth, they were captured. Even without knowing her profession, women hated her. And for good reason. After meeting Marla Mann, the majority of husbands reviewed their marriage certificates looking for loopholes. "Good morning, Marla. How are you?"

"Well, well. Gibson Stanford. It has been a while. I have missed you." Her soft Georgia accent with its hidden promises sent a shiver through the jurist.

Gib wasn't sure if she was still professionally active, but it didn't matter. He wanted her expertise in another area. "I do have a favor to ask." Her gentle smile was encouraging. "Are you still dabbling in the world of finance?" A little nod in answer. Although she was not a CPA or a licensed financial broker, Marla managed the investments and taxes of expensive call girls. "I was hoping you might offer insights on, shall we say, the economic implications of your unique profession."

"Yes, let's say." Marla laughed, enchanting him. "Would you like to see my home?" Gib gave in, knowing the way to gain her cooperation was through her passion for antique furniture. She used her cell phone's camera to give him a quick tour of her home. It was a study in good taste and expensive antiques. She finally arranged herself in the corner of an exquisite couch. The effect was as captivating as ever. "This is for the book, yes?"

He admitted it was. "With no attribution, of course."

Marla nodded. "Of course. I take it you want to know the mundane details of how much we make during our earning years, and how we deal with the IRS."

"Yes, something like that. In general terms, of course."

"Of course." Her voice changed. "But there is a price." Without waiting for a reply, she opened the door to the realities of her world. "Because of our clientele, our income flows follow a predictable pattern, and peak when the legislature is in session formulating a budget." She continued to talk as he made notes, and there was no doubt she was well versed in the economics of the sex trade in California's capital. He was surprised to learn that her clients made more than most doctors and lawyers did after taxes. Of course, that was the crux of it, tax avoidance without being nailed for tax evasion. It was a distinction he appreciated. "I estimate," she told him, "that if the aggregate income of all sex workers in California were taxed at the current rates, along with the tax-exempt campaign contributions our legislators collect, the total gain in tax revenues would retire the State's debt in approximately four years." She laughed. "But that will never happen."

"What an unusual linkage," he ventured.

"The two professions are closely related," she said. "But with one big difference."

"And that difference being?"

"Mine is honorable."

Common sense cautioned him not to pursue that subject. "You've been most helpful," Gib admitted. "And as to the price you mentioned?"

She fixed him with a long look. "Just an honest answer to a simple question. When are you going to marry me?"

* * * *

Caly's Island

Pete and Helena were engaged in a related activity, except no money exchanged hands. They spent the day in bed, and while some might describe their activities as love making, a more sophisticated observer would rely on sporting metaphors. Their activities did garner a noise complaint and the manager did knock on their door. But after a brief conversation with Helena, and as he did not receive hazardous duty pay, the manager ignored all subsequent complaints. Thereafter, the couple next door who had originally complained contented themselves by taking copious notes and sound recordings with their cell phone. It proved to be the highlight of their stay in Roche Harbor and the subject of countless conversations in their retirement years.

Unfortunately for Steve, conditions five miles to the north at Reid Harbor were not as conducive to entertainment, much less survival. The wind veered to the east late in the morning and reached hurricane force velocities. A seventy-five mph wind drove a tidal surge directly into Reid Harbor, sending wave after wave crashing over the dock. Fortunately, the Washington State Parks and Recreation Commission built sturdy floating docks. Unfortunately, *High Flyer* was tied stern on to the wind and waves. Steve soon realized his mistake, and being an intrepid septuagenarian, resolved to move his boat to the inside of the dock where calmer water prevailed and retie it bow on into the wind.

It went terribly wrong from the moment he untied the bow dock line. A wave swept down the harbor and over the dock, knocking Steve down. He dropped the dock line and skidded across the dock, straddling a creosote-soaked piling that saved him from going over the side. Painfully, he crawled back to his boat, which was now floating free except for the one stern dock line. Steve managed to pull the boat back to the dock, but not sure what to do, crawled aboard. Another wave washed over him and smashed the boat into the dock. *High Flyer* had a rugged hull, but no fiberglass boat could take that sort of beating for long. He had to get away from the dock.

On the edge of panic, he started the outboard and waited for a break in the waves surging down the harbor. When he saw a lull, he cut the stern dock line and gunned the motor. He tried to turn around at the end of the dock and head into the lee side next to the shore where the water was calmer. Just as he started to turn, another wave hit him. *High Flyer* rolled ninety degrees and, for a fearful moment, the boat was on the edge of turtling, rolling bottom up with its mast down. But Steve's luck held and the boat righted itself.

Steve gunned the outboard and used both the tiller and motor to turn, this time away from the dock. The boat slowly came around, its bow into the waves. Again, a wave washed over him. *High Flyer* pitched and rocked wildly as the motor stalled. Steve jerked furiously at the starter cord, but the engine refused to start. Another wave pushed him sideways towards the rocky beach at the far end of the harbor. Steve forced himself to remain calm and raised his jib. Immediately, *High Flyer* responded and he made enough way to steer as another wave pooped him. But this time, the push gave him more speed and control. Through the driving rain, he could make out the rocky beach, a hundred yards away.

Then he saw it. The storm had uprooted a large tree and washed it onto the far southern corner of the beach. But the tree had grounded in the shallow waters and debris had piled up against it, forming a breakwater of sorts and creating a small quiet pool in its lee. Rather than run aground on the rocky shore, Steve turned and shot across the waves like a surfer, heading for the small refuge between the tree and the shore. But his timing was wrong and the wave was carrying *High Flyer* into the tree.

Steve did the only thing he could think of and immediately put the helm over, heading up into the wave. Like a surfboard, *High Flyer* kicked out of the wave. Steve made a course correction and headed for the opening, but he wasn't going to make it before the next wave hit. Desperate for more speed, he jerked the outboard's starter cord. The motor roared to life and *High Flyer* shot forward. His keel dragged on the bottom when he punched through the narrow break. The wave crashed into the tree, but *High Flyer* was safe.

Steve was on the edge of exhaustion as he tied two lines to a thick branch, securing the boat in the little harbor. He crawled into the cabin, stripped off his foul weather gear, and slipped into his sleeping bag, totally exhausted and shivering violently.

SEVEN

It was a magnificent morning after. The storm had blown through and the air held the promise of good sailing weather. Blair, Gib, Zack, and Rufus headed for the Lime Kiln Cafe for breakfast where Sean was waiting. He was ravenously hungry, and as befitted a teenager whose energy intake the previous day was below two thousand calories, set to work devouring a sizeable portion of bacon, sausage, eggs, and pancakes.

"You must have gotten pretty tired of Spam," Blair said.

"It was okay," Sean said. "And the dog food wasn't too bad."

"You what?" Blair blurted. "Please don't tell your mother, okay?" The thought of what Helena would do to him if she learned Sean had shared Angus's food necessitated a quick mental review of his life insurance policy. "What did you do all day?"

"Read a book," Sean mumbled with a full mouth. He had the men's undivided attention. "I had to do somethin'."

Blair knew what was on board *Wee Dram* and couldn't imagine what had interested Sean for longer than ten seconds. "What did you read?"

"Ah, that funny story by Homer. The Odd-something. You know, the one about Odd-y-suss, or whatever they called him."

"The book is The Odyssey," Blair said, "and his name is pronounced oh-DIS-use. Sometimes he's called Ulysses."

"It's all Greek to me," Rufus quipped.

For the first time in his life, Sean was caught up in an intellectual conversation and he liked it. "Besides an old copy of The Odyssey, the Admiral's got The Iliad and a book about some Pillars of Wisdom."

"The proper title of the book is 'The Seven Pillars of Wisdom' by T. E. Lawrence," Blair explained.

"I never heard of him," Sean replied.

"He's better known as Lawrence of Arabia. There's a pretty good movie with the same name that's worth watching."

"Admiral," Sean blurted, "did you translate The Odyssey? It's got your name on the cover."

Blair shook his head, smiling slightly. "That was my grandfather, and I'm doing research for his biography. He was a classical scholar and rode with Lawrence in Arabia during World War I. They were good friends.

Gib took over. "Thomas Edward Lawrence and Hornsby Bradford Blair may have been the last Renaissance men to have walked the earth. They were a marvelous blend of poet, scholar, and soldier, and like our Hornsby Blair, both were short in stature, but not in spirit or intellect." The judge smiled mischievously. "And women were, and are, totally beyond their understanding." He laughed.

Sean wanted to know more. "In The Odyssey, what does 'she will unman you and you will be fit for nothing' mean?"

"Who is the she?" Rufus asked.

"Circus, or something like that."

"It's pronounced SIR-see," Blair explained. "In Greek mythology, Circe was a witch or nymph, depending on the story teller. Another god, Hermes, warned Ulysses that if he had sex with Circe, he would be totally subjugated by her."

Sean nodded. "You mean pussy-whipped. Why didn't Hermes just say that?"

"Because it sounds better the way Homer said it," Gib replied. "You'd be surprised what you can say if you use the right words."

"I had to read The Odyssey when I was in high school," Zack said. "I hated it. What a total load of crap."

"Homer is like Shakespeare," Blair explained. "He was meant to be heard, not read."

Sean munched the last piece of toast. "Ulysses sure fu . . . I mean messed around a lot. He shacked up with one woman for seven years on an island and cried a lot."

"That was Calypso," Blair said. He changed the subject. "By the way, was there any storm damage to the boats?"

Caly's Island

"We're okay," Sean replied. "There was a little damage to the docks. Oh, some dude asked where the boat with the red and white sail was."

Rufus's head came up. "Was it one of the guys from that big trawler?"

"Nope. He was off that big white yacht that says 'Saint Petersburg' under the name on the backend. He had a funny accent. I think he was Russian."

"What did you tell him?" Gib asked, recalling the times he had dealt with the Russian Mafia.

"I said Steve was over at Stuart Island."

Blair stood and walked over to the big windows overlooking the harbor. "The trawler and the yacht are gone."

Gib's inner alarm went off. "Perhaps we should check on our good friend." He pulled out his cell phone and punched up Steve's number. "There's no answer," he announced.

Blair heard the concern in Gib's voice. "We need to get going."

The four men were readying their boats when Pete and Helena ambled down the dock. "She certainly has a well-laid look," Rufus muttered to Blair.

"Pete looks unmanned to me," Blair replied.

"I like Sean's word better," Rufus said.

"Well, I better sort out Sean's things if we're going to get out of here this morning," Blair said. He walked back to his boat where Sean was sitting on a white dock box holding Angus. The teenager's eyes darted from his stepmother to Pete and then back again, not certain what was going on. They had arrived together and were much too friendly, which was very suspicious. Sean didn't say a word as Blair piled his bag and sleeping bag on the dock. Finally, the five captains raised their sails and were ready to cast off.

Helena walked over to Blair. "How's the weather?" she asked.

"The forecaster is calling for five clear days before the next front comes through. It should be good sailing."

"Where are you headed?" she asked.

"Over to Stuart Island to meet up with Steve. Not sure after that. The storm changed everything. We might head for Sydney on Vancouver

Island." He checked the other four boats. "Let's do it," he called. As usual, Pete cast off first and headed for the harbor entrance. Rufus was right behind him. "Sean is still welcome to come with us," Blair said.

For a moment, Helena hesitated. "Well, just don't sit there," she told Sean. "The man wants his dog back. Get on board if you're going."

Sean jumped up and gave her a quick kiss on the cheek. "Thanks, Mom." He quickly passed his gear to Blair and climbed on board *Wee Dram*. Angus was the last to board, and Blair followed the other four boats out of the harbor.

A gunshot woke Steve. For a moment, he wasn't sure where he was. His breathing slowed when he remembered. He unzipped his sleeping bag. He was still dressed and quickly pulled on his shoes and a heavy jacket before donning a dark watch cap. He found his glasses as a second shot echoed over the boat. Well into the drill, he drew the Judge from its hiding place and unlocked the hammer. Automatically, he checked the cylinder. It was loaded with two .410 gauge shotgun shells filled with birdshot, and three .45 caliber ACP rounds. Move! Move! he berated himself, rolling the revolver up in a towel and placing it in the rack next to the companionway. The hatch boards were quickly stowed and he climbed into the cockpit. For a moment, the bright sun blinded him. A third, much sharper, gunshot echoed over the harbor. That sounds like a high-powered rifle, he thought.

For the first time, he could see his surroundings. He was behind a huge tree and floating on a shallow pool of water barely large enough to hold *High Flyer*. He was close to the shore and could step onto dry land without getting wet. Above him, *High Flyer*'s masthead almost reached the top of the branches. Thanks to pure, blind luck, and the decision to move during the height of the storm, the boat was well concealed. He checked his cell phone. No reception. Then reality kicked in. He was in a fight up to his neck and his life expectancy had taken a sharp downward turn.

Steve forced himself to eat a power bar and drain a bottle of water. Feeling better, he ate an apple. The distinctive rattle of an AK-47 split the air followed by an explosion. "Don't panic," he told himself. "You always knew this could happen. Be cool." A wispy trail of smoke drifted over him. Was it time to abandon the boat and run for cover on the

Caly's Island

island? He didn't know, but the time to make a decision was growing shorter. He hung a set of binoculars around his neck and climbed into the tree for a better look. He worked his way through the thick branches, reached a spot with a clear view of the harbor, and slowly raised his binoculars. A sleek white motor yacht was anchored next to shore and looked unmanned. Further on, a big trawler was tied up to a mooring and on fire, sending billows of smoke down the harbor. He swept the scene, carefully adjusting the focus, and froze. A body was lying on the dock. A shot rang out and the body jerked from the impact. Steve lifted the binoculars and saw a shadow moving through the trees. It materialized into a man carrying a hunting rifle with a scope.

The man stopped and looked directly at him. Steve dropped the binoculars, afraid the shooter had caught a reflection off the lenses. Panic ripped at him. Get a grip! You've been in worse situations. Slowly, the panic died away and he was in control again.

Fairly certain that he was still hidden from view, Steve didn't move as he considered his options. The smoke from the burning trawler turned black as the fire set, and he chanced another sweep with his binoculars. There was no doubt the trawler was abandoned. He scanned the trees but couldn't find the man with the rifle. Another shot rang out answered by a burst of submachine gun fire. Someone was in a very serious firefight. He checked the dock again and caught a glimpse of a RIB bobbing on the backside of the dock. Certain there was a connection, he zoomed in on the body lying close by. The angle was bad, but he could see a mane of blonde hair. A woman. "Oh, no," he muttered. It was one of the Sirens.

Pete had barely cleared Roche Harbor when he saw the smoke rolling out of Reid Harbor over two miles away. He keyed his radio. "All FOGs, how copy *L'Amour*?" The other four boats quickly checked in. "Heavy smoke is pouring out of Reid Harbor. Something big is on fire. I don't see Steve."

"Copy all," Blair transmitted. "Press ahead. Steve is out there somewhere."

"We'll find him," Pete replied. "There's a fog bank forming around Spieden Island and moving towards Reid Harbor."

"That doesn't make sense," Blair replied. "The conditions are all wrong for fog."

73

"Well, there it is," Pete replied.

Gib's voice came over the radio. "I would venture we are experiencing a local abnormality and can easily avoid it. We need to concentrate on finding Steve."

"Roger that," Pete replied. "I'll call the Coast Guard and report the fire."

"Sean's already called it in on 9-11," Blair said.

"Well done," Zack radioed.

"Roger that," Rufus added. As one, the five FOG's started their outboards and raced for Reid Harbor.

A single muffled gunshot from the far side of Stuart Island echoed over Steve. "It's moving away," he told himself. His eyes were burning from the smoke and he could barely see the dock and the white motor yacht. "Time to get the hell out of Dodge," he decided. He climbed down out of the tree and quickly untied *High Flyer*. The motor started on the first pull and Steve backed out. He gunned the engine and headed for the harbor entrance, hiding in the smoke. Much to his dismay, the fire on the trawler was burning itself out and the smoke thinning. "Come on," he urged, twisting the throttle harder. The man with the rifle emerged out of the trees above the dock. He dropped to a shooter's crouch and carefully aimed, centering the crosshairs on Steve's head as he squeezed the trigger.

Pete heard the gunshot and keyed his radio. "I hear gunfire coming from Reid Harbor!" he yelled.

"This is the Coast Guard Cutter Stockdale. Vessel reporting gunfire, identify yourself."

Before Pete could answer, he heard another shot, but this one was much duller. "Roger, Stockdale. This is sailboat *L'Amour*. I just heard another gunshot. But this one sounded like a pistol."

"Copy all," the Stockdale replied. "Stay clear of Reid Harbor. Repeat, stay clear of Reid Harbor. We're headed your way, ETA thirty-five minutes."

Caly's Island

"Copy all," Pete replied. "*L'Amour* standing by on channel sixteen." He never slowed and headed straight for Reid Harbor. The FOGs were right behind him.

Steve crouched in the cockpit of *High Flyer* and steered with one hand as he squeezed off a second round in the general direction of the dock. He had no illusions of hitting anything with the Judge at that range, but hoped it would drive the shooter to cover. It did and he raced past the burning trawler. He checked *High Flyer* for damage. A single bullet had drilled through the port gunwale three inches from his head and continued out the other side. "The bastard can shoot," he growled. Now he could see the mouth of the harbor and the looming fog bank coming from Spieden Island. He headed for the fog bank and safety.

Pete was a mile short of Reid when he saw *High Flyer* emerge from the harbor. He hit the radio transmit key. "*High Flyer*, *L'Amour* has you in sight." There was no answer.
"I don't think he's monitoring the radio," Zack radioed. "It looks like he's headed for the fog bank."
"A RIB's chasing him!" Pete transmitted. "A half mile behind."
"What the hell is going on?" Zack shouted over the radio.
Blair took charge. "Everyone, cool it. Pete, keep Steve in sight." A gunshot echoed from the RIB.
"Admiral!" Pete shouted. "There's two guys in the RIB. One's shooting at Steve."
Blair's voice was cool and measured on the radio. "Gib, contact the Coast Guard and advise them of the situation. It looks like Steve is trying to hide in the fog bank."
"I see another RIB," Pete radioed. "It's chasing the first one down." The distinctive rattle of an AK-47 split the air followed by the sharp crack of a rifle. "They're shooting at each other!"
Blair's voice never changed. "Everyone head for the fog bank and hide there. I'm right behind you." Simultaneously, the five boats turned to starboard, away from the harbor entrance and towards the nearby fog bank. "Sean," Blair said, "take the tiller and keep your head down." Sean quickly traded places with Blair. "Head straight for the fog," Blair

75

ordered. He stood and scanned the scene with his binoculars. The lead RIB erupted in smoke and flames, driving Blair down. An explosion echoed over them. "Scratch two shooters," Blair said. He focused on the second RIB that was dead in the water and sinking. "Sean, head for that boat. I see someone in the water. I'm padlocked on the man overboard, you keep your eyes on our guys."

"Got 'em," Sean said, doing his best to imitate Blair's cool. Then, "I lost 'em. They're all in the fog now."

"They'll be safe there," Blair replied. He waited, counting down the minutes as they closed in on the motionless body. He could see long blonde hair trailing behind the body. "Almost there. Cut the engine." Sean retarded the throttle to idle. "Come to port five degrees. Good, good, five more degrees." Blair reached over the side and pulled the woman into the boat. She was unconscious and bleeding badly from her left side. "Okay, head for the fog bank but don't go into it."

Blair dropped the hatch board and gently lifted the woman into the cabin. Once inside, he quickly stripped off her PFD, heavy jacket, and outer clothes to prevent hypothermia. "Is that what passes for underwear these days?" he muttered, carefully examining her wounds. She had a nasty bruise on her left temple and a single bullet hole in her left side where age would grow a love handle. He shook out his first aid kit and found a packet of compress bandages. By using two compress bandages and wrapping an Ace bandage around her body, he managed to slow the bleeding to a trickle. Finally, he wrapped her in his sleeping bag before joining Sean in the cockpit. He snatched the VHF radio out of its holder and called Rufus. *"Nailing On, Wee Dram.* I've got an unconscious woman on board with a gunshot wound. I've got most of the bleeding stopped, but I need your help." There was no answer.

"What do we do now?" Sean asked.

"Wait for the Coast Guard," Blair replied. "They should be here in fifteen minutes or so."

"I don't think we got fifteen minutes," Sean said, pointing to Reid Harbor. The white yacht was bearing down on them at a high rate of speed, its bow high in the air.

Blair raised his binoculars and focused on the fast-moving boat. A man was crouched on the bow holding a submachine gun. "Head for the fog," he told Sean.

EIGHT

High Flyer punched out of the fog and into the sun. Steve cut the outboard and looked around. He was in a pocket, like the eye of a hurricane, and completely surrounded by fog. The glare reflecting off the water blinded him, and he raised his right hand to shield his eyes. Out of ideas, he backed his jib, let the main sheet go, and put the tiller to windward. The boat hove-to and he was dead in the water. Within moments, he was in a dead sweat and peeled off his jacket and sweater.

Long experience had taught him how quickly he sunburned, and he rummaged around in the cabin until he found a wide-brimmed hat and sunscreen. He slathered on the sunscreen and shed his shoes and heavy socks before checking the temperature. It was thirty degrees Celsius, which he easily converted to 86 degrees Fahrenheit. Then it hit him. "Warm temperature and fog? "No way."

He was caught in a meteorological impossibility, but there it was. He studied his compass. It was swinging back and forth, hunting for magnetic north.

Thoroughly puzzled, he turned on his GPS. It cycled and announced no signal. "That's strange," he muttered, checking the menu to see what satellites were overhead. Again, the screen was blank and the device continued to hunt. "That makes no sense." He turned on his VHF radio and hit the transmit button. "Any station, radio check." There was no answer and he cycled to channel one for a weather report. Again, there was nothing, only light static. Out of ideas, he checked his watch. The hour hand was jumping around and the number in the date window was stuck between what looked like 5 and 6. It jumped to 31 as he watched. He felt the sharp point of panic jabbing at him. "You're delusional," he told himself. He had been under enormous pressure since the telephone call at Bellingham and the bill had come due.

He took a long drink of water and tried to relax, but he failed miserably. *L'Amour* emerged from the fog with *Nailing On* close behind. The two boats turned together and headed for him. At least he had company in his delusional state.

"Ahoy, *High Flyer*," Pete called. He had already stripped down and was wearing shorts and a T-shirt. "Where the hell are we?"

"I was hoping you would know," Steve answered. "My GPS and compass aren't working."

Pete coasted to a stop on the down-sun side of Steve to take advantage of the shade from *High Flyer's* sail. "Neither are mine," Pete said.

"I can't raise anyone on the VHF," Steve added. He checked his GPS. "I'm not getting a satellite signal." They waited for Rufus to come alongside.

The blacksmith was much more upbeat. "We got to come here again!" The three boats rafted up in the gentle swells. "There's Gib," Rufus said, pointing to the fog bank. He quickly stripped down to his boxer shorts and went over the side for a swim. He paddled around the boats on his back, his knees pulled up to his chest. "Is there a warm current in the San Juans?" he asked.

"Not that I know of," Pete answered. "What kind of stroke is that?"

"Give me a break. I had a deprived childhood and learned to swim in a bathtub."

Gib reached the three boats and rafted up next to Pete. Like them, he had shed his heavy clothes and rolled up his sleeves. He sat in *Habeas Corpus* and stared at his GPS without saying a word. Rather than comment, he turned it off and tapped his compass. It was swinging back and forth. "I assume your radios are not working," he said.

"Afraid so," Steve answered, his voice tense. "And my watch keeps jumping around."

"Mine's spinning," Pete said. They exchanged worried glances, afraid to vocalize the panic that was stalking them. Pete stood on the foredeck of *L'Amour* and scanned the fog bank. "There's the Admiral," he said. Blair's blue and white sail emerged out of the fog. Rufus stretched out his stroke and swam a few yards away. "Rufe, my man," Pete called. "You might want to rethink that. I see a couple of dorsal fins

Caly's Island

coming our way." Rufus set a record in the panic stroke and almost flew out of the water and over the stern of his boat. He dried off as they waited for Blair to join them.

Sean guided *Wee Dram* towards the four boats. Blair's lips compressed into a tight line and his eyes darted back and forth as he tried to understand what was happening. The "No Signal" warning on his GPS was worrisome but not critical; however, his wandering compass and the spinning hands on his watch were of deep concern. Blair was a navigator of the old school, and he could do without the electronic gadgets so many relied on, but time and compass heading were the rock-hard constants of his life. A whisper of panic demanded to be heard, but he forced it into the walled niche that had served him so well flying combat. He keyed his VHF radio to see if he could raise anyone. Nothing. He calmly turned the radio off and dropped it in its holder on the bulkhead. What the hell is going on? he asked himself. For a brief moment, the panic was back. He stepped on it with a vengeance as years of experience flying fighters kicked in. "First things first," he muttered.

"Man," Sean said, "I've never seen fog like this."

"It is unusual," Blair allowed. He glanced at Sean, relieved that the teenager was calm and in control. "Let the main sheet go," Blair said. Sean released the line and the boat slowed, giving Blair time to think before they joined up. He took stock of his companions. They were all seasoned sailors and could handle emergencies. But this was beyond anything he had ever experienced, so how would they react? Set the example, he told himself. Don't let fear take hold.

"Ahoy, *Wee Dram*," Pete called from *L'Amour*. "Have you seen Zack?"

"I was hoping he was with you," Blair answered, forcing his voice to remain calm.

"Admiral," Steve blurted, "what's wrong with our GPS?" A chorus of shouts echoed over the five boats.

Blair whistled loudly, quieting them. "Hey! I just got here. First things first. Is anyone sinking?" They all shook their heads. "Good. Rufe, I've an unconscious woman on board, one of the Sirens, I think. She's been shot in her left side below the ribs, and I can't stop the bleeding. Can you patch her up?"

"I can try," Rufus said. He disappeared into his cabin.

"Okay," Blair said, working hard to stay the panic he could feel building in his companions. "I'm guessing we're caught in some sort of local magnetic abnormality that we can sail out of."

Sean perked up. "You mean like the Bermuda Triangle or a time warp?"

Blair nodded, thankful for the teenager's quick imagination. "Roger on the Bermuda Triangle, but time warp? I don't think so."

"Why aren't we getting a GPS signal?" Steve asked.

"Who knows?" Blair replied. "Just remember what they call folks who rely on a GPS." He paused before delivering the punch line. "They're called lost. Electrons and water don't mix." It was enough to break the rising tension.

Rufus emerged from his cabin with a large first aid kit and a thick manual. He tossed the book to Sean. "I'm gonna need some help." He crawled into *Wee Dram's* cabin and hunched over the unconscious woman. He opened his medical kit. "Sean, find the section on gunshot wounds." He scrubbed his hands with disinfectant.

Blair took charge. "Gib, crank up your shortwave-multi band radio. See if you can pick up a station – shortwave, FM, AM, anything. Pete, try to call someone, anyone, on your cell phone. Steve, work the VHF and try to raise anyone on any channel. Also, see if you can get a weather report on channel one, but I don't think we're gonna hear a thing until we sail out of this area. Everyone, check your boat from top to bottom. Check your bilge, rigging, motor, you name it. Go over everything with a fine-tooth comb. We don't need any nasty surprises like a rudder falling off."

Rufus pulled on Latex gloves and looked at Sean who was crouched in the companionway with the open first aid manual. "Okay, start reading."

"Call 9-1-1 as soon as it is clear a gun is involved."

"Can't do that," Blair said. "No phones – yet."

Sean continued reading. "Follow basic first aid. First, keep the airway open and clear. Insure the victim is breathing."

Rufus opened her mouth and held her head back to extend her neck. He probed her mouth with a finger and moved her tongue aside. She was breathing regularly. "Nice teeth," he allowed. "Twenty-four years old."

"She's not a horse," Blair said.

Sean read. "Next, control any bleeding."

Caly's Island

Rufus gently removed the compress bandages and examined the wound in her side. "That's a problem," Rufus admitted. "Hand me that bottle of Betadine antiseptic in the first aid kit."

"You ever treat a gunshot wound?" Blair asked.

"Nope," Rufus replied. "Sean, keep reading."

Zack Hilber was lost, but that was the least of his problems. He was caught in a storm and taking a ferocious beating. After a fierce struggle, he had doused his mainsail, and, thanks to roller furling, he was only flying a hanky of a jib. The waves kept growing, and he used his outboard to power into them. He tried to punch up a twenty-footer, but it broke before he could top it. The wave crashed down and *Wild Turtle* broached to port, finally rolling over. But the sturdy fifteen-footer popped to the surface like a cork and righted itself. Only the short lifeline Zack had snapped to his PFD kept him in the boat, and he came up, still in the cockpit, and coughing up copious amounts of water. He jerked at the motor's starting cord, but the engine wouldn't start.

Battered and tired, Zack turned and ran with the storm, surfing the waves on the wildest roller coaster ride of his life. He raced down the steep face of a wave and realized he was going too fast. He tried to angle off a few degrees as he bottomed out in the trough. But the bow dug in just as he put the tiller over and the stern came up, threatening to pitch-pole the boat forward, over the bow and onto its back. Somehow, the bow came up and *Wild Turtle* leapt out of the water as another wave overtook him. The sloop slammed into the water and shot down the wave. Zack sawed at the tiller, desperate to angle down the face of the wave. The wave broke behind him and the cascading water washed over him, again rolling the boat.

But *Wild Turtle* wouldn't die and righted itself, the cockpit full of water. The waterlogged boat lay abeam of the waves and rocked as a small wave rushed past. The bow dock line attached to the bow cleat uncoiled and whipped at him. "What the . . ." he shouted, brushing the line away. A larger wave bore down on him and he froze. Next in line was the mother of all waves, and there was no way he was going over it. He had to bring *Wild Turtle's* nose into the wave and hope he could punch through. The dock line whipped at him, again capturing his attention.

Dick Herman

Zack shook his head, forcing the cobwebs of hypothermia away. "Son of a bitch!" he roared, finally remembering the bucket Blair had given him. He opened the lazaret under the port seat and hauled out a five-gallon canvas bucket and fifty feet of line. He quickly closed the compartment before it flooded. As long as the bilge and cabin remained dry, he had a chance. First, he tied one end of the line to the bucket's rope handle and the other end to the bow dock line. Next, he punched a hole in the bottom of the bucket with his knife and tossed the bucket overboard, letting the combined eighty feet of line trail out. The improvised sea anchor dug in and *Wild Turtle* 's bow swung around. The wave washed under the boat and he slid down the backside of the wave. The line tightened and pulled the bow into the on-coming monster wave.

The wave bore down on him and a strange calm claimed Zack. *Wild Turtle* 's bow rose up in the wave, passing sixty degrees. "Angela, I love you," he whispered, now certain he was going to die. He watched the canvas bucket rise up in the wave and then disappear over the crest. Zack held on and prayed. "Forgive me, Father, for I have sinned and truly repent for those I have killed."

Sean read from the manual. "Aggressively irrigate the wound with antiseptic. Probe the wound with a finger and remove the bullet and as much debris and torn cloth as possible." Rufus flooded the wound with the Betadine and inserted his forefinger. "Agitate the fluid to flush the wound," Sean said. Rufus probed the wound with his finger and slowly extracted his finger. Blood gushed out. He jammed his finger back into the wound to apply pressure and stop the bleeding. It didn't work and he almost panicked. Fortunately, Sean's calm recitation kept him on track. "Probing and proper irrigation will momentarily increase bleeding; however, if not excessive, it is beneficial for mechanically reducing the bacteria count." Rufus forced himself to wait, and after a few moments, the bleeding tapered off. Within minutes, the wound was only oozing the last of the antiseptic.

"The bullet is in there pretty deep," Rufus said, "so I'm not going to mess with it." He closed the wound with a butterfly bandage to let it drain. He pulled off his gloves and surveyed his handiwork. "The bleeding's stopped," he announced. He wiped the woman's face with a damp cloth. "You are beautiful," he said in a low voice. Her eyes opened. "Hello, there."

"What are you doing?" she asked, her eyes fixed on Rufus's face.

"Applying first aid. You've been shot."

"Who are you?"

"We call ourselves the FOGs for Freakin' Old Guys. My name is Rufus, that's Sean, and the Admiral is behind him. And you are?"

"Alexandra, but I am called Sasha. Did you get the bullet out?"

Rufus didn't recognize her accent. "It's still in there, but the bleeding's stopped."

"Bullets are unpredictable," Sasha said. "Thank you, Mr. Rufus."

"Get some rest," Rufus said. He covered her with Blair's silk sleeping bag liner and crawled out of the small cabin. "It's getting pretty hot in there," he told the FOGs. "I've got more room and better ventilation on *Nailing On*. Maybe we should move her." The FOGs agreed and they carefully transferred Sasha to *Nailing On*. Rufus helped her settle into his cabin and opened the portholes and forward hatch. He climbed back into the cockpit. The other four men were huddled together on *Habeas Corpus* comparing notes. Their radios, cell phones, and GPS's were still not working, but their boats were sound.

"Oh, oh," Rufus said. The fog bank was lifting and all he could see was clear blue sky and an empty ocean.

"Gentlemen," Gib said in his best courtroom manner, "we are, if I may use a most appropriate phrase, in deep shit."

By any measure, Zack's situation was growing worse as the wave rose up above him. The line to the sea anchor straightened and snapped as it took the strain and cut down through the wave's crest. The wave broke and tumbled down on him. Much to Zack's surprise, the sea anchor pulled him through and he popped out the backside of the wave. Totally exhausted, he sat in the cockpit and braced for the next wave. But this one was much smaller and *Wild Turtle* bobbed over the top, its bow still into the waves. At the top, he saw the sea anchor. "What the . . ." he muttered. A calm slick of water spread out in a V behind the sea anchor, much like an oil slick, creating a lee shadow.

He was unbelievably thirsty and opened the lazaret under his bench, pulling out a water bottle. He quickly drained it, shivering uncontrollably from the cold. *Wild Turtle* crested another wave, now riding out the storm. Zack made a mental note to thank Blair for the bucket and teaching him how to use it. On the edge of exhaustion, he rolled up the last of the jib and crawled into the small cabin. He sealed the hatchway and stripped off his foul weather gear. Underneath, his clothes were soaking wet. He peeled them off and pulled on a set of sweats before crawling into his sleeping bag. An instant later, he was asleep.

Outside, the winds gusted past sixty knots and whipped the sea into a frenzy.

Pete sat in *L'Amour's* cockpit as the FOGs debated what to do next. He gave Blair high marks for the way he kept them focused and on task. Without doubt, Blair's priorities were right and they had to find land, but it didn't help that no one knew where they were. The lawyer made a silent promise to remain calm and supportive. He knew when it was time to follow. A fin flash caught his attention and he reached for his camera. He snapped a photo of the two dorsal fins cutting a circle around the boats. "Hey, Rufe," he called, doing his part to break the tension, "they're dolphins. They wouldn't have eaten you."

Rufus eyed the brown cetaceans moving gracefully beneath the surface. "Lost members of the Delphinidae family." Together, the dolphins shot off towards the horizon, only to return a few moments later. Again, they circled the boats. "I guess they like us," the blacksmith said.

"Or else they're hungry and waiting for you to go swimming," Pete said. After two orbits, the dolphins swam off in the same direction. "Later, alligator," Pete quipped.

Blair stood up in *Wee Dram* and held onto the boom. "They're coming back," he announced. "I wonder?"

"Wonder what, H?" Gib asked, also intrigued by the dolphin's behavior.

"I think they want us to follow them," Blair said.

Steve scanned the empty horizon. "What have we got to lose? The wind's picking up."

"And we can't just stay here in the middle of nowhere," Pete added. To make his point, he shook the reef out of his mainsail and raised a Genoa, the biggest foresail he had on board.

Caly's Island

"Gentlemen," Blair said, "my compass is alive and stable." Encouraging shouts answered him as the FOGs discovered their compasses were also working. "But my GPS is still hunting for a signal." The men quickly checked their individual sets, all with the same result. "That doesn't make sense. There's always a couple of satellites overhead. Turn 'em off and save the batteries."

"My watch has stopped spinning," Steve said. They compared times but none agreed.

"H," Gib said, "May I suggest you pick a common time for us to use." Like Pete, he was getting behind Blair.

Blair checked the sun. "I'm guessing it's late afternoon, say five o'clock." The men all set their watches to five p.m. "Our nautical friends indicate northeast is the preferred direction, so let's do it." He cast off from the other boats and sheeted in the mainsail. Within moments, the five boats were following the dolphins. "Sean, take the tiller and hold a compass heading of zero-four-zero degrees. I need to make a chart and plot our course."

"You can make a map?" Sean replied.

"Sort of." Blair dove into the cabin and emerged with his navigation bag. He pulled out a chart of the San Juans and turned it over to the blank backside. He drew a tic-tac-toe grid with his plotter and dividers and arbitrarily assigned thirty nautical miles to the side of each square. Next, he added a few vertical and horizontal lines to make the grid bigger, and marked the top of the vertical lines with 'Mag N' for magnetic north. Satisfied that he had a workable plotting grid, he drew a little circle, about the size of a dime, in the middle of the center grid. He dotted the center of the circle and wrote 17:00 beside the circle. "Okay, that's where we are now."

"But where is it?" Sean asked.

"I have no idea. I'm just plotting our course." Using his magnetic north lines as a reference, he plotted a vector at a forty-degree angle out of the little circle. "That's the magnetic course we're sailing." He wrote C-040-M on top of the line. "The C stands for course, the zero-four-zero for our heading, and the M for magnetic. Now how fast do you think we're going?"

"The speedometer says we're going three knots," Sean replied.

"It's called a knotmeter and tells how fast we're moving through the water." He wrote S-3.0 below the C-040-M. "The S stands for speed, and the three point zero for how fast we're going. Divide three into sixty and we're going a nautical mile every twenty minutes. So in forty minutes we'll have gone two nautical miles along the course line that I drew, if you can hold a heading of zero-four-zero."

Sean quickly corrected their heading back to 040. "Sorry," he said.

"Hey, this is all new, and you're learning," Blair told him. He spanned off two nautical miles with his dividers and placed a dot on the line two nautical miles from the circle. He drew a half circle around the dot and wrote 17:40 beside it. "That's called a DR position. DR stands for dead reckoning."

Sean was worried. "Dead?"

Blair laughed. "It has nothing to do with death. It stands for deduced. That's where I think we will be at 17:40. If we change our heading then, I'll draw in the new course line from that point, based on our new compass heading, and plot our next DR position along that line."

The proverbial light bulb came on over Sean's head. "So if I change heading at" – he thought for a moment – "twenty minutes from now, at 17:30, you'd plot a DR position one and a half nautical miles from where we started and draw in our new course from there."

"Well done," Blair said. "But you don't have to plot it immediately. All you do is keep track of the time when you turn, the new compass heading, and the speed." He showed Sean how to keep a log on the edge of the chart.

"Can I plot our DR position for right now?" Sean asked.

"You bet." He took the helm while Sean plotted a DR position and placed the time beside it. "That's where you think we are right now," Blair announced. "If our GPS was working, you could write our latitude and longitude beside it, make it a full circle, and you'd have a fix. Piece of cake." From the look on Sean's face, it was. "Okay, your turn to steer. Compass heading: zero-four-zero degrees." They switched places.

Blair stood and checked on his flock, determined not to let Sean see how worried he was. As expected, they were spreading out with Pete in the lead. Steve was well to the west, with Gib and Rufus less than a hundred yards to his starboard. He swept the horizon with his binoculars hoping to see Zack's red and yellow sail. But there was no trace of *Wild Turtle*, so he checked their rear quadrant. "I'll be damned," he said. The

Caly's Island

fog bank was back in the same place. He picked up the makeshift chart, shaded in the area around their starting point, and labeled it 'Fog Bank.'

Wild Turtle came off the crest of a wave and slammed into the trough. The jolt woke Zack from a deep sleep and he blinked, forcing himself awake. His watched glowed in the dark – 03:15. He had slept over six hours. Well, he decided, that's one way to ride out a storm. He held onto the center post and squinted out the porthole. It was pitch-black outside and the storm had subsided somewhat. A big wave crashed over the boat, squelching that idea. Time to eat, he thought, fishing around in the bilge for an MRE, Meal Ready to Eat. He opened one of the small packages and wolfed it down cold. A loud crack filled the cabin as the sea anchor's rode let go. The constant chafing where the line passed through a line chock had finally worn through the heavy Nylon line. *Wild Turtle* broached, side on to the wind and sea.

Zack held on as the boat slowly righted. He set a record pulling on his foul weather gear and PFD. The boat bucked as he struggled out of the cabin, but before he could slide the hatch back in place, a wave crashed over him and partially flooded the cabin. He sealed the cabin, snapped on his lifeline, and unrolled a corner of the jib off the roller furling. He grabbed the loose jib sheet and jerked it tight as he put the tiller over. Slowly, the water-laden boat responded. Fortunately, the waves had set down and he was sailing. A bolt of lightning streaked across the sky.

He shook his head. "Well, I'll be," he muttered. In the flash of light, he had seen a sailboat less than a hundred yards away. It was approximately sixty-feet long and sailing under bare poles, with a bank of oars stroking the water. The night enveloped the boat and it was gone. *Wild Turtle* crested a wave and, in the distance, he saw a beacon in the night. It winked at him as he came down the wave. He sailed up the next wave as another bolt of lightning split the dark. The strange boat was further away and barely making headway against the waves as it headed for the beacon. He blinked his eyes. The boat was a galley right out of a Greek epic with a pointed bow for ramming and a raised poop deck for archers. "Somebody's making a movie," he decided. Obviously, they had been caught in the storm like him.

Dick Herman

Wild Turtle surged over a wave and, again, he saw the light. For the first time, he checked his GPS. His agile fingers punched at the buttons, but there was no satellite signal. "These puppies never work when you really need them," he groused to himself. Frustrated, he turned off the offending instrument, threw it in the cabin, and checked his compass. His heading was due south, directly for the beacon and safety.

NINE

Because he was a natural worrier, Blair's main hobby was obsession and he was setting a new record in that department. He could explain the inoperative cell phones and lack of GPS satellite signals, but why were their radios dead? No matter how he analyzed their situation, he couldn't explain it. Somehow, the FOGs had sailed through the fog and emerged into a magnificent ocean, warm and calm, with gentle swells and a following breeze. Majestic cumulus clouds drifted across the sky, creating pockets of shade on the azure sea and breaking the heat. But it simply didn't make any sense, and he rejected the idea that they had died and gone to a sailor's paradise.

And where was Zack? And what about the woman who called herself Sasha when her name was Alexandra? Without doubt, she was a dangerous commodity. Was there a connection with Steve? He scoffed at the idea. Steve! Mr. Meek of the nonentity crowd threatened by one of the most beautiful woman he had ever met? That made no sense.

He forced himself to concentrate on their immediate problem. They had to make a landfall. He was confident they had enough food between them to last four or five days, maybe a week without fishing, and Gib had an emergency reverse osmosis water filter that would keep them all hydrated. First things first, he reasoned. Let's get through the night. He leaned against the cabin bulkhead and looked at Sean. Could he rely on him? The teenager was comfortable at the tiller with Angus curled up beside him. He was holding a steady compass heading, constantly adjusting the sails, and wringing out every bit of speed possible. They were making a steady four knots as the sun disappeared below the horizon. Without doubt, Sean was turning into an excellent helmsman.

"Hungry?" Blair called. Sean grinned and bobbed his head. "I can heat up some beef stew."

"Sounds better than dog food," Sean allowed.

"You're not going to let me forget that, are you?" Blair climbed into the cabin and rigged a gimbled one-burner propane stove to the center post. He opened a can of beef stew and poured it into a pan. Although it was smooth sailing and the stove swung gently back and forth, he closely watched it with a fire extinguisher at hand.

"*L'Amour* is coming back," Sean called.

Blair poured half the beef stew into a bowl and handed it to Sean along with a box of crackers. He opened a can of dog food for Angus and finished off the stew while waiting for Pete to join up. It was the end of evening twilight as the five boats rafted up and a beautiful starlit sky emerged overhead.

"What now, Admiral?" Pete asked. "Heave-to for the night?"

Blair considered their situation. "What happened to the dolphins?"

"Last I saw," Pete answered, "they were still headed to the northeast."

"Admiral," Sean said, pointing to the north, "where is the North Star?"

"Sean," Blair said, "thanks for reminding me of the obvious." He dove into the cabin and came out with a black plastic case. He snapped it open and pulled out a sextant. "Sean, can you update our DR position?"

The FOGs watched as the teenager mentally calculated the distance run since plotting their last DR position on Blair's makeshift chart. "We've averaged four knots since 17:40 so we've gone twelve nautical miles." He spanned off the distance and marked their current DR position along the magnetic vector Blair had already plotted on the grid. He wrote in the time, 20:40.

"If you're trying to make me look bad," Rufus groused, "you're doing a damned good job of it." Sean grinned at him. In his own way, Rufus was determined to keep cool.

"I thought you had to be able to see the horizon to get a celestial shot," Steve said.

"The sextant has an artificial horizon," Blair replied, "and I don't have to use the horizon-mirror assembly. Polaris is always within a degree of the celestial North Pole, so the altitude of Polaris above the horizon is the same as our geographical latitude, give or take a degree."

Caly's Island

He sighted on Polaris and moved the index arm on the sextant. "Got it." He read the apparent height of Polaris off the sextant's arc and corrected the number for sextant error. "We're at thirty-six degrees latitude, plus or minus a degree." Next, he pulled the Nautical Almanac out of his navigation bag, found the tables for Polaris, and extracted three numbers. "I'm winging this. I don't know our longitude or Greenwich Mean Time, but I can get in the ballpark because of the relative position of Polaris to the Chair of Cassiopeia."

"What's the Chair of Cassio-whatever?" Sean asked.

"The Chair of Cassiopeia is a constellation that circles around Polaris. It looks like a big W." He added the three numbers to the corrected sextant reading and then subtracted one degree. "We're at thirty-five degrees five-minutes north latitude." He drew a parallel line that ran east to west through the DR position Sean had plotted, and wrote N35-05 on it. "We're on that line, give or take fifteen or so nautical miles north or south."

"But the San Juans are around forty-eight degrees north," Pete said. "So how in hell did we get so far south?"

"Beats me," Blair replied.

Sean said, "Seven hundred and eighty nautical miles south." The FOGs turned and looked at him. "Well, more or less, I guess." He had to explain. "The Admiral said there are sixty nautical miles in a degree of latitude and we're thirteen degrees south of the San Juans. Thirteen times sixty is seven hundred and eighty. Right?" His face reddened with embarrassment.

"Well done, Sean," Gib said. "And never be ashamed for using your head. Our immediate and most pressing problem is that we can be anywhere at latitude thirty-five north in the eastern or western hemisphere, in the Pacific or Atlantic Ocean. So what do you recommend we do?"

"You're asking me?" Sean replied, not believing an adult would want his opinion. Gib nodded to encourage him. "I don't know . . ." His voice trailed off.

"I think you have an idea," Gib said. "I would like to hear it."

"Well, we got to go somewhere, so why not go north? Isn't that where we came from originally? And the dolphins are headed sort of that way, so why not follow them?"

Gib nodded. "I agree.

"I love sailing at night," Steve added.

"We got the wind," Rufus said. "Use it or lose it."

"Makes sense to me," Pete said.

They all looked at Blair. "We need to sail when we can to conserve our fuel. Let's follow the dolphins. Compass heading zero-four-zero degrees. Keep everyone in sight."

Within minutes, their navigation lights on and they were under way. "Admiral, why did Gib ask me what I thought?" Sean asked.

"Because your opinion counts." Blair took the helm and turned, heading directly for Polaris. "That's interesting. With Polaris on our bow, our heading is true north, and our compass heading is the same. That means there's no, or very little magnetic variation here. Variation in the San Juans is nineteen degrees east."

"So we're not in the San Juans," Sean said. "I thought we knew that."

"I really needed to hear that," Blair muttered. "You do the dishes and clean up."

"Ah, man," Sean moaned as he went to work.

"Then hit the sack. You've got the dog watch."

"Ah, man. That's not fair."

"Yeah, it is." Blair allowed a tight smile. The kid was doing fine. Blair put the tiller over and steered 040.

Zack crested a swell and saw the light still winking in the dark. The strange boat was a mile in front of him and pulling steadily away as it headed for the beacon. Feeling more confident as the storm tapered off, he untied his mainsail, put in a double reef, and hoisted it. *Wild Turtle* responded and the ride smoothed, stabilized by the sail. Encouraged, he unfurled a little more of his jib. The heel increased five degrees, but the ride was much smoother. Zack composed a mental letter to the makers of his boat. "Dear Ken, thank you." He had every intention of mailing it.

An hour later, the first glow of sunrise lit the dark clouds scudding overhead. "I'll be damned," he muttered. He was gaining on the boat and could clearly see the oars extending from each side, stroking in rhythm and pulling strongly for the beacon.

* * * *

Caly's Island

The upper limb of the sun was just breaking the eastern horizon when Pete yelled "Land ho!" at the top of his lungs. He put the tiller over and headed back for the other boats that were huddled together like lost sheep. "Land!" he shouted. The men were standing in their boats searching the far horizon. He pointed in the direction where he had seen a dark smudge.

Sean saw it before the others. "There!" He jumped up and down, rocking *Wee Dram*. "Over there!" Embarrassed, he stopped and shrugged, determined to act cool. "How far away is it?"

"Hard to say," Blair replied. "Check the Distance of Sea Horizon in Reed's."

"Check Reed's Nautical Companion," Sean groused as he opened the handbook and found the page. His eyes grew wide in surprise. "According to this, the horizon we can see standing up in the boat is less than three nautical miles."

"Check the next table," Blair replied. "Say we see a light on the horizon that is 450 feet above the water."

Sean worked the problem. "We can see it from twenty-seven miles away."

"So how far are we away from land?"

"Anywhere from three miles to twenty-seven miles, if the land was 450 feet high. Or further if the land was higher. So what do we do?"

Blair noted the time, 05:31 hours, and sighted on the dark mass with his hand-bearing compass. "Steer zero-six-five degrees" he told Sean. Still navigating, Blair plotted their DR position for 05:31 and drew in their new course line. He stood and checked on his flock. "Rufe, how's your passenger doing?"

Rufus waved at him and disappeared into the cabin to check on Sasha. He was back in moments, a worried look on his face. "She's running a fever," he called across the thirty feet of water that separated them.

"Do you have any antibiotics?" Blair asked. Rufus answered in the negative.

"I do," Gib called. He sailed over to Rufus and handed over a small bottle. "It's not much but better than nothing." There were six pills left, enough for two days. The five boats headed for the brown smudge on the horizon.

"Hungry?" Blair asked. Sean nodded. Blair opened the cabin and went to work. "Oatmeal with some raisins," he told the teenager.

"Ah, man. Even Angus eats better than me." Blair jerked his head, primed to issue a quick reprimand. Sean grinned at him. "And I should know."

"Grotty kid," Blair groused.

The wind had kicked up and lashed at Zack from dead astern, driving *Wild Turtle* towards the beacon. In the growing light and through the pounding rain, he could barely make out the landmass in front of him. More confused than ever, he checked his waterproof map and his compass. It had to be either Vancouver Island to the west, or the Canadian mainland to the east. But he was headed south, and even in his normal directional muddle, that didn't make sense. He retrieved his GPS from the cabin and turned it on. Again, there was no signal. "Screw it," he muttered, throwing the GPS back into the cabin. He would do what he always did – follow another boat until he reached safe harbor.

An hour later, Zack decided that was a bad idea. "Oh, no," he muttered. The beacon was a bonfire on top of a low bluff overlooking a shoreline that stretched out in front of him. To his horror, the high winds and waves were pushing both boats straight for the beacon and certain destruction on the rocks below. Then he saw it. Approximately half a mile to his left, to the east, the shoreline ended in a rocky point. Behind the point of land, he could see open water and safety. The strange boat turned in an attempt to beat away from the shore and round the point. Its oars furiously beat the water as the boat wallowed. Then four men tried to set an anchor, but the water was too deep. There was nothing the crew could do and they were driven onto the lee shore, the curse of mariners in the age of sail. Zack quickly refilled his outboard's small gas tank and pulled on the starter cord. Nothing happened. The motor wasn't going to start after twice turning turtle. "Don't panic," he told himself. "Sail out of it."

Zack crested a wave and saw the ship hit the beach directly below the still burning beacon. Men jumped into the pounding surf and struggled ashore. Fear was the spur and he shook out a reef and flew more of his jib. *Wild Turtle* heeled thirty degrees, clawing into the wind, fighting for sea room. At first, Zack didn't think he could make it, but he

Caly's Island

slowly gained distance away from the rocks and sailed parallel to the shore, making for the point. On the top of a wave, he chanced a quick glance. The ship had come apart and he saw more men scrambling ashore where two tall figures were waiting to rescue them.

The wind slacked and he saw more of the shoreline through the driving mist. The rocky point was a quarter mile in front of him and marked the end of a rocky shoal. The beacon should have been closer to the point. But he had a more pressing matter to think about. He had to beat clear of the point or suffer the same fate as the ship. He tacked into the wind and waves, slugging it out, fighting for every inch of sea room he could gain. The rocks and crashing waves loomed closer. "Not today!" he roared in defiance. He jerked on the starter cord again. The motor finally coughed to life.

Zack gave it full throttle and punched into the surging sea. "Come on," he urged. *Wild Turtle* dug in as he used the sail and the motor together to maintain his course. A wave crashed over the last rock in front of him. He sheeted in the jib and mainsail, increasing his heel and heading up a fraction of a degree. The next wave carried him onto the rock. In desperation, he pushed off, badly scraping his left hand. Then he was clear and around the point.

"Yes!" he shouted. Open water stretched out in front of him to the south and he saw land on both sides. The wind and current catapulted *Wild Turtle* into a strait that curved to the southwest, separating the two landmasses. The water calmed and he hugged the shore on his starboard, taking advantage of the wind shadow behind the point he had just cleared as he sailed southward. He killed his engine to conserve fuel. In the growing light, he saw a mountain peak far to the southwest. Fatigue and relief swept over him and he dozed, allowing *Wild Turtle* to drift into the middle of the strait. He came awake with a jerk and looked around. "Son of a bitch," he muttered. He had almost sailed past the entrance to a bay hidden behind a hook of land.

Zack headed for the opening but a line of breakers blocked his way. "What did the Admiral say? It's all in the timing." He eased the sheets, depowering his sails, and started the motor. The engine idled while he studied the breakers surging into the inlet. *Wild Turtle* coasted closer and he waited for the right wave to sweep under him and break a few feet in front. A set of two waves formed behind him and he gunned the engine, riding the first wave as it surged past. He raced for the entrance. Just when he was certain the second wave would poop him, *Wild Turtle* surged ahead and shot through the gap and into the bay.

For the first time in almost twenty-four hours, Zack was in calm waters. He cut the engine, released the sheets, and dropped an anchor a few feet from the shore. The lack of motion caused his internal gyros to tumble and he felt dizzy. He leaned over the side and regurgitated the remains of his last meal. Then he collapsed onto the seat, his body wracked with the dry heaves. Slowly, the nausea calmed and he slept.

The sun was nearing its zenith when Pete stood and studied the shoreline with his binoculars. He was three or four miles offshore to the southwest and headed towards what looked like an island. Automatically, he looked for the other boats. They were still to the west, two miles away, and closing on him. For the next hour, he worked his way towards the island, finally heaving-to just offshore. He rigged a tarp for shade and drank deeply from his water bottle. Feeling better, he devoured a Power Bar and settled down to wait. Always hopeful, he turned on his shortwave radio and searched for a station. Nothing. Only a little static. Next, he tested his VHF radio. The results were the same and a wave of despair washed over him.

An inner sense warned him to stay busy and concentrate on something else. He reached for his journal and made the first entry since Sunday at Fossil Bay. The memories of the sail from Sucia Island to Roche Harbor and how they had outrun the storm on Monday were bright and easily captured. Being a gentleman, he only mentioned that Helena was waiting for them at Roche Harbor and that they had talked on Tuesday while waiting out the storm. What a day! he thought. He didn't need a journal to remind him of Tuesday's activities with Helena. It was burned into his memory and he hoped it would trump the ravages of Alzheimer's. He had visions of becoming a legend in a retirement home when he babbled about it. Then he got to Steve.

I though I heard gunfire coming from Stuart Island right after clearing Roche, but I wasn't sure at first. The second time there was no doubt, and those guys in the first RIB were definitely shooting at Steve. Luckily, he hid in the fog, otherwise it would have been curtains. We need to sort it out with Steve. And we have a definite problem with

Caly's Island

Sasha. Rufe is a jack-of-all-trades and stopped her bleeding, but she needs medical help. Why can't we get a radio or GPS signal? I almost lost it when we came out of the fog, but nothing seems to upset the Admiral. If he can handle it, so can I. Thank God for those dolphins that led us in the right direction. But where are we? Hopefully, the Admiral will figure it out. On the good side, the sailing doesn't get much better. On the bad side, there's still no trace of Zack.

He closed the journal and put it away.

The lawyer swept the shore with his binoculars, looking for a place to land. The shoreline was rocky with low scrub growing in shallow crevices. It reminded him of Baja California when he had cruised the Sea of Cortez. Further back, he could see thick stands of trees, which was totally unlike Baja. *L'Amour* rode up on a swell, and a break in the shoreline caught his attention. By standing in the cockpit, he could make out a small bay behind a big rock. "So where's the entrance?" he mumbled to himself. He settled down to wait for his friends..

Steve was the first to pull alongside, and gestured at the island. "Well, that's encouraging," he allowed. Rufus arrived next with Gib and Blair close behind. The five boats bumped together in the gentle swells. "Have you seen the dolphins?" Blair asked.

"Not since last night," Pete replied.

Blair plotted their DR position on his makeshift chart and marked the time: 14:00. He wrote 'Island' beside the circle and spanned off the distance to his first plot. "Not bad," he announced, passing the chart around. "We sailed eighty-four miles in twenty-one hours."

Steve examined Blair's handiwork. "Well, we now know 'Fog Bank' and 'Island' are eighty-four miles apart."

"And where they are in relation to latitude thirty-five north," Pete added. "But that doesn't help much, does it?"

Sean came to Blair's defense. "Well, it's something, isn't it?"

"Sean," Gib said, "you are absolutely right."

"Gentlemen," Blair said, "we've got about six hours until sunset. I think it's time we make landfall. Any ideas?"

"I don't think we can land on the beaches here," Pete said. "But there's a little bay behind that big rock over there. The trick is getting to it."

"Let's go take a look," Blair said. "Pete, would you take the lead?"

97

"Will do, Admiral." Pete snapped a salute and sheeted his sails in. He headed for the island. Steve and Gib fell in behind.

"Rufe," Blair called, "how's your patient doing?"

"Her temperature's up to a hundred and one and she's sweating," the blacksmith said.

"We need help," Blair conceded. "The sooner the better." He fell in behind Rufus, bringing up the rear.

Pete closed to within two hundred feet of the rock and turned due south. "Got it!" he shouted. He put the tiller over and headed for the gap between the rock and the headland. A gentle swell pushed him through the entrance. The other FOGs followed him into a beautiful lagoon approximately a quarter-mile wide. Large schools of fish darted beneath them in the clear blue water. "Fish for dinner tonight!" Pete called. He headed for the beach on the north side of the lagoon where a little stream flowed down to the water. *L'Amour's* centerboard was up when it ran aground on the golden sand. Pete hopped over the side to plant an anchor before running back to the water's edge. He spread his arms wide as the others approached. "Mi casa, su casa," he called.

High on the headland above the lagoon, a woman watched the five little boats run onto the sand. Her eyes narrowed when the men set their anchors. She had never seen boats or equipment like that. A breeze ruffled her long gray hair and the soft fabric of her white gown caressed her body. She smiled, and her lips formed a word. But after years of silence, it didn't sound right. Words she had never heard before came to her. "Welcome to my island." Her smile hardened into a deep frown when two of the men carried a woman ashore and sat her in the shade of a low araar tree. "What is she doing here?" She turned and disappeared into her cave.

TEN

Rufus hovered over the glowing coals and turned the three fish on the grate. The FOGs were gathered around on the sand, sitting in their camp chairs and sharing a bottle of wine. Gib had an extra chair for Sasha and she was bundled in a blanket sitting next to Steve. Sean was parked on the sand with Angus, his knees drawn up to his chest as he watched the sun go down and a magnificent sunset play out. "I can make great charcoal with this wood," Rufus said. He rooted the last of his potatoes out of the embers and filleted the fish. "What kind of fish is this?"

"It's a sea bass," Pete replied. "I caught 'em just off the rocks outside the entrance in less than twenty minutes. I don't think this place has been fished in years, and the water gets pretty deep, fairly fast." He waited while Rufus parceled out the fish and potatoes. "Rufe, my man, this smells delicious. You should have been a chef."

Rufus handed a plate to Sasha but she shook her head. "You need to eat something," he told her. Again, she refused. The five men and Sean attacked the fish and potatoes with gusto. When he finished, Sean took Angus for a walk to do his thing. "Take a flashlight," Rufus called. The night was turning unusually dark. "And stay on the beach."

Blair waited until Sean was out of earshot. "We need to talk," he announced. "I'd like to take it in order. First, Steve. What's going down? It's obvious you're in some sort of trouble and Sasha is part of it."

Steve leaned forward in his chair and clasped his hands, not sure what to say. "Steven," Gib urged, "we've formed conclusions based on what we've observed, and none of them are favorable. Now is the time to clear up any confusion. I, for one, would like to help, if I can." Only Sasha did not nod in agreement.

Steve looked at his hands. "For the last six years, I've been very low profile. Let's just say I'm involved in a certain matter the Russian Mafia is very interested in, but they've been looking at the wrong people, in the wrong places. I only learned last Saturday they were on to me and had issued a hit contract."

"That explains a few things," Pete said.

"I figured I was safe enough for a few days," Steve continued. "But I wanted to put some distance between you and me, in case they found me."

Pete looked at Sasha. "Which they did."

In the growing dark, Steve missed the implication. "Yeah, they did – at Stuart Island. Luckily, Sasha and her sister had my back."

Pete was confused. "Sasha's not with the Russian Mafia?"

"I am Ukranian," Sasha announced.

"We know that," Blair said. "But we thought . . ."

Sasha snorted in contempt. "You thought I was Russian Mafia? Russians are pigs."

"I hired Sasha and her family for protection," Steve said. "That was the last phone call I made before we left Squalicum."

"So that's why the Sirens were at Portage Island," Pete said, fitting the pieces together. "They were guarding you."

"Actually," Steve replied, "they were coming to get me. But it all got delayed when I ran aground off Portage Island. I was going to sink *High Flyer* and radio the Admiral that I had a family emergency back home."

"And then disappear," Blair added.

"Something like that," Steve admitted. "But things got complicated when the Cigarette ran aground, the Coast Guard showed up, and we had to run from the storm."

"It all came apart," Rufus said.

"I was playing it by ear."

"To protect us from harm if the Russians found you," Gib said. Steve nodded, thankful the judge understood.

"I have a question," Blair said. "When I made that first Mayday call rescuing Angus, who answered? It didn't sound legit at all."

"It was Russian Mafia," Sasha replied. "That was how they knew where to look. But when they go to Sucia Island, you are gone. The storm also cause them troubles, but they hear you tell Coast Guard you go to Roche Harbor. They go there, but Mr. Coyote is at Stuart Island."

"Mr. Coyote?" Rufus asked.

"The surname I adopted," Steve explained, "is from the scientific name for the coyote, Canis Latrans. The Sirens caught it immediately."

"No doubt," Pete scoffed, "a tribute to European education."

"In Ukraine," Sasha said, "students must learn or they have no future."

Blair asked the question they all wanted to ask. "So what's your real name?"

Steve leaned forward in his chair. "Garrison S. Williams. The 'S' is for Steven, which I kept." He needed to talk and unburden his soul. "I never married and was a CPA for thirty-four years, a solid, dependable pillar of the community. Good old Garrison, always good for some civic project. Then I stumbled onto a chance to make real money. It was a sure thing and I knew I could pull it off. Do you know what it's like to walk on the wild side after a lifetime of stodgy respectability? For the first time in my life, I was truly alive."

Pete had defended the Russian Mafia in court and knew how dangerous they were. "How did you avoid them at Stuart Island?"

"Because of the storm and pure luck," Steve answered, "I was anchored in a hidey-hole and they couldn't find me."

"And the Sirens were still trying to pick you up," Pete added.

"We had special plane waiting on Vancouver Island," Sasha explained. But when we go to Stuart Island to pick him up, Mafia is there. They see us and start shooting. They burn our boat and kill Natalka, my sister, and my cousins, Taras and Pavlo. Now I will kill them."

"You got two of them already," Blair said.

"There are others," Sasha replied, her voice steely calm.

Blair made the last connection. "Then the white motor yacht that chased us into the fog was the Mafia."

"Yes," Sasha said. They are dead men." The quiet resolve in her voice sent a collective shudder through the FOGs.

Years of judicial experience had honed Gib's logic and analytical powers to a sharp edge. "Steven, the services of Sasha's family obviously do not come cheap, and the cost of all this must be immense.

Apparently, money is not a concern for you, which, I suspect, is the common denominator in all this. Please enlighten us."

"It's complicated," Steve replied.

"I'm quite sure you can un-complicate it," Gib said. The authority in his voice could not be denied.

Steve took a deep breath. "I was the comptroller for a small Savings and Loan. It wasn't much of a job and didn't pay very much. But I had time for my hobby, you might say my obsession, with cryptology – making and breaking codes." He came alive with a passion his friends never suspected lurked beneath his placid exterior. "Cryptography is a form of mathematics that uses information theory to create codes. Think of it as a unique mathematical form of communication. If a code can be created by mathematical theory, it can be decrypted by mathematical theory." At last, Steve had a captive audience and he turned into a fire hose gushing out information. But explaining was like trying to fill a washbasin with the fire hose at full pressure.

Gib smiled. He knew when he was being hosed down, even when it was not with a malicious or evil intent, but by a superior mathematical intellect that exceeded any he had ever encountered. Who would have ever suspected? he thought. "Steve, you are far beyond us. When it comes to math, we're mere mortals. We struggle to balance our checkbooks."

Steve came back to reality. "Anyway, I was doing a routine audit, and noticed that one of our S & L members used coded messages when transferring money in and out of his account. Mind you, nothing very large, only small sums, never more than a few thousand dollars. Being curious, I tried to break the code. But it was the devil itself to break and extremely complicated, which really piqued my interest. Then I stumbled into one of those breaks cryptologists dream about."

"Not to mention orgasm over," Pete added.

Steve caught the sarcasm and smiled. "Well, it is a rush. By pure luck, I discovered it was a cipher overlaying a code. Once I had stripped the cipher away, I got my second lucky break. I intercepted two messages sent out the same day, one in code, the other in clear text. I assumed the coded message had the same meaning. It turned out to be my Rosetta Stone. After that, it was relatively easy to break the code. I was in cryptology heaven. Like I said, I had the time."

"The devil's playground," Gib said.

Caly's Island

"Once I had broken the code, I discovered my Savings and Loan was part of a huge money laundering scheme run by the Russian Mafia, and the chairman of the S & L was in it up to his neck."

It was the old story of temptation that Gib had seen many times before. "But you didn't tell the authorities."

"That's correct. But I couldn't let it go. Once inside, I was able to follow the electronic trail, and I cracked the entire scheme. It was an extremely complex system that led to a Swiss bank."

Now Pete was fully on board and filling in the blanks. "So you diverted some of the Russian Mafia's ill-gotten gains your way."

Steve nodded unhappily. "Like I said, it's complicated. The Swiss were very accommodating with secret accounts, and it worked beautifully, all on autopilot, so to speak. After that, it was easy for me to disappear into the woodwork."

"But you got greedy," Pete added.

Steve shook his head. "I had created a monster. The money just kept flowing in, and I couldn't shut it off. So I ignored it."

Pete understood. "Because to shut it off, might reveal who set up the secret accounts."

Rufus was fascinated. This was not the man he knew. "So if Steve sticks his head up to shut off the money flow, said head gets lopped off."

"Quite painfully," Gib said. "I take it the redirected amounts became too large, and garnered someone's unwanted attention."

Steve nodded. "A Swiss auditor. He figured it out. But rather than report me to the authorities, he sold me out to the Russian Mafia."

"So much for Swiss integrity," Blair groused. One of the constants of his world just went onto the trash heap.

"So how do you get hold of the money?" Rufus asked.

"Once the money was in the accounts, I used a cutout to siphon off the interest into another secret account in the Ukraine. Again, all automatic. My Ukrainian account manager learned the Russians were looking for me, he didn't know why, and warned me. He told me about Sasha's family and gave me their phone number."

"Ah," Gib said, "the source of the phone calls at Squalicum. May I ask how much you have realized so far?"

"The last time I checked, the Ukrainian account was over forty million euros. That was a year ago and the money is still coming in. The Russians know I'm behind it, but they can't figure out how it works or how to shut it off." Sasha's hand came out from under her blanket and held Steve's hand. She smiled at him.

Pete caught it. "Women and money," he muttered. Then, louder, "Steve, with those amounts of money involved, did you really think you could stay off their radar scope?"

"I did until last Saturday." He looked at his friends. "I had created an electronic trail that led back to the chairman of my S & L."

"A certain justice there," Rufus said.

"Anyway," Steve continued, "I thought I was safe. I guess that was very naïve of me."

"Indeed it was," Pete told him.

"I may be able to help," Gib said. "That is, if you want help, and if we get back to civilization. Which brings us to the next subject. Where in God's name are we?"

Blair didn't answer at first, taking time to form an answer. Making landfall had helped break the tension and given them hope. Now he had to build on it. "I'm working on it. First things first. We made safe harbor and are not in any immediate danger. Other than Sasha, we're well. The boats are fine, we've plenty of food and water, and the weather is cooperating."

"So what do we do now?" Rufus asked.

"We take it one step at a time. For now, we build a fire and get a good night's sleep. But we're going to need a sentry to stand guard, just in case. I'll take the first shift until midnight. Pete, will you take it until zero four hundred, and Gib after that?" Both men readily accepted their assignments. "Thank you, gentlemen. Please excuse me, I need to shoot Polaris. And may I suggest we all offer a prayer for Zack?"

Zack blinked and woke in a dead sweat. His first conscious thought was to strip off his foul weather gear and cool down. Slowly, he came alert, shaking off the cobwebs of sleep and fatigue. The depth and richness of the night sky captured him and he looked up. "Oh, my God," he whispered. The Milky Way marched across the sky in sharp relief, and he had never seen so many stars. The faint aroma of cooking meat caught his attention. He sniffed, trying to catch it, but it was gone. Suddenly, he was thirsty and ravenously hungry. "First things first," he muttered to himself, sliding back the cabin hatch. The storm had

Caly's Island

pounded *Wild Turtle* unmercifully and he was worried. He reached around to the inside bulkhead and flicked on the cabin lights.

There was a little water in the bilge and his bedding and cushions were soaked, but other than that, he couldn't see any damage. Lady Luck had been kind, but common sense warned him to tend to business and make some luck on his own. A full water bottle was lying next to the centerboard trunk. "Keep hydrated," he warned himself, draining the bottle. His survival instincts kicked in and he calculated he had enough water to last three or four days. "Catch some rain or find a stream," he said. Thinking out loud definitely helped. "Where am I?" He quickly checked his GPS. No signal. Next, he turned on his radios and scanned the frequencies. Nothing. Frustrated, he tried his cell phone. No service. "What the hell?" he muttered.

Fortunately, his appetite was still working and he rummaged through the cabin, finding another MRE. Again, he caught the faint aroma of cooking and, as quickly as before, it was gone. He made a mental promise to find the source in the morning. Rather than eat a cold meal, he lit his stove. Attracted by the flame, bugs swarmed around him and one took a healthy bite. "Mosquitoes," he grumbled, quickly applying repellant. But the spray only seemed to attract more mosquitoes. "Hungry little buggers," he allowed. It was time to move. The motor started on the first pull, and he went forward to weigh anchor. Again, he smelled the cooking meat. "Its got'a be fairly close," he told himself.

He crawled back into the cockpit, motored into the center of the bay, and set an anchor. A warm breeze drifted over him, and thankfully, the bugs were gone. Famished, he heated the MRE and settled against the cabin bulkhead to enjoy the meal. It never failed to surprise him how good an MRE tasted when warmed to the proper temperature. Feeling better, he relaxed and took in the magnificent sky. The Belt of Orion was directly above him.

The three stars winked at him.

"What are you so happy about?" he groused. Loneliness was taking its toll and he was talking to the stars. "Oh, no," he groaned. Orion the Hunter with his shield and raised club were clearly visible and hovered over him. "Fatigue will get you every time," he muttered. He crawled into the cabin and fell asleep.

* * * *

Dick Herman

Blair sat in the cabin of *Wee Dram* and worked the sight reduction of Polaris. It had been easy shooting the star and he had four good sights, two with the artificial horizon bubble, and two with the horizon-mirror assembly. Normally, it was impossible to calibrate on the horizon at night, but the moonrise made it possible. All four sights were close and, once averaged, placed them at 35 degrees, 49 minutes, 12 seconds north latitude. He drew a horizontal line on his chart just north of their last DR position and labeled it N35-49-12. Underneath, he wrote 'by Polaris.'

A sip of Scotch worked its magic and he sat back, studying the chart. If only he could determine their longitude and fix their position. It was the problem that had vexed mariners until the Eighteenth Century and the invention of accurate chronometers. If he knew Greenwich Mean Time, he could shoot the stars or the sun and fix their position. But he had winged it setting their watches and didn't even have an accurate local time. A stray thought niggled at him.

An old, grizzled navigator he had flown with when he was a first lieutenant in the Air Force had a shortcut for determining the true azimuth of Polaris without looking it up. "The Chair is the right one," he had told Blair, meaning when the Chair of Cassiopeia was to the right of Polaris, Polaris's azimuth was 001. As the Chair of Cassiopeia was to the left of Polaris when Blair took his sightings, that meant Polaris's azimuth was 359 degrees. With that number, and the rough latitude from the shot, he had worked backwards in the Polaris tables in the Nautical Almanac to determine their latitude. While not totally accurate, he was well within the ballpark. What was he missing? He poured himself another dram of Scotch as his frustration ratcheted up a notch. "Better go easy on the good stuff," he told himself. The FOGs needed to practice conservation.

"Admiral!" Sean shouted from down the beach. "Where are you?" Blair heard the panic in his voice and bolted out of the cabin as Sean ran up to the beached boat. The teenager stumbled in the dark and bounced to his feet. He ran, only to stumble again and fell to his knees. "I lost Angus!"

ELEVEN

Sean knelt in the sand and held his hands up, trying to explain. "We were walking down the beach, over there." Tears coursed down his cheeks as he pointed to the eastern end of the lagoon two hundred yards away. "We were just above the rocks, and I could see real good in the moonlight, and we heard a sound, sort of like an animal, and Angus takes off chasing it. I followed him as far as the trees but couldn't see where he went. So I came back to the rocks and waited. But Angus never came back."

Blair sat beside him, shoulder to shoulder, looking out over the lagoon. "You did the right thing. Don't worry, he'll come back."

"He will?" The relief in Sean's voice was obvious.

"Oh, yeah. Jack Russell terriers are hunters, and he was probably chasing a small animal. One time he took off and was gone for three days, but I think he was chasing a bitch in heat that time."

The levity was enough to ease the guilt and worry that bound the teenager. "I thought you'd be mad at me."

"For what? Angus is just doing his thing."

Sean was still worried. "But what if he gets hurt, or, or . . ." The thought was too painful to finish.

"Or is killed," Blair said. He reached out and clamped Sean's shoulder. "It happens. That's life. When I was flying in the Air Force, I lost a lot of good buddies, most in accidents, a few in combat. Sure, I was sad and really broken up in a couple of cases. But they were all doing what they wanted to do – and they knew the risks. Look, we all die. When you're young, it's a matter of when. When you're older, it's a matter of how. Angus is twelve years old, that's getting up there for a dog."

"My Mom said one year for a dog is like seven for a person."

"There's a better formula. Figure ten and one-half dog years for the first two human years, then four dog years for every human year after that." He let Sean do the math.

"So Angus is sixty-one. That makes him a FOG like you guys."

Blair laughed. "You got it. Always remember, he's out there doing what he wants to do. He'll come back. Not to worry."

Sean stared into the night. "Aren't you worried? I mean worried about all this?"

If only you knew, Blair thought. He was strung tighter than the proverbial banjo string, but hard experience had taught him how to handle the unknown and stress. Combat did that, if it didn't kill or maim you. But this was totally off the scale. "Oh, yeah, but we'll get through it. The secret is to take it one step at a time and not panic."

"So what do we do now?"

"Get a good night's sleep. Tomorrow's going to be a busy day."

"I wish I could do something. Like now."

"You might want to wish Zack good luck, maybe offer a prayer for his safety."

"I don't know how to pray."

"Just think good thoughts. Someone will hear you."

Blair woke to the aroma of Gib's coffee and poked his head out of *Wee Dram's* cabin. It was still dark and he saw a lump on the sand that was Sean bundled up in his sleeping bag. "Good morning, H," Gib called. "Coffee?" Blair pulled on a pair of shorts and a light sweatshirt and walked barefoot over to *Habeas Corpus*. He climbed on board and Gib handed him a mug of the potent brew. For a few moments, they drank in silence. "It was very quiet last night," the judge told him. "I think we are perfectly safe here." The two men sipped their coffee in silence. "May I ask what you make of all this?"

Blair pulled into himself, straining for a rational answer. "The most logical explanation is that we've died and gone to this place. Nothing else makes sense."

"The evidence," Gib replied, "suggests that we are still very much alive. I still creak and ache as before." Skepticism flashed across Blair's face. He liked the 'died and gone to heaven/hell (cross out one)' theory. Gib stepped on his bare toes.

"Ouch!"

"See," Gib said, "we're very much alive." By the simple act of causing a little pain, he had focused Blair on reality. "So what are the other options?"

"We're hallucinating?"

"Possible," Gib replied. "But what are the chances of us all sharing the same hallucination? Besides, everything is real. My watch is now keeping time, my laptop works, and our compasses and VHF radios are working as they should, although I can't raise any stations on shortwave or AM-FM, or on my cell phone."

"Neither can I," Blair said. "We'll figure it out."

Rufus joined them. "I couldn't sleep," the blacksmith said. He had spent a fitful night, trying to rationalize all that had happened. He was an intensely practical individual and not given to self-pity or flights of fancy, but this was totally beyond him. He lived in a world of fire and steel where hard labor, skilled hands, and an artist's eye were the common currency. When Cheryl, his young and beautiful ex-wife, was putting him through pure hell he found solace and comfort at the forge, banging on metal and creating art in wrought iron.

His link to the past was in his tool collection, and he saw the future in children, which Cheryl rejected. Rufus dealt with the world as it came at him, and being on the water with a working catboat with a single large sail responding to his command was a simple joy. It was an experience many men could not relate to, yet his companions understood all to well. Of all the FOGs, he was the least worried about the strange turn of events because his faith in his companions was absolute. Together, they would get through it. Gib handed him a mug of coffee. Rufus took a sip and made a face. "Now that will curl your toenails."

"How's Sasha?" Blair asked.

Rufus was worried. "Her fever is still over a hundred and I think her wound is infected. I'll give her the last of the antibiotics today, but we need to get her to a doctor." The three men sipped their coffee as the first light of dawn cracked the horizon. "Any idea where we are?" Rufus asked. Blair and Gib shook their heads in unison. "So, what do we do now?"

"Wake Steve and Pete," Blair said. "Time to get organized." Rufus walked down the beach and knocked on the cabin tops, waking the two men. Within minutes, the five men were all gathered at Gib's boat. "Here's the drill," Blair said. "First, we need to conserve our food, fuel, and batteries. That means we fish and live off the land, sail when we can, and use solar panels to recharge our batteries. If you can't recharge it, don't use it."

"I can make a list of all our supplies," Steve said. "Like a fleet commissary."

"Fishing is a piece of cake here," Pete said. "But we're gonna get awfully tired of three squares a day of our finned friends."

"Until we get sorted out," Blair added, "we only eat two meals a day. Also, a source of fresh, clean water would be convenient and save us a lot of pumping on Gib's water filter."

"What's wrong with the stream over there?" Rufus asked. He gestured at the little brook that ran down to the lagoon.

"Anyone got a test or purification kit?" Blair asked. They all shook their heads. Rufus walked over to the stream, scooped up a handful of water and drank.

"Let's see if I get sick," he said.

"Some test," Pete muttered. "I've tasted your chili. They don't call you 'Old Iron Guts' for nothing. So what's next?"

"We need to reconnoiter," Blair said, "and find out all we can. Are we on an island? Are there better places to camp? Is this place inhabited? Pete, I want you and Steve to take *L'Amour* and *High Flyer* and sail north along the shore. Keep track of compass headings and distances, take photos, and make a map. Go as far as you can today, anchor or heave-to tonight, and sail back tomorrow. You know what to look for."

"People, fresh water, and a better place to camp – in that order," the lawyer said.

"Rufe and Gib," Blair continued, "I want you to do the same to the south." Another thought came to him. "And everyone, keep playing with your GPS, cell phones and radios. See if you can pickup a commercial station. I'll stay here with Sean, take care of Sasha, and explore the local area. Any questions?" The men answered with headshakes and steadfast

Caly's Island

looks. The worry that held Blair hostage eased a fraction. As long as the FOGs had a purpose, they could cope, and activity was the antidote to despair and panic. "Super. Breakfast today is any food that might spoil. Let's do it."

Breakfast went quickly and they set up a sunshade on the beach to move Sasha ashore. Rufus and Gib were the first to launch and sailed out of the lagoon shortly after sunrise. Steve walked over to Blair and handed him a bundled up towel. "You might need this," he said. Without another word, he boarded his boat and followed Pete out of the lagoon. The two boats turned to the north and disappeared along the shore.

Blair unwrapped the towel and handled the heavy revolver. "I'll be damned," he said to himself. He dropped the weapon inside *Wee Dram's* cabin and walked over to the canopy to check on Sasha. She was wrapped in a blanket and her forehead glistened with a light bead of sweat. Blair handed her a pill. "Better take this," he said. There was only one left.

"Thank you," she said. Blair watched her swallow the antibiotic. Even pale and running a fever, she was beautiful. Beautiful women were easy to find, as he well knew from the outrageous number of beauty pageants inflicted on the American public. But pretty and intelligent women were not as common, and it was rare to find one who was beautiful, intelligent, and talented. Sasha would be a top contender in any beauty pageant as Miss Ukraine, but he wondered what particular talent she would showcase. Do they allow pole dancing? he wondered.

Sasha gazed calmly at him, as if fully aware of what he was thinking. "You don't like me, Mr. Admiral."

"I don't know you." She didn't reply and fixed him with a look he couldn't read. "We need to get you to a doctor," he told her.

Again, she drilled him with the look. "Can you shoot?" she asked. "I saw Mr. Coyote give you the gun."

Blair's inner alarm bell went off. She didn't miss much. "How did you know?"

She smiled. "Your face says more than words. Besides, bundle was the right size. It is good Mr. Coyote gives it to you. He cannot shoot." Blair didn't answer and she sighed. "He shoots at Mafia at Stuart Island when he is too far away. But he was lucky and Mafia duck heads." She snorted. "Amateurs. Mafia bury heads and he escapes. But he wastes

111

ammunition and warns them he has gun. Mafia get more cautious and he loses surprise. If I shoot, I kill. Otherwise, never use gun."

Blair was surprised she was being so upfront with him. "Would Steve have escaped if he hadn't shot at them?"

"Mr. Coyote escapes because I shoot Mafia when they expose themselves to shoot at him."

"But Steve didn't know that. He had to do something, even if it was wrong."

She conceded the point as Sean joined them. "Good morning," she said, turning her full attention onto the fifteen-year old. Her voice was soft and melodious, raising visions of soft summer evenings in Blair's imagination. "I hear you talk about Angus last night." She reached out and took the teenager's hand. "It was not your fault. Dogs run away all the time. He will come back." Sean nodded, eagerly accepting her words. She gently stroked his tattoos with her fingers. "You have beautiful skin but need a better artist." She smiled at him. "We can make better."

"Do you like tattoos?" Sean asked.

"I like pretty things," she told him. Sean blushed at the compliment.

Blair stared at Sasha, trying to understand her. Without doubt, she manipulated men to get what she wanted, and she was charming Sean the same way she had charmed Rufus and Steve. "Sean, you need to get some breakfast," he said, anxious to distract the teenager.

Sasha smiled. "Do not worry, Mr. Admiral. I will not harm your young friend."

Suddenly, his inner Klaxon was clanging in full alarm. Sasha was off the danger scale. "Mind reading and sharp shooting," he said. She arched an eyebrow, not understanding. "Your talent in a beauty contest."

The sun was well above the horizon when Zack finally stirred and lifted his head above the gunwale. *Wild Turtle* was anchored in the center of a natural harbor formed by a hook of land that curved around to the north and almost touched the shore, creating a very narrow entrance at the extreme northern end. "Okay, where am I?" he asked himself. Again, he checked his GPS, radios, and cell phone. Nothing. He concentrated, determined to get his bearings. "I'm in a bay on the western side of a strait that runs north and south." It got easier as he verbalized his

Caly's Island

situation. "I sailed south about two hours after rounding the point at the northern entrance." He stood and swept the bay with the binoculars Angela had given him for Christmas. The bay was a half-mile long and a quarter-mile wide with marshes at the southern end. Far to the southwest, he could barely see a mountain.

A warm breeze ruffled his hair, warning him that it was going to be a very hot day. "Time to change clothes." The cabin was still a jumble and he rooted around, finally finding a pair of running shorts, a sleeveless top, and a pair of running shoes. As a precaution, he slathered sun block over his bare arms and legs and jammed a wide-brimmed hat over his gray hair. His confidence surged and he knew he could survive, thanks to *Wild Turtle*. "You did good, old girl." He weighed anchor, lifted his mainsail, and sailed back to the shore.

A little cove, hardly more than a dent in the shoreline, beckoned and he headed for it. The closer he got, the better it looked and he ran *Wild Turtle* aground. Rather than set an anchor on the shore, he tied the bowline to a low tree. "Time to dry you out," he told the boat. He set to work, emptied the cabin, and spread the cushions and his sleeping bag over nearby bushes to dry. Next, he pumped out the bilge and checked for storm damage. Other than a slightly warped mast and two loose stays, the boat was fine. "Okay," he muttered, "time to check the motor." *Wild Turtle* had rolled twice in the storm and he was worried that seawater had contaminated the motor's engine oil. He removed the cover, tentatively checked the dipstick, and breathed a loud sigh of relief. The oil was a clean black and not a milky color. His luck was holding.

Feeling better by the moment, Zach spent the next four hours repairing the damage to the rigging and cleaning *Wild Turtle*. Satisfied he had done all he could, he ate the leftovers from the MRE and plotted his next move. "Sail south and follow the shore." Long experience had taught him it was always best to follow something or someone, and the shoreline should lead to a fishing village or settlement. Again, the faint smell of cooking meat caught his attention. "Change of plans," he mumbled to himself. "Follow the smell." It was the logical thing to do.

"What would Angela take?" he wondered, recalling the many times they had gone hiking. His fanny pack was stuffed in the forward locker with a first aid kit. He added a small compass, a water bottle, and a pair of binoculars. To be on the safe side, he stowed the dry cushions and sleeping bag and locked the hatch and companionway. Ready to go, he pulled foliage and a few tree branches over *Wild Turtle* for concealment. He looked around, making one last check. *Wild Turtle* was securely tied to the shore and well camouflaged. He checked his compass. "Go north, keep the shore on your right. *Wild Turtle* is south, with the shore on your left."

Zack was a man who knew his limitations and had no intentions of going far. Buoyed by a strong determination to not get lost, he set out. He constantly checked his compass, and about every hundred yards turned and looked back, memorizing the way he had come. It was easy going as he pushed through the low scrub and scattered trees. An animal trail looked promising and he followed it to the top of a low hill. He looked around in wonder – he knew where he was! Approximately five miles to the north, he saw the northern entrance to the strait and the point he had rounded in the storm. The strait itself was about three miles wide, and the bay where he had left *Wild Turtle* was about three miles to the south. Well inland and to the south, a majestic mountain reached high into the sky, its peak shrouded by a white cloud. Automatically, he took a bearing – 220 degrees from his hilltop – and estimated the distance at fifty miles. The white cloud started to dissipate, much like steam. "It's a volcano," he said, remembering Mount St. Helens on the drive to Bellingham. The association was enough to trigger an image of Angela and home. He forced it back into the carefully guarded niche of memory where he held it close.

A thin column of smoke near the northern entrance to the strait captured his attention. He raised his binoculars and swept the shoreline as it turned to the west. "Nothing but ocean to the north," he told himself. The memory of how he had almost wrecked on the northern shore was still vivid and sharp. "Don't want to go there." A tingle of fear mixed with loneliness played on his emotions and he zoomed in on the thin column of smoke. "But that way is help."

Zack's confidence slipped away as he made his way toward the smoke. It was further than he thought and the nagging worry about finding his way back to the bay and *Wild Turtle* grew stronger. Only the aroma of meat roasting over an open fire drew him on. "How far can a smell carry?" he wondered. A gust of wind carried the strong odor of burnt meat and the sharp sound of a hammer beating on metal echoed over him. "Bingo!" A sense of relief cascaded over him and he plunged

Caly's Island

into the brush, following the sounds and smell. The brush grew heavier and scratched his bare legs, but he pressed ahead, eager to reach safety.

Zack broke into the open.

Without thinking, he dropped into a deep crouch and pulled back into the brush. His breathing slowed and his eyes narrowed as he scanned the scene in front of him. A large open area overlooked the shore where the strange sailing ship had run aground, and the remains of the beacon still smoldered at the edge of the low buffs. A corral with a fence made of the same thorny scrub Zack was hiding in filled the clearing. A large number of bearded men, most of them naked, were huddled together in the center of the corral. In the far corner, a pile of pottery jars, boxes, and bags were dumped along with debris from the ship. The wind shifted and the smell of urine and human waste blended with smoke from the cooking fire to create a sickening stench.

Zack pulled back into the bush when he saw the dogs, or what he assumed were dogs, that were guarding the men. They were huge with shaggy, matted coats encrusted with dirt and blood. Their snouts were broad and flat like a pit bull with vicious fangs that reminded him of saber-toothed tigers he had seen in a museum. It was a breed he had never seen and reduced mastiffs to gentle lapdogs. One of the dogs caught his scent and charged into the corral's fence, shaking the thicket, and barking. It was a howl straight from the depths of hell, and sent a jolt of pure fear through him. Five more dogs, all huge and from the same litter, charged into the fence, and for a moment, Zack was sure the animals would break through.

The clanging stopped and a voice shouted in a language he had never heard. The tone was deep and guttural but definitely belonged to a woman. Then he saw her. She was a hulking brute, well over seven-feet tall, with a roughly woven short skirt wrapped around her waist. Her legs were approximations of tree stumps, and a crude leather vest encased her upper torso, exposing most of her breasts and bare arms with biceps larger than his thighs. A wide mouth and crooked broken teeth scarred her face. Her flat nose separated wide-set eyes under a single heavy brow, and her long hair matched the dogs' coats as if they cohabitated the same den. There was nothing feminine about her, yet the creature was a woman. She charged into the dogs, a crude mallet in her hand, swinging and shouting at the animals. One snapped at her and, raging with fury, she kicked it, launching it into the air. The animal slunk away. All of

Dick Herman

Zack's training was back as he fought the fear that threatened to consume him. He crouched lower. Don't move, blend in with your surroundings, he thought. The dogs were in a pure frenzy as they charged around the woman.

The dogs finally quieted and the woman shook the fence to ensure it was still intact. If she looked up, she would see him. But she turned and stomped back to her work where she waded into the men and grabbed one by his hair. With a quick flick of a knife, she cut the last of his clothes away. She dragged him to the fire and, for a moment, Zack was sure she was going to cut his throat. Instead she threw him onto his stomach and planted a gnarled foot in his back, pinning him to the ground. The creature bent over and jerked his right foot over a flat rock next to the fire. She fitted a shackle over his ankle and fished a heated rivet out of the burning coals with a crude set of tongs. Zack couldn't look away as she deftly shoved the pin through the shackle's lock, raised the hammer and banged on the rivet, sealing the shackle. She stood and laughed. There was no humor in it and the sound would haunt him until his dying day.

Zack was horrified when the monster squatted over her handiwork and urinated on the hot rivet. A cloud of steam drifted over the compound. She pulled the man to his feet and shouted a name Zack couldn't make out. There was no answer. "Ka-rib!" she yelled again. A similar creature stood up in the middle of the men and rubbed her eyes, driving the sleep away. How can anyone sleep in all that? Zack wondered. But these were beasts from a hell beyond his worst nightmares. The second monster lumbered over to the man and grabbed him by the hair. Without a word, she dragged him to another group of men and ran a chain through a ring on the shackle, binding him to the others. Zack's eyes opened wide as the pieces came together. The men were sailors and the women had lit the beacon to lure them onto the rocks below their compound. Then he knew. The two monsters were slavers. Never in his innocence had he understood what that word truly meant. This was the working definition of barbarism and the shell of his civilization crumbled around him.

Satisfied with her work, the woman called Ka-rib lumbered over to a walled-off section of the corral and reached over the low wall. She pulled a large pig over the wall by a rear foot, deftly cut its throat, and sat on it as it bled out. Her knife flashed as she gutted the animal, spilling its

Caly's Island

entrails on the ground. Then she dragged it over to the fire and skewered the carcass with a stake. She hung the pig over the fire while the other monster dragged a man over and set him to work turning the carcass. Zack didn't move and studied every move the two creatures made. From the shouting back and forth, he learned the other's name – Silla. There was a clear division of labor in the compound. Silla was the master of the six dogs, and Ka-rib the slave master. An overpowering urge to run swept over him.

Ever so slowly, Zack inched his way backwards, pulling deeper into the scrub. Just when he was sure he was safe, one of the dogs came over to the fence. The beast looked directly at him, it's eyes burning with a ferocity that would never be dampened. Zack waited for it to bark and raise the alarm, but the dog just looked at him. Zack looked away, watching it with his peripheral vision, anxious to avoid direct eye contact that might send the beast into a frenzy. The dog raised its head and started to howl, high-pitched and keening. Slowly, it modulated into a human-like moan. The woman called Silla stomped over to it and drove her fist into its forehead, driving it into the ground. Zack was sure she had killed the dog, but it came to its feet and slunk away. Silla looked up and saw Zack. For a moment, they stared at each other.

"Ka-rib!" she bellowed. The other monster came running. Silla pointed directly at Zack and uttered three words, totally foreign to Zack. But he knew "Loose the dogs" when he heard it. He came to his feet and ran, deliberately turning to the west and away from *Wild Turtle*.

Pandemonium broke out in the corral as the two women ran for the gate. They quickly pulled back the thorny thicket and yelled at the dogs. All six of the animals ran through the opening in hot pursuit. At the same time, the men who were still unshackled bolted for the opening before the two brutes could close it. Silla yelled at the top of her lungs. The dogs skidded to a halt and came running back. Each one lunged at an escaping man and dragged him to the ground, savagely ripping at his neck. Zack never saw the six men die as he ran for all he was worth.

The women waded into the dogs, pulling them off. They were barbarians in the truest sense of the word, but they understood the basics of the slave trade. The men were too valuable as trading commodities to use as dog food. But the dogs were in a feeding frenzy. Silla beat on the smallest dog until she was able to pull it off a mangled corpse. She dragged the dog out the gate and pointed in the direction Zack had fled.

She issued a command and the lone dog raced after Zack. It let out a howl that echoed in the still air.

Two miles away, Zack heard the dog's cry. There was no doubt it was baying for him and in hot pursuit. He hugged the shoreline and put on a burst of speed, only to stumble and fall. Then he was up and running again, but it was only a matter of time until the dog caught him.

Sean held the whisker pole from *Wee Dram* upright as Blair anchored it in the soft sand. The older man used a plumb line to make sure it was vertical, and stood back about fifty feet to the south. He sighted on it with his hand-held bearing compass, looking due north. "Sean, draw a line in the sand straight north from the base of the whisker pole. About three feet long should do it." Blair used his left hand to give directions. "A little to the left, there. You got it." The two worked together and turned the line into a narrow trench, two inches wide and four inches deep. "Now we wait for the shadow from the whisker pole to fill the trench," Blair said. He stopped his watch and set the hands at twelve o'clock. They sat in the sand and waited as the sun reached its zenith. When the shadow from the whisker pole filled the narrow trench, Blair depressed the stem on his watch, starting the time. "It's high noon local time, give or take a few seconds."

"Why do you need to be so accurate?" Sean asked.

"I want to see if there's a star I can identify lined up with Polaris at exactly midnight. I might be able to find our longitude."

"Can you do that?"

"I don't know," Blair confessed. "I read a book on how the Chinese determined longitude eight hundred years ago. Maybe I can do the same thing. Who knows? There's a lot of knowledge in the group. I'm pretty good at math, but Steve is in a league all his own. Gib's got a computer, and Rufe can make things. It's just a matter of using what we got." He stood and pulled up the whisker pole. "Are you up for a little exploring on your own?"

"I'm hungry," Sean answered.

"I know, but we need to ration our food for now. We'll eat this evening. I'd like you to look around and see if you can find any fruit or anything that looks edible. Don't taste it but bring it back here. Who knows? You might find Angus." Sean nodded. "Good. Take a VHF radio and only turn it on to check in. We need to conserve our batteries." He thought for a moment. "Check in on the hour." They synchronized their watches and Blair fitted him with a backpack, baseball cap, and water bottle. "Don't go too far." He handed him a pocket compass. "Off you go." He watched Sean until he disappeared into the low trees to the east. Blair retrieved the whisker pole and checked on Sasha. She was sweating and he took her temperature – 102 degrees.

"You like him very much," Sasha said.

"He's a good kid."

"Do you have children?"

Blair shrugged. "Not that I know of."

"You never married?"

He pulled into himself, recalling that time. He doubted that Sasha would understand how his love of flying had doomed his marriage. Unless they had been there, few people did. How could he describe the pure joy of flying a modern jet fighter that could dance on the head of a pin as it maneuvered or reached for the heavens? Or what it was like to takeoff and punch through a heavy overcast only to break out on top with a clear blue sky that reached to eternity? At times, it was like riding a whirlwind, defying all laws of gravity. Yet the aircraft were infinitely demanding, challenging you to match their performance. And if you were found lacking in skill and judgment, they could kill you.

The jets were the ultimate efficiency-machine with no quarter given, but the rewards were beyond imagination, and capped with the knowledge that you walked with a select few. And how could he ever describe combat, the ultimate challenge where you pitted your skill and your aircraft's performance against a deadly enemy? It had taken everything he had, and his marriage had shattered under the strain. Blair caught her studying his face. Did she sense what he was thinking? He focused on the moment and answered her question. "I was married once. It didn't last long. I was in the Air Force and loved the flying. The Service was my life, but it was too much for her. I never blamed her for leaving me. Before I knew it, it was over. I retired and taught college for a few years. Meteorology."

"I studied meteorology in Kiev," Sasha said. "I wanted to be a weather forecaster on the television. I was first in my class." She humphed in contempt. "But men only want to sleep with me, not give me a job."

"So you came to the States and became a hit woman."

Sasha didn't take offense. "It pays well, and I do other things." She gave him the look. "Why don't you want to sleep with me?"

Blair laughed. "Well, you are taller than me."

"Is that important?" Again, the look. "Are you gay?"

"No. I just never found the right woman."

"The Judge is back," Sasha said.

Blair turned in time to see *Habeas Corpus* clear the lagoon's entrance. "That was quick." He walked down to the water to beach the boat. "Where's Rufe?" he asked.

"Right behind me," Gib answered. The two men pulled *Habeas Corpus* onto the sand. "I think we're on an island," Gib announced. There was an odd sound in his voice. "We headed south, but after a mile the shoreline curved around to the southeast. We'd gone ten or twelve miles when we saw a break in the shore. At first I though it was a bay, but it was a pass, maybe two miles wide, with clear ocean on the other side – to the north. There was a small island in the center of the pass." He clicked on his camera and hit the review button, showing Blair what he had seen.

"So why didn't you keep going? You'd have probably run into Pete and Steve coming towards you."

"There's Rufe," Gib said. His words were as drawn and tired as his face. "We tried to sail into the pass but a hellacious current and a fierce headwind came out of the north and pushed us back. Once we were pushed back, the current and headwind completely died away. We tried it three times. The last time, Rufe started his motor but the current and wind just got stronger. So we came back while things were still under control."

The two men caught *Nailing On* as it beached. Rufus hopped off, a very worried man. "That was weird," he said.

"Did you see anything, smoke, animals, buildings?" Blair asked.

"Nothing," Gib replied. Rufus nodded in agreement.

"Any luck with the GPS or radios?" Blair asked.

Gib shook his head. His ordered and rational world had taken a serious hit since coming out of the fog and he was shaken to the core. As a judge, he had been in control, the master of those in his courtroom. It had been a giddy ego stroke, yet a humbling experience at the same time, but this was different and he would never be the same.

Caly's Island

"I hope Pete and Steve are okay," Rufus said.

TWELVE

Zack had been running for over two hours when he hit "the wall" and collapsed. His body's glycogen was depleted and had to start burning stored fat, but his system wasn't delivering the energy fast enough. The baying grew louder and Zack raised his head. It had been a long run and he had shaken off the dog twice, first by wading up a stream, and then by darting through a lava field. But each time the animal had ranged until it picked up his scent. Now the chase was nearing the end game; however, he had one more trick to play.

He fumbled through the first aid kit in his fanny bag and found the small stainless steel tube left over from his days in the CIA. He cracked it open. Inside was a go-faster pill. Zack hesitated before swallowing it. His trainers had warned him what it could do to his liver, but it guaranteed a sudden burst of energy that was good for thirty or forty minutes. After that, "the wall" would be nothing compared to the crash landing he would suffer. He washed the pill down with the last of his water and stumbled to his feet, discarding his fanny bag. The pill kicked in and the chase was on again.

Twenty minutes later the baying stopped. The hunt was over and he twisted around, looking for the beast. A loud crashing sound echoed from the thicket, but he couldn't see the animal. He searched for a tree, but there was nothing high enough that was out of the reach of the savage jaws that could rip a man apart. Again, he heard the crashing sound as the dog closed in. Where was it! Out of ideas, he ran for the water and waded into the low surf. It was not a rational decision, and he was certain the dog could swim. He was swimming within a few feet and the cool water temporarily revived him. The dog broke from the thicket and bounded into the water with huge leaps. It came to the surface and paddled relentlessly for him. Zack rolled onto his back and backstroked, looking directly at the animal as it closed on him, paddling furiously, its eyes fixed on him. A white-hot anger surged through Zack. One of them was going to die and it wasn't him. He took a deep breath and dove.

Zack stroked for the bottom, kicking hard. He turned and looked up in the incredibly clear water. The dog was trying to dive but only descended a few feet before lack of breath, or its buoyancy, forced it to the surface. Zack exhaled slightly and watched the animal as it circled, waiting for him to come up for air. His rising bubbles excited the dog and it tried to dive, but it only descended a few feet before popping to the surface. The odds had slipped in Zack's favor.

Zack stroked for the surface, timing his ascent to blindside the dog. The dog stopped circling and Zack kicked furiously as he exhaled, surfacing behind the dog. He gasped for air and dove. The dog was right behind him. Once again, it only descended a few feet before surfacing. Years before, Zack had learned how to kill a dog at 'The Farm,' the CIA's training school at Camp Peary, Virginia, but this dog was beyond anything in the CIA's manual. Zack timed his ascent and shot for the surface, this time coming up beside the dog. He grabbed a handful of hair, swung a leg over the dog's back, and tried to lock his ankles in a scissors grip under its belly. The animal was too large and he could only ride it like a bucking bronco. Fighting to stay on, he threw his arms around the dog's neck. His legs flapped like a rag doll as the dog twisted and rolled in a desperate attempt to throw its rider.

Zack forced his right shoulder against the back of the animal's massive head and tried to force it under water. But the dog threw its head back and forth, and he was lucky just to hold on. The dog rolled and he lost his grip. He managed to grab an ear with his left hand as he fell free. It saved his life as the downward pressure turned the animal's massive jaws away from him. The dog pawed at him with its rear legs and a claw raked his stomach in a single slashing stroke. Blood mushroomed in the water as Zack's gut exploded in a searing pain.

Somehow, he managed to grab a handful of loose skin on its neck with his right hand and remount the dog. He clenched the dog's ears and clamped his knees against its massive body, forcing the animal's head underwater. The dog reared up to take a breath and Zack threw his weight forward. Now they were in a rocking horse motion, down and up.

Caly's Island

Slowly, the dog tired and Zack was able to hold its head under for longer periods. Finally, he held it there. The animal went limp as it drowned.

He rode the dog and held it under water, afraid that it wasn't dead. Zack's head barely broke the surface and he blinked to clear his vision. A huge fin cut the water left to right then back again as it ranged on the scent of blood. Zack was at the apex of the scent triangle and the shark was swimming along the base, but each leg was shorter as it closed on Zack and the triangle grew smaller. A second fin surfaced behind the first, then a third and fourth. Zack panicked and swam for shore. He flailed at the water in a blind rush. His hand touched the bottom and he tried to come to his feet, but his legs cramped and he collapsed into the water.

Behind him, the first shark hit the dog and ripped a huge hunk out of the carcass. The sharks went into a feeding frenzy and tore at each other and the dog. Zack pulled himself into shallower water and tried to stand. Again, he collapsed. This time he rolled sideways until he was on the sand. He turned onto his back and held his stomach, trying to staunch the flow of blood. He looked up into the clear blue sky. "I could use some help down here!" he cried. A welcomed warmth swept over him as he sank into unconsciousness.

Sean held the compass Blair had given him and walked due east through the trees. It was easy going and he wasn't worried about retracing his steps as he climbed a low ridge. Behind him, the headland overlooking the lagoon where they were camped served as a constant reference, pointing the way home. Encouraged, he followed the ridge and came to an overlook. The terrain dipped away and a low dale spread out in front of him. He checked his watch. It was time to check in, and he fumbled with the radio, finally turning it on. "Admiral, this is Sean."

"Read you loud and clear. How's it going?"

"I'm on a ridge east of you and can see the rocks over the lagoon. I found a little valley and see a path."

Blair heard the enthusiasm in Sean's voice and knew the teenager wanted to follow the path. But all his warning flags were flying. "Hold on for a moment before you charge off. Do you see anyone down there? Any signs of smoke?"

"It's just a path."

Blair heard Sean's frustration and anger in those simple words. The teenager was up against adult authority and Blair was the problem. The older man sensed they had come to a watershed in their relationship and it was all about trust. However, Blair was worried that the teenager might be in harm's way. "There could be some mean dudes down there. You're on your own so engage your brain. Make sure you know what you're headed into, and always check six."

"It's okay for me to go?"

"It's your decision. I'm not there. I can't see what you see. But stay on the path so you don't get lost. Rufe will be really pissed off at me if that happens. If you see anyone, be careful and run like hell at the first sign of trouble. If you see anything spooky or strange, get back here ASAP."

Sean's confidence and morale went over the moon. His brain kicked in and he remembered what Blair had told him about their radios: they were line-of-sight and short range. "I might be out of radio contact down there."

"Take a couple of hours before you head back." He was already having second doubts and was worrying like a good parent. If he were a religious man, he would have had prayer beads out and worrying them.

"I'll be okay," Sean assured Blair. He turned off the radio and scrambled down the path, heading into the valley. The undulating path hadn't been used in a long time and the chirping birds fell silent at his approach. A fruity smell caught his attention and he followed the scent into a wild stand of pear trees. He picked one off a low hanging branch and sniffed it. Normally, he would have curled his lips in disdain, but his hunger got the better of him and he took a bite. It was the perfect pear, not too hard or woody, yet firm and sweet. He wolfed it down. Even though he was alone, he was embarrassed by the juice dribbling down his chin and took a quick swipe at it with his left hand.

A soft giggle teased him from behind. "Are you left handed?"

Sean twisted around and froze. He was looking at a vision. A girl his age stared back at him with big green eyes, her head cocked to one side. Her long blonde hair was swept back and around, gathered in a loose ponytail over her left shoulder where it cascaded down her back. Her full lips were slightly parted revealing perfect teeth, and her faultless complexion did not need makeup. Starlets would have gladly sold their soul to a plastic surgeon for her nose and firm breasts. The girl was

Caly's Island

exactly Sean's height and wearing a short, cream-colored, off the shoulder dress cinched at her narrow waist with a golden cord. Her arms were bare, and the short hemline revealed perfectly shaped legs. Simple leather sandals protected her small feet. Like any good healthy teenager, Sean fell instantly in love. She smiled at him and he was undone.

"Cat got your tongue?"

Sean nodded dumbly, certain in his teenager's heart that anything he said would be totally uncool.

She laughed and his heart did a flip-flop. "You are silly." She sat on a rock and beckoned for him to join her. They sat close, but did not touch. She smelled sweet and he thought of wildflowers, or the sea, or of lemons. To say he was confused was simply acknowledging the eternal truth of every teenager in love. She turned and flicked her hair and batted her thick eyelashes as she looked at him. "I'm Caly, welcome to my island."

Somehow, Sean found the courage to answer and used a line from the movies he had practiced in front of a mirror. He pitched his voice low. "My name is Homes, Sean Homes."

"Sean. That's a nice name. Is your family name important? Homes?"

Suddenly, he had to talk. "My stepmom says it is. My dad's a senator."

"I don't know what 'stepmom' or 'senator' means. But I don't trust adults who think titles are important." Again, she flashed the smile that melted his brain. "Let's not talk about that. Are you hungry?"

"Oh, yeah! Sometimes, I'm hungry all the time. Once, I even ate dog food. It was pretty good."

She laughed. "You must have been very hungry. Come." She stood and took him by the hand. Together, they walked into the grove. "Let's pick some pears for your friends. I've got a picnic. Not much, just some bread and cheese. Oh, and some grapes. You'll like them."

"I liked the pear."

"But you normally don't eat pears."

It never occurred to Sean to ask how she knew that. He was just happy to be with her.

* * * *

Dick Herman

The sun was low in the west when Zack opened his eyes. His entire body ached, which was reassuring as it indicated he was alive. He blinked, urging his eyes to focus, and came up on one elbow. Something felt strange and he glanced at his stomach. A thick bandage was wrapped around his torso covering most of his wound. The gashes had been cleaned and a yellow-like salve smeared over the long scratch marks that extended above and below the bandage. The pain was gone. "I'll be damned," he muttered. Confused, he looked around. He was lying under a tree above the sand where he had passed out, and skid marks in the sand marked his path. How did I get up here? he asked himself. His mind was a blank and he couldn't remember crawling. Yet, he was in the shade and that had saved him from a bad sunburn. His water bottle was beside him, filled to the brim. He took a long drink. It was cool and refreshing.

"Whoever you are, thanks," he called, coming carefully to his feet. The after-effects of the go-faster pill still burned in his body and he wobbled. The ocean was in front of him and the setting sun was to his left – he was looking north. He shook his head, hardly believing that he had finally gotten his bearings on his own. Angela would be proud of him. He scanned the calm waters looking for any sign of the sharks, but only the dog's carcass was washed up on the shore, a grisly tribute to nature's justice. He walked down to the shore. The dog's head and three legs had been torn off and large chunks ripped from its underside. But what was left was still huge and he tried to envision it whole. It was more the size of small horse than any dog he knew. The image of the monster kicking it came back, putting her size in perspective. He made a mental note to avoid the two monsters at all costs.

"So which way to *Wild Turtle*?" he wondered aloud. His survival depended on finding his boat. "The volcano, that's the clue," he reasoned, scanning the far horizon. The edge of panic touched him when he didn't see it. "Find high ground." The decision made, he walked along the beach, towards the setting sun. He wasn't sure why he went in that direction, but it felt right. He saw a big rock jutting into the ocean and headed for it. It was an easy climb to the top and he looked around. "Which way to the bay?" he asked himself, his eyes squinting. A jolt of fear hit him when he saw a thin trail of smoke far to the east, rising into the air. It had to be coming from the monsters' slave stockade. "Don't go there." But that was the way back to *Wild Turtle*.

Caly's Island

Far to the south, he saw the volcano rising into the sky, its summit bathed in a dull red glow. At first, he thought it was the sunset. Then, "I'll be damned, it's really active now." He sat on the rock and took a swig of water as he stared at the volcano. He was on the verge of collapse and had to find shelter for the night. His head came up when he saw a thin wisp of smoke rise above the low trees less than a hundred yards away. An image of the two monsters flashed in his mind and the fear was back. "I don't think so," he rationalized. It had to be the Good Samaritan who had dressed his wound and dragged him into the shade. He tried to stand, but lost his balance and had to sit to scoot off the rock. After resting for a few moments, he headed into the trees.

Zack picked his way slowly through the long shadows, stopping every few feet to gather his strength. The trees opened up into a wide, grassy clearing with a cottage in the center surrounded by a kitchen garden. The small house was made of a granite-like stone with a slate roof. A grape vine encircled the open door, and the window shutters were thrown back. Smoke drifted from a chimney at one end, and he smelled the fragrant aroma of cooking. He hesitated, not sure what to do, and almost retreated into the trees. Then he knew – this was not the barbarism he had encountered with the slavers. Besides, he was out of options. "Hello, the house," he called.

A figure appeared in the doorway, indistinct in the long shadows, and Zack staggered towards the house, each step more tiring. It was a young woman wearing what looked like a long T-shirt tied at the waist. She waved at him and he took a few more steps as she stepped out of the house and into the light. The girl was slender and young, and looked vaguely familiar, an image from his past. Zack stopped and stared at her. "Angela?"

She smiled and he passed out.

The radio squawked at Blair. "Admiral, Sean. How copy?"

The relief Blair felt was palpable as he keyed his radio. "Read you five-by."

"Roger," Sean answered. "I'm okay. RTB in thirty minutes."

"Copy all," Blair replied. "See you then."

"Sean out."

Blair allowed a tight smile; Sean was using correct radio discipline. Sasha gave him the look. "You were worried for nothing."

"I shouldn't have let him go off on his own."

"That is how he learns," she replied. She pointed to the lagoon as Pete and Steve sailed through the entrance. "They are back."

Blair walked down to the water's edge and waited with Rufe and Gib. They caught the boats and dragged them up onto the sand. Pete released his main sheet and let the sail flap. He climbed off *L'Amour* holding a map, his face strained and haggard. Steve just sat in *High Flyer*, on the edge of collapse. "We're definitely on an island," Pete announced. "Nada on people, radios or the GPS." He walked to the canopy where Sasha was sitting and collapsed into a camp chair. Blair, Gib, and Rufus were right behind him.

"We ran into some pretty tough conditions and had to come back," Pete said, his voice cracking with fatigue. "We were damn lucky to make it." He spread out the chart he had sketched. "We sailed north for four miles, maybe two hundred yards off shore." He pointed to the northwest corner of the island. "We saw two hills here, I'd guess about five-hundred feet high. We turned east, still following the shoreline, and found a stream here." He pointed to a spot on the north shore. "That was the only fresh water we found. Not as good as what we've got here, so we headed out again, still going east. After four miles or so, the shoreline turns to the southeast. We made good time and discovered a few coves and beaches, but they're all open to the north and not protected from the weather. After sailing southeast for about ten miles, we reached the end of the island. There's another island about a mile further to the southeast and a big landmass a mile beyond it. I'm guessing that's an island too. Anyway, we turned south to go through the pass and round the island. We were making a good five knots, and I was sure we could be back here in four or five hours."

Pete paused and his friends had never seen him look so haggard and drawn. "That's when the shit hit the fan. I'm maybe a quarter mile in front of Steve. The moment I got near the tip of the island, I got hit with a headwind and current you wouldn't believe. The wind came out of nowhere, maybe fifty knots, and knocked *L'Amour* over. I'm in the water and *L'Amour's* on her side. Luckily, the companionway boards are in and the hatch closed, otherwise *L'Amour* would've swamped or turtled. I

Caly's Island

lost my GPS and camera, but my radio floats so I grabbed it. Anyway, I held onto the centerboard and the current pushes me back to Steve.

"Now it really gets weird. Steve is fine, no wind, no current. We're talking a couple of hundred yards and the conditions are like night and day. Steve gets a line to me and we right *L'Amour*. I'm wet, but OK, and the cabin's got a little water in it. Steve figures it was a weather phenomena called a microburst. Airplanes get hit with 'em occasionally and crash. He figures the current going through the pass is causing a cold water upwelling, which creates all sorts of weird conditions. Like idiots, we figure we've got it all worked out and try again. We head into the pass and all hell breaks loose. I mean sixty-knot winds this time. We both get knocked down, but our luck holds and the boats come up on their own, but Steve is overboard and the current is pushing us back to the north. The wind is still blowing like hell, but I manage to get Steve on board. *High Flyer* takes off on her own, and we have to chase her down. I'm afraid to start my motor because it was under water and the oil needs to be flushed. We're halfway back here before *High Flyer* heads up into the wind and we catch her."

The men set in silence, trying to understand what it all meant. "When we tried to round the island in the same place," Gib finally said, "we ran into a strong headwind and current that blew us back."

"That doesn't make sense," Pete said. "You came from the south and we were coming from the north so the wind and current should have been behind you and pushed you through."

"They got there a couple of hours before you did," Blair explained. "Maybe the tide or current had changed."

"I think I know where we are," Steve said. As one, every head turned. They hadn't seen him get off *High Flyer*. "That big landmass Pete talked about could be the island of Malta. If it is, we're on an island called Gozo. Sorry, no photos. I lost my camera when we capsized."

Blair lit up like a Green Bay Packers fan who had finally gotten season tickets. He was supercharged and in overdrive. "We need a map of the Mediterranean. Everyone, get your GPS. One of 'em might have a European map database we can call up. Gib, does your laptop have an atlas or a trip planning program?" The FOGs ran to their boats. Moments later, they were all back, fingers frantically pressing buttons, but without an uplink to a NAVSTAR satellite or a connection to the internet, they came up dry. "Someone must have a map of Europe

131

somewhere," Blair said. "In a book, someplace you wouldn't expect." He worked to keep their spirits from crashing.

Now it was Rufus's turn to light up. He ran for *Nailing On* and rummaged through the cabin, finally finding what he wanted. He ran back, waving a pocket planner and address book. He thumbed to the back and found a map of Europe. "It's not much," he said. He touched a dot in the Mediterranean south of Sicily labeled 'Malta,' but there was no second dot for Gozo.

"Gozo is on the western side of Malta," Steve said.

"You've been here before?" Blair asked.

Steve shook his head. "Not to Gozo, but I've been to Malta."

"How sure are you?" Blair asked.

Steve held up his hands and shrugged. "It looks right."

"It's something," Blair conceded. He thumbed through the other maps in the pocket planner.

"Well, well," Blair chortled. "Looky here." He squinted at a very small time zone map in the pocket planner. "Malta's longitude is approximately fifteen degrees east."

"How do you know that?" Pete asked. "There's no longitude on the map."

"Each time zone is fifteen degrees wide and Malta is in the middle of time zone Alpha. Alpha is on the eastern side of time zone Zulu. The Greenwich Meridian, zero degrees longitude, splits Zulu right down the middle, so Zulu extends seven and a half degrees of longitude west and east of Greenwich. Alpha runs from seven and a half to twenty-two and a half degrees east longitude."

"And as Malta is in the middle of Alpha," Gib concluded, "we are at fifteen degrees east longitude. But more germane to the discussion," he said in his somber and stately way, "how did we get here?" – his voice hardened – "and how the fuck do we get back?" They all looked at him in shocked silence.

"And where are all the people?" Blair finally added. "I thought these islands were heavily populated."

"They are," Steve answered.

"Here's your young friend," Sasha said. Sean was running across the sand.

"I met a girl," he said breathlessly. "Her name is Caly. We're on her island and she lives here all alone."

THIRTEEN

It was a new experience for Sean. He had often been the center of adults' attention, but never like this. The frustration and anger that marked his normal reaction to adults was gone, and what he had to say was truly important, not only for the men, but for himself. "She's my age and lives in a cave."

"Did you go there?" Blair asked.

Sean shook his head. "We just hung around and talked."

"What did you talk about?" Gib asked.

"Ah, nothing. You know."

Rufus laughed, fully understanding what 'nothing' meant to a teenager. "Yeah, I do. She's pretty nice, right?" A shy nod answered him. "Sean, she may be able to help us. Sasha needs medical attention and we need to get to a phone to call for help."

"I don't think she's got a phone," Sean replied. "Things are pretty simple here."

"Sean," Pete asked, "don't you think it's strange that a girl lives here all alone?"

Sean was very confused. No one was angry or doubting him, but they raised questions he couldn't answer, and a voice deep inside told him that he should know the answers. "She seems pretty cool with it."

"Tell us how you met and what you did," Pete said, gently interrogating him. "Take your time, start from the beginning, and try to remember everything that happened." Sean sat on the sand and methodically recounted his entire afternoon, encouraged by their undivided attention. For the most part, it was the age-old story of two teenagers meeting and stumbling around the edge of intimacy, oblivious to their surroundings and reality. Pete's years of courtroom experience helping witnesses reconstruct an event paid dividends as he carefully separated fact from emotion. Finally, Sean was finished. "Did she say how to contact her?" Pete asked.

"She said to come to the same place tomorrow and wait." Sean fidgeted, suddenly very uncomfortable. "I got'a take a leak." He stood and headed for the slit trench Blair had dug for a latrine.

Once Sean was out of earshot, Pete asked, "What do you think?"

"She was in control from the very first," Gib said. "They did what she wanted, she revealed little, and Sean responded the way she desired."

"That is true," Sasha said. "This Caly is much older than Sean thinks."

"He couldn't have been too far off," Blair replied. "Kids know kids."

"How old do you think I am?" Sasha asked.

"Early twenties," Pete answered. His friends nodded in agreement.

"I'm forty-two," Sasha told them. They looked at her in stunned silence.

"You have damned good genes," Pete allowed. He turned to Blair, eager to change the subject. "What's next on the agenda?"

"We eat dinner," Blair replied, "and tomorrow Gib goes with Sean to meet Caly." The expression on Pete's face demanded an explanation. "Gib's the ultimate father-figure."

"H, I think you should go," Gib said. "I may look like a father-figure, but in Sean's eyes, you are the real McCoy and he will react accordingly. Based on what Sean has told us, I believe she will sense that immediately." He arched an eyebrow in anticipation. "I'm hungry. Let's eat."

They were a well-organized team as Rufus built a fire while Pete cleaned the fish Blair had caught earlier. Once the coals had set, Rufus grilled the fish, Blair prepared a pot of rice, and Steve opened two cans of vegetables from their common larder. They ate in silence. Afterwards, Sean helped Blair clean up and the men went their separate ways.

Rufus sat alone on a rock and watched the sunset as twilight enveloped them. The old ache was back as he thought about Cheryl, his ex-wife. An inner voice warned him he had to move on, but he couldn't let go. When he had finished with his chores, Sean joined him, bringing

Caly's Island

the blacksmith back to the moment. "Mr. Gunnermyer, may I ask you a question?"

"Sure. Have a seat. And you can call me Rufus or Rufe, like everyone else."

Sean sat beside him. "When I was talking on the radio today with the Admiral, he said you would really be pissed off at him if I got lost." He studied his feet, not exactly sure what he wanted to say.

Rufus sensed what was bothering the teenager. "And you're wondering if it was true." Sean nodded, thankful the older man understood and he didn't have to explain. "Yeah," Rufus continued, "I'd have been pissed off, really pissed off." Sean didn't understand. "Me and the Admiral need to have a 'come to Jesus' talk. He made a bad decision. He let you go off on your own without a buddy to cover your back. If you got lost or hurt, I'm the guy who would have to find you, or your body. You ever see a corpse?" Sean shook his head. "Trust me, you don't want to. Look, when the Admiral was flying fighters and getting his ass shot off, he always had a wingman to cover his backside. So who was your wingman today? He made a bad decision." Rufus reached out and clasped Sean's shoulder. "But you did good."

"I did?"

"You made contact with a person and got back safe and sound. Go talk to the Admiral about it." He turned and walked to *Nailing On*, leaving a very confused teenager sitting in the dark.

Sean pulled into himself, fighting the emotions raging inside. It bothered him that he hadn't told them everything about Caly. She had warned him not to trust any adult and be careful what he told them. Still confused, he decided to take Rufus's advice and talk to Blair. He walked over to *Wee Dram* to get his sleeping bag and bed down for the night. Blair was sitting in the cockpit studying the northern sky. "Are you looking for Polaris?" he asked.

"Nope." Blair pointed to the North Star. "There's Polaris. I'm looking for a red glow on the horizon. If we're on Gozo, we're south of Sicily. It so happens that Mount Etna, one of the world's biggest and most active volcanoes, is on Sicily."

"How do you know that?"

Blair laughed. "I was the only student awake in my high school geography class. You never know when you'll need something you learn. If Etna erupts, we might be able to see it, especially at night. That would tell us a lot."

"Admiral," Sean blurted without thinking, "you said something about 'check six' today. What's that mean?"

"Don't get blindsided from the rear. When I was flying fighters, it was the guy you never saw who shot you down from behind."

Sean was amazed that the short, bald, skinny old man had flown jet fighters in combat. "People were shooting at you?"

"Oh, yeah."

"Why?"

Blair flung his hands up and rolled his eyeballs in mock frustration. "Because I was dropping bombs on them and doing my damnedest to kill them." He played it like a good fighter pilot. "For some reason, they took offense. No sense of humor, I guess."

Sean caught it and laughed. Then it hit him; Blair was an aerial assassin and had killed people, apparently quite a few. It was a revelation for Sean as he reevaluated the man in front of him. Blair didn't fit his image of a fighter pilot and his brain was engaged, overriding his turbocharged emotions. "Commander Charles and those Coast Guard guys, do they get shot at too?"

"Probably. You'd have to ask them, but they won't like talking about it. I know I don't."

"And cops?" He was thinking about Officer Roberts of the Bellingham police force.

"Cops get killed all the time. It's a pretty dangerous job."

Sean fell silent. He needed time to think. Being fifteen years old didn't help, as well as the aforementioned emotions that kept getting in the way. "Why did you let me go off on my own today? Wasn't that dangerous?"

"It sure was. Not my smartest move. I thought you could handle it and it was time to find out if you could. You did."

"But what if something had happened to me? Like if I got killed."

They had come to the crux of the matter. Is he ready for the truth? Blair thought. He decided to take the chance. "That would have hurt very much and I would've blamed myself, but I would've learned that there was a definite danger out there." Blair grinned, making light of it. "On the plus side, there would've been one less mouth to feed. Seriously, you were on the point today and could have been in harm's way. You did good."

"I did?"

"Sean, if you had screwed up, I'd be the first to tell you. Trust me, you did good out there."

Sean nodded, picked up his sleeping bag, and turned to go. Another thought came to him and he stopped. "I didn't find Angus."

"He'll come back," Blair said, not at all sure that he would.

Pete bailed out *L'Amour's* cabin from the capsize and hung out his wet gear and cushions to dry in the warm night air. He made himself as comfortable as possible in the bare cabin and pulled his journal out of its watertight bag. For the next hour, he recaptured all that had happened since making landfall on the island. Satisfied the facts were in place, he slowly wrote an addendum.

Everything about this place defies logic and no jury would ever buy it. Fortunately, nothing seems to bother the Admiral and he just pushes ahead, taking it one step at a time. There is no way we can be on Gozo, and who is this Callie, or Caly, that Sean met. A beautiful young girl living alone on an island makes even less sense. All things considered, everyone is holding up well and no one has panicked. I worry about Steve, he's not that strong. Growing old sucks. Sasha dropped a bombshell about her age. What else have we misjudged about her?

Pete zipped the journal back into its bag and stretched out under the blanket Gib had leant him. "Thanks guys," he murmured, drifting off to sleep.

Zack slowly came awake and forced the fog back. He sensed that he was still lying on the ground in front of the little cottage house and covered with a blanket. Every instinct he possessed urged him to surrender to the warmth and go back to sleep. A soft hand touched his cheek and his eyes snapped open. The young woman was sitting beside him, patiently waiting. He blinked his eyes. The resemblance to his wife when they were young and first met was uncanny. The after-effects of the go-faster pill were still playing havoc with his mental processes and he had slipped a cog, convinced that she was Angela. "I thought I would never see you again." She only looked at him, not understanding what he was saying. Another thought came to him and he panicked. "Please don't tell me I'm dead."

Her laughter rang like a bell, clear and pure. She bent over and kissed him lightly on the cheek. He certainly didn't feel dead. She spoke a few words in a language he had never heard. "Okay, so we're experiencing a failure to communicate." He pointed to his chest and said "Zack" before pointing to her with a puzzled look. No response. She laughed as he struggled to his knees to face her. He flexed his muscles and tried to look manly as he spoke in a deep voice. "Zack." Again, he pointed to her, but this time flipped his hair and batted his eyelids, asking the unspoken question. This time, she understood.

She pointed to her breast. "Circe."

It sounded like 'sir-see' to his ear, sweet and melodious, but he knew, without doubt, she was Angela. He pantomimed as he talked. "I am hungry and thirsty." She laughed, delighted with the game, bounced to her feet, and ran into the house. Her backside wiggled at him like Angela. "Oh, boy," he breathed. "I'm in trouble." That was exactly what he had said on a beach years ago when he first met Angela. Circe was back with a beautiful glazed bowl filled with a delicious smelling stew and a jug of water. She knelt in front of him and spoon-fed him, murmuring softly in the same language.

When she had finished feeding him, she leaned back and studied his face. "Hungry?" Her voice was soft and filled with music. He shook his head. Circe pointed to him. "You" – she pointed to his eyes – "see" – she pointed to her breast – "me."

He repeated the gestures. "You see me." Her smile was beautiful as she leaned forward and kissed him again, this time on the lips. She helped him to his feet. He was weak and very unsteady. "Fever." He touched his cheek and then his forehead.

She touched his cheek and looked at him in alarm. "Fever."

He nodded in answer. "Yes."

She nodded and said "yes." They were definitely communicating.

"You are a quick study," he replied. She came up on tiptoe and kissed him again. "I love your language lessons," he told her. She helped him inside.

Caly's Island

* * * *

The coals glowed in the fireplace as the fire died. The woman sat in a rough-hewn rocking chair, creaking back and forth on the flagstone floor. A slight draft drifted over her, providing the ventilation needed to draw the smoke up the chimney. She pulled a shaggy wool rug over her lap to break the cool temperature of the small cave. It was a comfortable chamber. Small alcoves were chiseled into the wall for storage, and a much larger one for her bed, a straw mattress covered by a down-filled duvet. A heavy wool curtain sealed the sleeping alcove off for warmth. At the back, a wooden bench held a stone basin for washing and pottery jars for storing water. An antechamber served as a lavatory. The plumbing consisted of a small rivulet that flowed into a deep cavern that was flushed by the changing tides. The entrance was sealed by a heavy door that rolled out of a hidden niche, but she couldn't remember how long it had been since the door had closed.

"He's awfully young," she said. "Too bad about the tattoos on his arms. They're terrible." The fire glowed with warmth. "But he is nice." The fire cooled. "Don't be jealous. I wonder what his friends are like." The fire flared. "Not to worry, I'll be careful." The fire settled down. "It has been a long time, and I am lonely." The coals glowed with understanding. She rocked and brushed her long hair. "No one said there was a woman." Her voice was filled with reproach, and the fire went out. "So they didn't tell you either. You're forgiven." The fire came back. She cleaned a few long gray strands of hair from her brush. "Thank them for sending someone." The coals glowed red as she laid her brush aside and picked up Angus.

FOURTEEN

Rufus carried the dry logs to the beach and dropped them on the sand. He brushed his hands and watched the long shadows of twilight surrender to the morning. It was his favorite time of day. The lump on the sand stirred and Sean stuck his head out of his sleeping bag. "Rise and shine," he told the teenager. "I can use some help."

"Whatssup?" Sean grumped.

"Making charcoal. Can you dig a pit about three by three?" Sean nodded and Rufus trudged back into the trees.

Sean used a stick and a small flat rock to scoop out a hole. Satisfied with his work, he washed his hands in the lagoon. He ate a pear while he waited for Rufus to return. Movement in the trees caught his attention, but it wasn't Rufus. Hoping it was Angus finally back from whatever he was doing, Sean ran for the trees, searching for the terrier. A feeling of disappointment swept over him until he saw two large hunks of cheese and four loaves of bread on a rock. Like most teenagers, Sean existed in a perpetual state of hunger that wasn't getting any better since they had landed on the island. He tore at the bread, but suddenly stopped, remembering what Blair had said about having one less mouth to feed. "Thanks, Caly," he muttered. Then, much louder, "Thank you." He carried the cheese and bread back to *Wee Dram*.

Rufus was back with another load of wood. "No shortage of wood. I found a couple of dead trees. Pretty well dried out. Some kind of oak." He methodically split the wood with a survival ax and arranged the wood and kindling in the hole Sean had dug. Then he piled in dry leaves and set it afire. Together, they sat back and watched it burn as the other FOGs woke up and joined them.

"Why the fire?" Pete asked.

"He's making charcoal," Sean answered.

"Why do we need charcoal?" Pete wondered.

"I might need to make some tools," Rufus replied.

Blair stretched. "Where did the bread and cheese come from?"

"I found it over there," Sean replied, pointing to the rock. "I think Caly left it."

"Looks like a mouse got to it," Blair said. He reached over and gave Sean a playful slap on the back of his head. "I hope you said thank you."

"I did," Sean said. "Sorry I took a bite. I wasn't thinking."

"You're thinking," Gib said as he joined them. "How's our patient doing?"

"Her temperature is up," Rufus replied. "It's over a hundred and two."

"So what's on the agenda today?" Steve asked as he ambled up.

Blair ran down the mental list he had created. "*L'Amour* turned turtle long enough yesterday for its motor oil to be contaminated."

"I've got a quart of oil," Rufus said. "I'll take care of it and check all the engines."

"Super," Blair said. "While you're at it, we could use a decent latrine. Gib, can you take care of that?"

Pete laughed. "A judge digging an outhouse. I'm not going to touch that one."

Blair ignored the lawyer. "Rufe, you take care of Sasha while Sean and I see if we can find his friend. Pete and Steve, I want you to go exploring. See if you can find those hills you saw yesterday and get to the top. Take a good look around. I'm hoping you can see a mountain or something to the north." He opened the Army survival manual he was carrying. "Everyone, keep your eyes open for anything to eat." He pointed to the photos of different plants. "Things like a carob tree. Its seed pods make a good cocoa." He thumbed through the pages. "I hope you know how to recognize mushrooms."

"I went mushroom hunting with Zack and Angela a couple of times," Gib said. "He really knows his mushrooms and she can navigate. I think I can recognize a King Bolete or Chicken of the Woods."

"Everything tastes like chicken these days," Rufus grouched.

"Like double-breasted wart-headed clams?" Sean asked.

"Mind what you say, gentlemen," Gib warned. "Master Sean forgets nothing."

Caly's Island

"A mind like a sponge," Steve added.

"More like a steel trap," Blair mused. Sean grinned at the men.

Rufus looked into his fire pit. "I think the coals are ready. Sean, Pete, can you help me move that big rock over the pit?" They worked to roll a rock over the fire pit, and Rufus packed sand around the edge to seal the coals in. He poked four vent holes to provide ventilation and wisps of smoke trailed out. "Give it a few days," he explained, "and, voila, charcoal."

"We have bread, cheese, and pears for breakfast," Blair announced.

"And some leftover fish from the barbeque last night," Steve said.

"So how does a judge dig a latrine?" Rufus asked.

"Can we discuss that after we eat?" Gib replied.

Zack woke to the smell of cooking. He was lying on a bed covered with a thin flokati blanket. He cringed with panic when he realized he was naked under the blanket. Just to make sure, he sneaked a peak. "What the hell?" he muttered, coming up on one elbow to get his bearings. The bed was tucked in a corner of the only room in the house next to two carved chests. The room was not overly large, but comfortably furnished with two deck-type lounging chairs, a table with two regular chairs, and a stone counter under one of the windows obviously used for cooking and washing. A hibachi-type pot stood in the big fireplace that also held a bronze brazier with glowing coals and a skewer across the top. The top half of the Dutch door was open and he was alone.

"Angela," he called. Within seconds, the door opened and Circe came in, equally naked and holding a pumpkin-like gourd. She nonchalantly pulled a shift over her head and tied it at the waist. "Ah, did we?" he asked. She gave him a confused look. "You know." He pointed to his groin and clapped his hands.

Circe laughed. "No. You sleep." She imitated him snoring, and pulled her mouth into a little pout. "Ugh."

"At least we're communicating," he muttered. He definitely felt better and touched his cheek. It was cool to the touch. "No fever," he announced. She nodded, held up a small green-colored flask, and made a drinking motion. "You gave me something to drink?"

"Yes. You drink." She placed the little jug on a shelf. She looked at him and concentrated, working to get the words right. "Are . . . you . . . hungry?"

"Am I hungry? You bet!"

Circe smiled and walked gracefully over to the fireplace, enchanting him with the way she moved. She pulled a skewer off the brazier and pushed chunks of meat and vegetables onto a wooden platter. She handed it to Zack with a large piece of bread. "You eat."

He wolfed it down. "This is really good. Thank you."

"You are welcome."

"When did you learn that?"

"We talk when you sleep. I listen and learn."

"That's an understatement. Where are my clothes?"

She jumped up and ran outside. She darted back inside with his washed and mended shorts and T-shirt. She handed them over and he examined the shirt the dog had shredded with its rear claws. It was expertly mended with tight, small stitches. He pulled his shorts on under the blanket as she laughed at his modesty. "Okay, what's so funny?" She cocked her right little finger downward in the time-honored way signifying lack of male performance. "Very funny," he groused.

Suddenly, Circe's head came up and she ran to the door, quickly closing and bolting it. Then she shut the heavy shutters and slipped a bar into place, securely locking the windows. She held a finger to her lips, warning him to be silent as she ghosted silently to the fireplace. She knelt and stared into the burning coals in the brazier. Her lips moved rapidly, but no sound came out as her brow knitted in concentration. Something crashed against the door. A dog barked furiously as it smashed repeatedly into the door, shaking it violently. Circe only stared into the coals, her mouth moving in a silent chant. Again, the door shook as the dog threw its weight against it. One of the slavers' dogs had found the little cottage. Zack looked around for a weapon.

He heard a shout and a bolt of pure fear speared him. It was one of the monsters. His heart raced at the thought of being trapped and he started to warn Circe. She waved him to silence, never taking her eyes off the fire or stopping her chant. The monster was at the door, yelling and kicking at the dog. He ran to the door and threw his body against the heavy oak in a pathetic attempt to reinforce it. He chanced a look through the peephole and froze. Less than a few feet away, the monster

Caly's Island

Silla kicked and yelled at the dog, finally dragging it away from the door. The dog broke from her grasp and ran for the trees, making for the beach. Silla stomped after it, bending to avoid a branch as she disappeared into the trees, still yelling and cursing at the dog.

Zack took a deep breath in relief and collapsed onto one of the chairs. Circe sat beside him and placed a hand on his chest. His heart was racing. Ever so slowly, she guided his right hand to her breast and held it against the thin fabric of her shift. Her heart was beating as fast as his. Slowly, she calmed, but continued to hold his hand over her heart. "You have some very dangerous neighbors," he said.

"Silla not see. Dog see. Silla . . ." She pointed to her right ear. "

"Silla hears," Zack said, pointing to an ear, "but she cannot see the house."

"Yes. Silla hears, but she cannot see the house."

"Because you cast a spell." He pointed at the brazier and pantomimed her chanting.

She nodded. "I cast spell. Silla cannot see house."

Zack gestured as he spoke so she would understand. "Can you cast the spell outside?" She shook her head. "So you can only cast the spell if you are inside the house and looking at the fire." She nodded. "It must be terrible living with them so close," he told her. Circe collapsed against him, shaking with fear. He held her tight and stroked her hair. "It'll be okay, Angela. I promise."

Blair sat beside Sean on the rock. "Is this where you met her?" he asked. Sean nodded. "How long were you here before she spoke to you?"

"Not long. Maybe a few minutes. I was eating a pear."

"Now that's a plan. Let's eat one and see what happens." Blair picked a pear off a nearby tree and cut it with his knife. He handed Sean half and they ate in silence. "This is the best pear I've ever eaten," he said when he had finished. Sean nodded in agreement. They sat on the rock and talked as the sun reached its zenith. "I don't think she's coming," Blair said. "I'm gonna take a nap. Why don't you go look around before we head back? You might find Angus." Sean slipped off the rock and disappeared down the path. Blair stretched out on the warm rock and slept.

"You snore," a woman's voice said, rousing Blair. "Very loudly, I might add."

"It goes with getting older," Blair said, sitting up and studying the woman standing in front of him. Her head was cocked to one side as she took his measure. As Sean had described, she was blonde, beautiful, and wearing a short, cream-colored, off the shoulder dress cinched at her waist. He was struck by her similarity to Sasha, and they could have been sisters. He wondered why Sean hadn't mentioned it. "Caly, I presume."

"You presume correctly," she said. She leaned back against the rock and crossed her arms over her breasts. She looked straight ahead, not at him, and presented a perfect profile.

"You're older than I thought," he told her.

"How kind you are." Hurt filled her voice.

"I'm sorry. I didn't mean it that way. I misunderstood Sean. You know what teenage boys are like." His words seemed to sooth her hurt feelings. "May I ask a question?" She nodded. "Where are we?"

"My island is called Ogygia."

Blair stared at her, not believing what he had heard. "Ogygia? Like in The Odyssey?" She didn't answer. "The Trojan wars . . . Odysseus?"

"That bastard," she said, her voice low and intense.

"Right, and your name is really Calypso."

"Do you doubt everything, Colonel Blair?"

"How did you know my name?"

"Sean told me."

Blair never talked about his rank in the Air Force and wracked his brain trying to recall if he had inadvertently mentioned it to Sean. He must have said something as there was no other explanation. "Of course he did."

She walked away without looking at him. "When you accept what is, perhaps I can help you."

"Have you seen my dog?" he called. "His name is Angus."

"But perhaps not," she replied as she disappeared down the path and into the shadowy grove.

Blair almost followed her but decided not to. He didn't need to make her any more angry than she was. "Why do I always piss women off?" he wondered to himself. He liked women, but it was the story of his life – they simply didn't like him. He picked another pear and was

Caly's Island

still dicing it when Sean came up the path Caly had taken only moments before. "Did you see her?" he asked.

"Nah," Sean answered.

"That's strange," Blair mumbled under his breath. "Sean, when you met Caly did you tell her my rank?"

"Sure. Everyone calls you the Admiral."

"The Navy has admirals, I was in the Air Force. The Air Force has generals."

"Were you a general?" Sean asked.

"Nope. My mother was married to my father."

Sean laughed. "I get it. That's funny."

Zack shoved the end of the long pole into the brazier's burning coals and slowly turned the sharp point. The trick was to heat the hard wood to just the right temperature before plunging the tip into a crock of cold water, and it took three times before he got it right. He gingerly touched the point. It was much sharper and harder than he expected. Satisfied with the spear, he tested it for balance. It was eight feet long, a little over an inch in diameter, and fit his hand perfectly. "That should do the trick."

"What trick?" Circe asked.

"I'm going to kill a few dogs." He propped the spear beside the still bolted door.

Circe's eyes filled with worry and she shook her head. "The dogs will kill you."

He changed the subject. "You are a fast study when it comes to learning a language."

She wouldn't be sidetracked. "If you go outside, I cannot hide you. Stay in the house."

Zack shook his head. "That's where my boat is " – he pointed to the east – "where they are. Besides, you'll be safer." Tears flowed down her cheeks. "What's the matter now?" She rushed into his arms and held him tight. He felt her breast heaving and heart beating against his chest.

"Please, don't go." She showered his face with kisses.

Zack didn't stop her. "Hey, kiddo," he protested, "I'm forty years older than you."

She threw her arms around his neck. "You not older," she whispered in his ear.

He didn't push her away. "Come on, give me a break. You need a young stud to stir your juices and keep your bed warm."

"No one else is here," she told him. Zack gently pulled her arms away and unbolted the door to leave. Without a word, Circe rushed over to the bench and scooped up two knives. She joined him at the door and handed him the spear and a knife. "I go with you," she announced. Together, they walked outside, and she bolted the door. "Spell lasts long time and Silla not see the house." Her head came up and she pointed to the beach. "I smell fire. Meat burns."

"You've got a good nose," Zack said. "I can't smell a thing." They headed for the water but stopped at the tree branch Silla had ducked to avoid. It was at least eighteen inches above Zack's head. "Good grief! How tall is she?"

"Silla is tall," she said. "Sister Ka-rib is . . ." She made a sign signifying Ka-rib was taller.

"Taller," Zack said. She repeated the word and kissed him lightly. "I do like your language lessons." She smiled at him and held his hand as they walked down the path.

"Silla and dog are gone," she told him. She pointed to her nose and an ear. "Nose and ears tell me." Now he could smell the fire and whatever was burning. They came out of the trees above the beach where Zack had drowned the dog. The remains of a fire smoldered near the water with blackened lumps piled on top. He poked at the lumps with his spear and lifted one out. "Dog," she said. She drew her knife and cut into the scorched hide, exposing a bone. A shark's tooth was embedded in the bone. She looked around the sand, examining the gnawed bits and pieces. "Silla eat dead dog," she announced. "Ugh!"

Zack laughed at the way she expressed her disgust, and they walked down the beach, towards the rock Zack had climbed. "My God! What's that smell?" he asked. Circe pointed to a dark pile of dung and held her nose. "That is one potent dog." She shook her head and imitated a constipated woman having a bowel movement. Zack roared with laughter. "Silla took a dump, went potty."

She came up on tiptoe and kissed him lightly on the lips. "Silla took a dump. I go potty." She led him around the dark pile to the downwind side. The smell was acrid and overpowering.

"Now that's contaminating the environment," he told her. "I hope the tide takes it out." He imitated waves washing it away.

Caly's Island

"Kill many fish," Circe said. He almost laughed, but she was too serious.

They reached the rock and scrambled to the top where they could see the volcano. "Does the volcano have a name?" he asked.

She rattled off two or three incomprehensible words. "Name means 'home of Hephaestus.' Hephaestus is god of fire and volcanoes." The god's name sounded like 'Hee-fess-tus' to Zack's ear.

"Right," Zack said. "The Romans called him Vulcan." He laughed.

She was very serious. "He is the son of Zeus and Hera. Hephaestus is home now."

Zack looked at the smoke streaming from the volcano. "Is Hephaestus a friendly god?"

"Oh, yes. Hephaestus likes to talk."

"How do you talk to a god?"

"Talk to a fire."

"How do you talk to a fire?"

"Just talk," she said.

Zack looked eastward to where he had left *Wild Turtle*. A plume of heavy smoke drifted upward in the still air. "Judging by the smoke," he said, "I'd say Silla and Ka-rib are also at home." She rushed into his arms and he felt her shake with fear. He knew what he had to do. "I got'a do this one alone. Please, Angela, go home."

"I'm not Angela," she murmured. Zack held her tight, not listening.

The two men pushed through the heavy brush and emerged on top of the hill as the sun hovered above the western horizon. "That was harder than I thought," Pete said. He brushed bits of twigs and leaves off his shirt and looked around, taking in the view. "At least its open on top. Any idea what the elevation is?"

Steve checked his pocket barometer and compass. He made a face as he punched at the buttons. "Well, according to this, we're about six hundred feet above sea level."

"Nice gadget you've got there," Pete conceded. "How does it work?"

"It's a barometer. I reset it at the lagoon and it measures the decrease in barometric pressure as we climb. For every twenty-five feet in elevation change, it decreases one millibar. According to this, the millibars dropped 23.6, which means we're 590 feet above sea level."

Pete was impressed with the easy way Steve ran the numbers in his head. He pointed northward. "If the Admiral is right, there's a volcano to the north."

Steve pulled an expensive pair of binoculars out of his bag and swept the horizon, turning a full 360 degrees. He focused on the north. Without a word, he handed the binoculars to Pete. The lawyer adjusted the focus and studied the horizon. He could barely make out a cone-shaped mountain. "I'll be damned. It looks like a volcano."

"Look around," Steve said. "You can see the other island."

Pete pivoted, looking towards the south. "Does it look like Malta?"

"I never got a good look at it from the air," Steve confessed. "We landed and took off at night. But it all fits."

"We?"

"I was with a friend."

"A Tootie LaRue?"

"I assure you, she was not a Tootie LaRue, but she was expensive."

Pete roared with laughter. "Steve, my man, you are full of surprises. Who would have thought?" He checked his watch. "Time to check in with the Admiral." He returned the binoculars and turned on his VHF radio. "Base camp, base camp," he transmitted. "Steve and Pete checking in."

"Read you five-by," Blair replied. "Where are you?"

"We're on a low hill, approximately six hundred feet high. We can see a larger island to the south that Steve says looks like Malta, and we can barely see the peak of a mountain to the north. It's a long way away."

"Can you see us?" Blair asked.

"We can see the headland, but not the lagoon. I'd estimate we're maybe six miles away."

"Well done. Take some photos before it gets dark. I'd recommend you camp there for the night rather than risking a descent in the dark."

"Will do," Pete said. "We'll check in at six tomorrow morning." He signed off and turned off the radio. "Let's build a fire," he told Steve. "There's lots of wood around here." Steve took a few photographs with a borrowed camera and helped gather some wood. Within minutes, they had a fire going as the sun set. They sat on two low rocks and shared some beef jerky, a large baked potato, and two pears for dinner. "It does get dark here," Pete allowed.

Steve stood and looked to the north where a dull red glow lit the horizon. "That is definitely a volcano," he said.

"It could be Mount Baker," Pete said, "or maybe Mount Rainier. I hear that Rainier is one of the most dangerous volcanoes in the world." Both volcanoes were fairly close to the San Juan Islands.

"Pete, we're nowhere near Washington. I think its Mount Etna on Sicily. We're on Gozo and that other island to the south is Malta. It all fits."

Pete couldn't accept it. "So how did we get here? And what happened to all the people?"

"I'd say we went through some kind of time and spatial warp in the fog."

Pete was a modern man, educated, and trained with all the preconceptions, prejudices, and skills of his generation. What Steve was suggesting went totally against every law of science and reality. "Yeah, right."

Steve sensed what his friend was going through, and his voice was gentle. "Like Sherlock Holmes said, 'When you have eliminated the impossible, whatever remains, however improbable, must be the truth.'"

"Steve, my man, what you are suggesting is 'the impossible.' That way lays insanity."

"'There are more things in heaven and earth, Horatio, than are dreamt of in your philosophy.'"

Pete laughed. "Now you're throwing Shakespeare at me! There is a logical explanation for all this. I'm guessing we're caught up in some sort of mass hysteria or delusion."

"What about the girl Sean met? Is she a product of his delusion?"

"Bet on it, my friend. No hot chick lives alone on this island." He stoked the fire. "It might get cold up here tonight."

Steve pulled two small packets out his shoulder bag and threw one to Pete. "Survival blankets. Never leave home without them." They shook out the lightweight thermal blankets and wrapped up, settling in for the night. Within minutes, Steve was snoring peacefully.

Pete mentally composed an entry for his log to recapture their second full day on the island. Finding the volcano was definitely important, but he refused to believe they were in the Mediterranean. We'll get through this, he told himself. He rolled over and slept.

Pete came awake with a start. The fire had gone out and his bladder was sending him a very strong signal that he couldn't ignore. "Damn," he muttered. Normally, it took two beers to trigger a midnight call of nature. He stumbled into the darkness accompanied by Steve's irregular honks. "He must be having a nightmare." Finished, he followed the sound back to the dying campfire. "What the . . .?" he muttered. A shadowy figure was sitting on a rock next to the fire. "Hello?" he called softly.

A woman answered. "Are you the one Sean calls Pete?"

"Guilty," he replied. "Caly?" She didn't answer as he gathered up some branches and kindling to restart the fire. "Nice night." He dumped the wood on the coals.

"There are many nice nights here," she said.

He squatted by the fire but the wood didn't catch. Frustrated, he searched his pocket for his lighter. Then he remembered; Steve had it and he was sound asleep. Pete pulled out his key ring with its small LED flashlight, and hit the button. He wanted to see the woman. She held her hand up and the light went out. "Please, don't do that."

"I just wanted to see if you are as beautiful as Sean said."

"Since you are all delusional, does it matter?" She reached out and touched his cheek. Her hand was warm and soft. The fire flared for a split second and he got a better look. She had dark curly hair, not blonde, and was older than Sean had said, and to Pete's eye, much more beautiful. She was wrapped in a large shawl, exposing a great deal of bare skin. "Do you always doubt what you see?" she asked.

"When it is too good to be true, yes."

"You are very clever with words. Is that all you are clever with?" She patted the rock for him to sit beside her. She laughed. "Don't worry, your friend will not wake."

He sat down. "So, I am dreaming." She turned and licked his ear. Her tongue was warm and her breath fragrant. "Okay, I'm not dreaming." He sensed she was smiling at him but couldn't be sure in the dark. "Where are we? Can you tell me that?" He felt her take a deep breath.

Caly's Island

"You're on my island."

"Caly's Island. Does it have another name?" She didn't answer. "What's the date?"

She didn't answer at first. Then, "I really don't know. I lost track years ago."

"You've been here a long time?"

"All my life." She leaned against him and he felt the warmth of her body through the thin shawl. "It's very lonely here."

"Why don't you leave?"

She shook her head and stared into the fire pit. "I am not allowed to leave." She reached out and took his hand. "Sean is very upset with you. He says you banged his mother. I don't know what that means."

"It means I had sex with his mother. Believe me, it was her idea, and there are not many men who could refuse her and live to tell about it. I came damn near dying anyway."

"Is she beautiful and demanding?"

"She's not as beautiful as you." She beamed at the compliment, and he sensed she was responding to him. "She is very demanding." He smiled to himself. "But she has ways of encouraging one on, shall we say, to greater accomplishments."

"I can be very demanding, if you want." She stood as the fire flared.

Pete sucked in his breath. She was the most beautiful woman he had ever seen, and there was no doubt that she was only wearing the shawl. "Are you a witch?"

Caly laughed. "No, I'm a Nereid." She gestured towards the red glow on the northern horizon. "She's the witch." Caly extended her hand to Pete and the shawl fell to the ground. "Come."

Pete came to his feet in record time. "Where are we going?"

"I know a place, not far." She scooped up her shawl and led him into the trees. "You can use your light now to find the way."

Pete flicked on the light and found a path.

Steve came up on an elbow and watched them disappear into the night. "Good grief, Pete," he muttered to himself. He turned over and went back to sleep, not fully crediting what he had just witnessed.

FIFTEEN

Blair and Gib sat under the canopy on the beach sipping coffee and savoring the early morning. "This place does grow on you," Blair admitted. "The climate reminds me of San Diego."

"Does Malta have the same type of climate?" Gib asked.

"It does. And I think Steve is right. We're on Gozo."

"You've discovered something?"

Blair appreciated the way Gib thought and carefully chose his words. "I met Caly yesterday. I didn't mention it because she's not the way Sean described her. She was more like the mother of the girl he described. I asked her where we were, and she said we were on the island of Ogygia."

"As in The Odyssey," Gib said.

"I said the same thing. When I mentioned Odysseus, all she said was 'The bastard.' She didn't answer when I asked if her name was really Calypso. All very strange. I pissed her off, but I do that with most women. What's the opposite of enchanting?" He humphed. "Unchanting?"

Gib laughed. "Disenchanting is the word you're seeking. I assume you didn't mention all this earlier for fear of upsetting Sean."

"I'm having a hard time handling this, Gib. So what can we expect from a fifteen-year-old? Here's Rufe." They fell silent as the blacksmith joined them. The worry on his face was hard to ignore. "Are you okay?" Blair asked.

"It's Sasha," Rufus replied. "Her temperature is over 104 degrees, and the wound is infected. The bullet must've punched a lot of dirt and shreds of cloth into the wound that I didn't get out. I hoped disinfectant would sterilize the wound but until the bullet is removed . . ." His voice trailed off as he stared at *Nailing On* where Sasha was sleeping.

"Can you get it out?" Blair asked.

Rufus shook his head. "It's in there pretty deep. I'd have to cut it open, and . . . and . . . I don't know." He hung his head in despair.

"We need to talk to her," Blair decided. Without waiting for a reply, he stood and walked to *Nailing On*. He climbed on board and sat in the companionway to the small cabin. One glance and he knew she was burning with fever. He felt her forehead, and her eyes came open at his touch. They were large and glassy. "Your fever is getting worse," he told her, not pulling any punches. She nodded. "Rufus says your wound is infected and we need to cut the bullet out."

"Why are you waiting?" she asked.

"Because we don't know how, we don't have the instruments, and we don't have any anesthetic."

She thought for a few moments, never taking her eyes off him. "Tell Rufus to do it."

"He says he can't."

She snorted in contempt. "He's the only one I trust to do it. Let me talk to him."

Blair climbed off the boat and motioned for Rufus to join them. The blacksmith walked slowly over. "She wants to talk to you," Blair said, leaving them alone. He walked back to the canopy and sat down. The two men waited as Rufus crouched by the companionway, talking to Sasha. "I wonder what she's telling him?" Blair wondered.

"We'll soon know," Gib replied.

Rufus climbed off the boat and joined them. He was a very unhappy man. "She's pretty weak and is drifting in and out of consciousness. If I understood her right, she says she would rather bleed to death with my hands in her, trying to dig the bullet out than spend days screaming with fever and then die. I told her that would probably happen anyway, if I tried to cut the bullet out." He took a breath. "She told me that was okay, as long as I tried." Rufus looked at the two men, his eyes pleading. "I told her I couldn't do it. She called me a coward and said, 'tell the dwarf to do it.'"

"H," Gib said, "I do believe she meant you."

Blair's face was grim. "I will if I have to, but Rufe, I think you are the best one to do it."

Caly's Island

Gib nodded. "Mr. Gunnermyer, you know he's right."

Gib's solemn confirmation carried weight with Rufus. A lesser man would have turned away, but Rufus had sailed with these men for years and they were his friends. They would never fault him for failing, only for not trying. "Okay, let's do it before I lose my nerve."

They rigged a stretcher made from *Wee Dram's* boom, a long straight tree branch, and Gib's big Genoa. Satisfied the sail was stretched tight enough to serve as an operating table, they piled up rocks for a platform. Next, they opened the communal first aid kit Steve had assembled and inventoried what they had: one bottle of Betadine antiseptic, a bottle of grain alcohol, a pair of latex gloves, a scalpel, two suture kits, lots of compresses and bandages, a medical staple gun, and a pair of sponge packing forceps. The forceps looked like long tweezers with open triangular pads for tips. Rufus added a Phillip's head screwdriver to the pile as they built a fire to heat water and sterilize the instruments. "I wish we had some painkillers," Rufus said.

"I've got some Vicodin," Gib said. He dove into his cabin and quickly returned with his medicine bag. "At my age, I take so many pills that I need a red one for stop and a green one for go."

Sasha was weak with fever and drifting in and out of consciousness when Gib and Blair helped her off *Nailing On*. They carried her to the makeshift operating table under the canopy, and Rufus handed her two of the Vicodin tablets. "These will help with the pain," he said. She barely managed to swallow the pills.

"I've got some Scotch," Blair offered.

"We don't need a drunk patient puking her guts up," Rufus said. "We need to scrub her torso as best we can." He looked at the two men. "That means we have to undress her."

"Gib can do it," Sasha whispered, still with them. "Don't be embarrassed." Gib gently removed her shorts and briefs. "Save my shirt," she whispered. Gib pulled her T-shirt off and peeled away the bandages covering the wound. The area was swollen and red. Rufus handed him a sponge and soap, and he set to work as Sean finally woke and crawled out of his sleeping bag.

"Sean," Rufus called, diverting him, "we need some privacy."

"Don't be stupid," Sasha said, barely audible.

"Sean," Blair said, "get a couple of towels off our boat, okay?"

157

"And the first aid manual," Rufus called as he scrubbed his hands. Sean returned with two towels, his eyes wide, and handed them to Gib who covered her for modesty. Blair helped Rufus don the latex gloves and he was ready. "Okay," Rufus said, "pour half the Betadine all around the wound." Gib doused her skin with the yellowish-brown liquid. "Sean, start reading."

Zack crouched in the brush above the small cove where he had left *Wild Turtle*. He knelt on his left knee, his head up, the spear in his right hand resting on the ground. Only his eyes moved as he stalked the sleeping dog guarding his boat. The brush hiding his boat had been stripped away, and it was now floating thirty feet off shore at the end of its dock line. Why did they do that? he wondered. As best he could tell, the hatch boards were still locked in place and the boat undisturbed. So why is the dog tethered where *Wild Turtle* was beached? he asked himself.

The answer was a slight rustling sound in the brush behind him. "Because it's a trap!" He was up and running for all he was worth as a second dog broke from cover. He chanced a glance and looked back. He had thirty, maybe forty yards lead and only seconds before the dog was on him.

The huge dog was a trained hunter and came at him silently, covering ten yards with every bound. Zack skidded to a stop and braced the butt of the spear against the base of a huge rock. He stepped on the base of the shaft to hold it against the rock as he turned to face the fury coming at him. He held the spear with both hands as the dog leaped at him, its forepaws clawing the air, its jaws open as drool trailed behind. Zack aimed the point of the spear at the dog's chest, never wavering. The dog came down, impaling itself on the spear. But the dog kept coming at Zack, its weight and momentum thrusting its body down the spear. Zack muscled the spear to the right, trying to deflect a slashing claw. The claw raked the outside of his left forearm as Zack forced the dog to the ground. The giant rear claws pawed the air as he rode the spear, swinging back and forth over the dog's head as he pinned the dog to the ground. Twice, a rear claw raked his calves. But he wouldn't let go as the beast twisted, trying to free itself. A massive spasm wracked the animal's body and the spear snapped in two.

Caly's Island

Zack rolled away still holding onto half the spear as the dog staggered to its feet, the broken shaft still protruding from its broad chest. Before Zack could come to his feet, the wounded dog was on its feet and came at him. Lying on the ground, Zack jammed the end of the broken shaft into the dog's mouth. The dog fell on him, pinning him to the ground as it finally died. Zack struggled to roll free, surprised that the dog's claws had not touched him in its last slashing attack. He crawled away and sat on the ground, his back against a rock as his breath came in deep pants.

Zack finally came to his feet and staggered as he retraced his steps. He found his water bottle and drained it as he studied the barking dog tethered near his boat. "Two down and you're next, Fido."

"Sasha," Rufus said, "hold onto something." She reached out and grabbed Blair's hand as Rufus deftly sliced the infected wound open. Her teeth ground as she clenched her jaw and squeezed Blair's hand. Blood started to flow, but she didn't move. "I'm going to let it bleed to clear out the infection," Rufus told her. He inserted a finger into the opening and probed. "I can feel the bullet. Forceps." Gib handed him the long tweezers.

Sean continued to read. "Slip the forceps into the wound using the finger as a guide." Rufus did as he said and clamped the bullet.

"Got it." He pulled hard and dislodged the bullet. He pulled it out and dropped it in a cup. "Nice little souvenir," he said.

"Save it," Sasha ordered, her voice amazingly clear. Blair knew she was in pain from the way she squeezed his hand.

Rufus probed the wound with his finger, feeling for debris. He touched something hard and used the forceps to remove it. It was a bone chip. "I think it's off a rib," he said. He added it to the cup and stirred the wound with his finger, still probing as the blood flowed. Bits of thread flushed out.

"Irrigate the wound with antiseptic," Sean read.

"Pour the rest of the Betadine in the wound," Rufus said. Gib emptied the bottle into the wound, adding to the yellowish-brown stain marking her smooth skin. The blood changed color as flecks of debris and infection flushed out. Rufus felt around one more time and withdrew his finger. Now the blood gushed. "Screwdriver," he said.

Gib used a rag to grab the handle of the Phillips head screwdriver that was jammed in the coals of the fire. The shank glowed red as he handed it over. Rufus inserted the tip in the wound and carefully cauterized the wound. Steam and the stench of burning flesh filled the air. Sasha groaned and passed out. "My God, she's brave," Blair said.

"Indeed she is," Gib conceded.

"Almost done," Rufus said. He carefully removed the screwdriver as the flowing blood died away. "Irrigate it with the alcohol," he told Gib. Again, the jurist emptied the bottle into the wound, flushing it out.

Sean's eyes were full of tears as he read. "If available, use staples to loosely close the wound to allow the wound to drain and tissue to weep." Rufus did as he said and finished by taping a large compress bandage over the wound. He looked down at the unconscious woman and ripped off his latex gloves, his face sweaty and pale. He stood there shaking, not able to move.

Gib threw an arm around his shoulders to help steady him. "You did good, my friend. Very good." There was no higher compliment he could give another person.

Sean closed the first aid manual and stood there, proud to be part of the small band of men.

Zack sat on the ground, his hands clasped in front of his knees as he studied the dog and planned his next move. It was a straightforward tactical problem: how to kill the animal. The deep scratches on his left forearm and calves were stinging and that worried him. Then it came to him. "Of course." He berated himself for missing the obvious. How long is the leash? he wondered. "Only one way to find out." He stood and walked down to the water's edge.

The dog went into a frenzy and charged him. It came to the end of its tether only to be jerked back. It snarled and charged again, and for a split second, Zack was afraid the leash would snap. But the woven leather rope held. "Fido," he called, "you are one ugly dude." His voice goaded the dog into a howling rage as it strained against the tether. Zack studied the angle and decided the tether was long enough to allow the dog to swim about half way to *Wild Turtle*. He walked into the water and swam for his boat as the dog ran back and forth on the shore, barking and snarling.

Caly's Island

When Zack reached the stern of *Wild Turtle*, he pulled at the boarding ladder, unfolding it so he had a foothold, and climbed on board. Everything was as he had left it and his morale went over the moon. "Basics first," he told himself, reaching for his first aid kit. Hard experience had taught him how quickly infection set in, and he scrubbed the scratches with soap and water before dowsing them with disinfectant. He finished by smearing an antibiotic cream over the wounds, but an inner voice warned him that he needed to get back to the cottage and treat his wounds with whatever was in that little green flask. "Okay, Fido, what are you up to?" He checked on the dog, which was contenting itself with an occasional yelp and snarl.

"You are one ugly mutha," he muttered, taking a long drink from a water bottle. "So what are the angles?" Whoever had shoved his boat into the bay had tied the dock line to a tree stump about twenty feet from where the dog was tethered. He constructed a mental triangle with *Wild Turtle* at the apex, the dock line forming one leg, and the dog's leash the other leg.

Zack smiled as he started the outboard. It idled smoothly and he let it warm up as he went forward to untie the dock line. Rather than drop the line overboard and motor away, he walked the line back to the stern and tied it to a second line, adding another fifty feet. He secured the bitter end to a cleat on the transom and spun the boat around, its stern now to the shore. He gunned the engine to see if the long line could take the strain. It did and *Wild Turtle* was still tied securely to the shore.

"You could use a bath," he called. The dog barked and ran to the edge of the water, sending up a loud cry. "Come on in, the water's fine." The dog stood there barking. Zack looked for something to throw at the animal. "Damn," he muttered. He jumped over the side and dove to the shallow bottom. He scraped up a few rocks and pebbles and dumped them into the cockpit before diving again, collecting more rocks. He climbed back on board and wiped himself off. The dog had settled down and seemed content to just look at him. "We'll change that," he promised. Zack chucked a rock at the beast, but it missed. He selected another rock, took careful aim, wound up, and let go. This time, the rock hit the dog in the forehead, sending it into a frenzied howling that carried for miles.

"Good boy," Zack called. He peppered the dog with stones, driving the animal into a raging fury. "Come to poppa, Fido." The dog charged into the water and paddled towards its tormentor, its eyes blazing with hatred. Zack twisted the throttle as he put the tiller over. The little boat spun around and headed for the swimming dog, the line trailing behind it in a wide arc with the far end still tied to the shore. Just as the dog reached the end of its tether and stopped dead in the water, Zack tightened the turn and cut between the dog and the shore, still trailing the line from his stern. He kept the turn coming and circled the dog, running over the dog's tether and then his own line, forming a loop around the dog. He jerked the engine up so the prop would clear the lines and dropped it as he headed away from the shore. The loop closed on the dog and snared it around the neck. Zack gunned the throttle and headed out to sea. The line snapped tight.

It worked better than expected. The dog's leash held the animal in place while Zack's line pulled it the other direction. Zack gunned the engine, his eyes hard and remorseless as he strangled the dog. He didn't take any chances and kept at it. Satisfied the animal was dead, he retarded the throttle and let the line go slack. He stood and watched the floating, lifeless mass for a few minutes. "Three down, three to go," he told himself.

Silla broke from the thick brush like a Rhino in full charge with a dog in close trail. "Damn," Zack growled. "You must'a heard all the barking." She picked up a bowling-ball sized rock as Zack cut the line holding him to the shore and the dead dog. He gunned the motor as the rock soared over his head. She heaved an even bigger rock. *Wild Turtle* shot forward as the rock splashed in the boat's wake, soaking Zack. She was getting the range. He looked back as she threw a third rock, but it fell short. He eased off the throttle as Silla pulled the dead dog ashore by its leash. The dog ripped into the carcass as Silla watched him motor out of the cove and into the bay.

"Time to get the hell out of Dodge," Zack muttered. He raised sail and shut off his motor to conserve what little fuel he had remaining. He sailed out of the bay and turned south to follow the shoreline that curved to the southwest, towards the volcano and away from Circe's cottage.

Rufus gently pulled the thermometer out of Sasha's mouth and held it up in the fading light. Without a word he handed it to Blair who frowned as he read, "One hundred and four." The two men exchanged glances. "At least it hasn't gone up."

Rufus couldn't be consoled. "But she's delirious."

"Rufe, give it time. It's only been twelve hours since we operated."

The blacksmith nodded and stoked the fire. "We need to move her closer." He called for help and they all gathered around the makeshift stretcher to move her next to the fire as the evening twilight turned to night. "Sean," Rufus called, can you get my pillow? It's in the cabin." Sean bolted for *Nailing On*, anxious to help.

"Ah," Steve said, "the prodigal son returns, finally." The FOGs sat down and waited for Pete to join them. His clothes were washed and fresh, and he was smoothly shaven. "I take it that was Caly."

"You take it right," Pete said. He handed Steve a bag. "Goat jerky, cheese, yams, and bread. Compliments of our hostess."

Steve opened the bag and looked in. He nodded. "We can make this last a few meals. I do hope you rewarded the lady accordingly."

"Indeed," Pete replied, not missing the sarcasm in his friend's voice. "I sacrificed myself."

"Did you fuck her, Pete?" Sean said. They had not seen him return in the dark.

Rufus took the pillow the teenager was carrying. "Thanks, Sean." He placed it under Sasha's head and wiped her face with a moist cloth.

Sean stood in front of the men, shifting his weight from foot to foot in his anger. "You banged my girlfriend. What is it with you?"

Pete tried to explain. "It's not like that."

"The fuck it's not!"

"Sean, the woman I was with is much older than your Caly and had dark hair. She could be her mother." Pete knew it was the wrong thing to say the moment the words were out.

"You got a thing for mothers? I guess that makes you a mutha . . ."

Gib interrupted him. "Sean! Stop." There was an authority in his voice Sean had never heard and he fell silent. "Calm down and we'll discuss it in the morning." Sean shook with fury. Then he turned and ran into the night. Blair started after him. "Let him go," Gib commanded. "He needs time to cool down." Blair sat and stared at the ground.

The jurist fixed Pete with the look he used to scold errant lawyers in his courtroom before he administered a reprimand. Courtroom legend held that most of the recipients would have preferred a week in the slammer rather than the tongue lashing that was duly recorded in the public court record. One particularly scathing reproach was memorialized in a textbook on legal ethics and quoted at cocktail parties and fraternal roastings. Gib motioned for Pete to sit in an empty camp chair. "Our young master Sean overheard Peter telling us of the circumstances surrounding his sojourn with Caly." He looked around the group. "Gentlemen, I specifically warned you earlier to choose your words carefully around Sean. Please learn from this." He focused on Pete. "Would you be so kind as bring us up to date on the events of the last eighteen hours?"

Pete wasn't having any of it. "It's not really anyone else's business, is it?"

Gib turned up the heat. "Under normal circumstances, I would agree with you. However, our circumstances are far from normal, or are you in a state of denial? Peter, you may have discovered something of vital importance of which you are not aware."

A hard silence came down as the air crackled with tension. "Please," Rufus pleaded, breaking the quiet, "I had to dig the bullet out of Sasha this morning. I butchered the job and she's delirious. Maybe Caly can help."

Pete exhaled. "Gib, you're right. Please forgive me for mouthing off. The woman I met is not the one Sean described and is much older. She lives in a cave you would not believe, and is very lonely. She claims she's a Nereid, whatever that is."

"According to Greek mythology," Blair said, "a Nereid is the daughter of Nereus, a Titan who lived in the Aegean Sea, and Doris. That makes her a sea nymph."

"So what is she doing on land?" Pete asked. Blair didn't have an answer and shook his head. "I got to admit," Pete continued, "that she is the most beautiful woman I have ever met, but she is also one narcissistic bitch." He clasped his hands between his knees as he related everything that had happened between them. It was the predictable story of two lustful people sharing a bed and exploring each other's sensuality. Afterwards, there was small chitchat before round two started. Because he paid attention, Pete soon discovered which buttons to push, which led to round three, then round four as he perfected his technique. When he was finished, he stared at the ground. "I'm not sure she would help Sasha."

Caly's Island

"So what are we going to do?" Rufus asked.

"I'm not sure," Blair answered. "Sean, me, and Pete, in that order, have met Caly, and each of us has had a different experience. I'm forced to believe we have met three different women."

"I'm not so sure," Steve said. They all looked at him. "I saw her talking to Pete by the campfire."

"Did you see a different person?" Gib asked. Steve nodded, reluctant to say anything. "Steve," Gib cajoled, "what did you see?"

"She was an old hag."

Pete came out of his chair. "You're pulling my chain." Steve shook his head in reply. Pete sat down, his face ashen. "What have I done?"

"Maybe she's hypnotizing us," Rufus offered.

Gib pulled into himself and fell silent. Then, "Gentlemen, we are dealing with an unknown quantity. I need to reread The Odyssey. It may provide a clue to her behavior. H, may I borrow your copy?" Blair nodded. "For now," Gib continued, "I think it would be best if we made no further attempt to contact this woman until we have devised a strategy."

"I agree," Blair said. He thought for a moment, considering what he had to do. "Okay folks, try to get a good night's sleep." Pete led the procession back to the boats, anxious to bring his log up to date, while Blair dropped another log on the fire. He moved his chair next to Sasha and felt her forehead as he settled in for the night.

SIXTEEN

The first light of the new day broke the eastern sky and Blair came awake. He checked on Sasha and frowned. Her temperature was still high, and he stoked the fire, breaking the early morning chill. Being the worrier that he was, he added Sean to his angst list. "He'll be okay," he kept reassuring himself. It was their fourth day on the island and he automatically checked his watch. It was 04:45 local time. "I wonder," he said to no one. He walked up the low rise behind the beach to see the eastern horizon and waited for the lower edge of the sun to clear the horizon. The time was exactly 04:58. He walked back to the camp muttering to himself. "As I suspected."

"Suspected what?" Rufus asked, startling Blair.

"I didn't see you," Blair replied. "You're up early."

"I was worried about Sasha."

"I checked her temperature twenty minutes ago. No change. But to answer your question, sunrise occurs at the same time every morning at exactly two minutes before five. Unless I'm totally wrong, sunset will happen at twenty past seven this evening, the same as yesterday."

"That doesn't sound good to me," Rufus allowed. "What does that mean?"

"I think it means we're frozen in time, September fifteenth to be exact, which is the date we entered the fog bank in the San Juans."

Rufus stared out across the lagoon. "Does that mean we're dead?"

Blair's lips compressed into a tight line. "Gib doesn't think so. It just means we don't understand what's happening. We'll figure it out."

"We got to, don't we? Or we'll never get home." Rufus, in his uncomplicated way, had come to the heart of the problem.

Blair nodded. "First things first. How do we bring Sean in from the cold?"

Rufus grinned wickedly. "Food. He's a normal teenager and that means he's a walking, talking grocery destroyer. Nothing smells better than bacon frying and coffee perking over an open fire. I got a pack of irradiated bacon I was saving for a special occasion, and Gib's got the coffee. That'll bring him in." The plan worked different than expected, and within minutes, the FOGs were all gathered around the fire as the bacon sizzled. Unfortunately, there was still no sign of Sean. Rufus portioned out the bacon with bread and coffee, saving the largest portion for Sean. "Be patient," he told Blair.

When they had finished, Blair cleared his throat. "Gentlemen, there's something we need to do. I need two volunteers to sail north and see if they can reach Sicily."

"That would be me," Pete said. "Hey, I'm the logical choice." Blair agreed with him. Pete was, without doubt, the best and most experienced skipper. "Steve, are you up for it?" the lawyer asked. "We make a pretty good team."

"I'm game," Steve said. "Any idea how far it is?"

"Without a chart," Blair said, "I can only SWAG it."

"Ah," Steve said, "the dreaded scientific wild ass guess."

"If I remember the formula right," Blair said, "1.22 times the square root of the first height plus the square root of the second height equals the line of sight in nautical miles. Assuming Mt. Etna is 10,000 feet high, and you were at 600 feet elevation, you can see Mt Etna from . . ."

Steve easily ran the numbers in his head. ". . . from 150 nautical miles, give or take a mile. As I recall, Mt. Etna is on the northern side of Sicily, and Sicily isn't that big."

"So it's maybe sixty, seventy miles away," Pete ventured. "Let's do it. The day isn't getting any longer."

"If you don't see land by noon tomorrow, turn around," Blair said. "Take three days food." The two men hurried down to their boats to make it happen. Blair watched them for a few moments and turned back to the fire. Sean was walking towards him. "Hungry?" Blair called. Sean shrugged his shoulders and joined them, eyeing the bacon. Without a word, Rufus scooped the bacon onto a plate and handed it to Sean with a hunk of bread and cheese.

Caly's Island

The teenager wolfed it down as he watched Pete and Steve prepare to launch. "Where are they going?"

"They're sailing north to see if they can find Sicily," Blair told him. "It's a crap shoot and could be dangerous." He tried to read the emotions racing across the teenager's face but failed miserably. "Sean, they may get us home, or this could be the last time you'll ever see them. Why don't you go and make peace with Pete?" He still couldn't read the boy. "What happened is not what you think. I'm not asking you to be friends, just listen to what he has to say. Okay?" Sean grumpily answered and walked down to *L'Amour*.

Pete saw him coming and stopped rigging his boat. "How's it going?" There was no answer. "Sean, the woman I met was not your Caly, please believe me."

"Sure," Sean muttered, not really believing him.

"Talk to Gib and see what he says, okay? He'll play it straight." He let it sink in. Finally, Sean nodded. "Good. Mind giving me a push? We have to find a volcano."

Sean grabbed the bow of *L'Amour* and rocked it, breaking it free of the shore. He pushed the boat into the lagoon as Pete raised his sail. He waited as Gib launched Steve, and then shuffled over to the tall judge who was standing by his boat. "Pete said I should talk to you."

Gib climbed aboard his boat and watched the two boats slowly make their way out of the lagoon. He motioned for Sean to join him. "I reread The Odyssey last night. You read The Odyssey when we were at Roche Harbor. What do you remember about Calypso?"

Sean sat down beside him. "Wasn't she a nymph, or something like that?" Gib nodded. "And she lives forever. She promised Odysseus immortality." Sean's brain kicked in. "If she can do that, she must be pretty powerful."

"She would certainly have the power to change her appearance and become the creature of your dreams," Gib added. "What better way to lure someone into captivity."

Sean's eye's opened wide. "And captivity means forever."

"That almost happened to Odysseus."

"Bummer," Sean muttered. He stood up. "I got'a talk to Pete." Gib handed him his VHF radio. Sean punched it on and cycled to Channel 16. "*L'Amour*, this is Sean. How copy?"

"*L'Amour* reads you five by," Pete answered.

"I'm sorry for what I said. I didn't understand."

"No problem, Sean. I should have talked to you before I shot off my mouth."

"Can I go with you?"

At first there was no answer as *L'Amour* came about and headed for shore. "You bet. Tell the Admiral and get your gear." Within minutes, Sean was aboard *L'Amour* and Gib pushed the boat around. He watched them sail out of the lagoon before joining the others under the canopy.

"I take it Sean is doing much better," Blair said.

Gib found a seat. "Considering what he's dealing with, he's doing better than us." Rufus handed him a cup of coffee. "He's very intelligent and has an agile mind not encumbered with the prisms that bend our perceptions. He readily accepts we are dealing with the Calypso from The Odyssey, even though that is pure nonsense."

"He's a teenager," Rufus said. "They'll believe most anything."

"I accept believing she is Calypso is not rational," Gib said. "But for the sake of argument, let us assume that she believes she is Calypso."

"So what are you saying?" Blair asked.

"To put it in the vernacular," Gib replied, "we need to get with her program if she is going to help us."

It was mid afternoon when Zack anchored twenty yards off a magnificent sandy beach and collapsed in the cockpit, aching with fatigue. He let the sails flap, too tired to douse them. His left arm throbbed with pain and the deep scratches were turning red. "Damn," he muttered. He scrubbed his wounds and rubbed in the last of the antibiotic from his first aid kit. "This ain't gonna hack it," he muttered. It was time to head back to the cottage and let Angela do her magic, but that meant sailing back into danger. The plan he had worked out was simplicity itself: sail south to lose Silla and lead the monsters away from Angela. Unfortunately, he had to retrace his steps to reach the cottage, and that meant sailing past the monster's compound. "Do I have a choice?" he asked aloud. "Wrong question. When do I head back?" Common sense said to do it at night. Zack mentally calculated the distances and times. A freshening wind whipped at his sails, swinging *Wild Turtle's* bow to the north. "I guess that's a sign," he said. An overpowering urge to sleep swept over him. "Sleep later," he mumbled, struggling to stay awake.

He weighed anchor and headed north. "There be monsters there." He made a mental promise to stop talking to himself.

Much to his surprise, the sail was uneventful, and under any other circumstances, would have been a delightful night voyage. The sea was flat and he had an offshore breeze, which meant he was downwind from the monster's compound. Even the moon cooperated and hid behind a cloud when he rounded the point and sailed westward past the compound. The sun was rising when he found the beach where he had drowned the dog. He beached *Wild Turtle* and secured it with two lines.

It was deathly quiet when he reached the cottage, and he held back in the trees, checking it out. The shutters were thrown back and the door open, but there was no smoke coming from the chimney. He sat down and waited, wondering where she had gone. He didn't have to wait long before he heard her humming a strange melody as she emerged from the trees. She was holding a fishing spear and three small fish. Her short tunic was wet around the bottom and she was carrying her wet sandals. His heart did a little flip-flop as he watched her clean the fish. He gulped as he stood. "Hello there."

Her head came up and she saw him. She dropped her knife and ran into his arms, cooing in the unfamiliar language. Tears filled her eyes and he could feel her heart thumping against his chest. "I was afraid . . ." her words trailed off.

"That I wouldn't come back?"

She answered with a little nod and broke the embrace. She held his face with both her hands as she looked at him. Then she saw the scratches on his arms. "Oh!" She held his hand and led him into the cottage. She sat him down at the table and bathed his arms before having him drink from the small green flask.

"I wish I could patent that stuff," he told her. "What is it?"

"It is a gift from the gods."

"Can I get some?"

"Perhaps, but first you must believe." She bent over him as she bathed him with warm water and a gentle, sweet-smelling soap while he recounted his fight with the dogs and how Silla had bombarded him with rocks before he lost her. "Come, you must rest." She led him to her bed and helped him lie down. She sat beside him until he was gently snoring. Satisfied he was sound asleep, she moved silently and bolted both the outside and inner shutters before closing the door and lifting two heavy beams in place. She slipped out of her tunic and knelt before the fire, bringing it to life. She chanted softly and rocked back and forth.

Zack came awake with a jerk. Circe's hand was over his mouth, but he couldn't see her in the dark. "Shush," she whispered. In the far distance he heard dogs baying in the night. "Silla is back."

"My God, how many has she got with her now?"

"Only two." Her hand came down harder, urging him to be quiet. He gently kissed her palm as he worked the problem. Silla was a relentless hunter, and after losing him, was backtracking with reinforcements. Zack felt her move away and heard her blowing on the coals in the brazier. The fire came to life and he could make out her silhouette as she bent over the glowing coals. Her soft chanting was barely audible over the baying sounds coming from outside. He held his breath as the howling grew louder and circled the cottage. Silla's loud grunts and curses echoed over the clearing and slowly the barking faded into the night as the hunter and her pack moved on. She lit a candle and he saw the black soot marks she had drawn on her cheeks. From her look, he knew the spell would not work again.

"So how do I kill them?" he asked.

She didn't answer and only stared into the fire. Finally, she looked at him. "Hephaestus says you must bring Silla to his house."

"So why is the god of fire and volcanoes willing to help?"

"You asked for help and he likes your friend who uses fire."

Zack was confused. "My friend who uses fire?" Then it came to him. "Right. Rufus. So what's the best way to get Silla to the volcano?"

She answered with one word. "Sail."

Rufus stared into the coals and clenched the mug of coffee in his big hands. He stared at Sasha in the early morning light. She was drenched in sweat and delirious. Gib wiped her face with a damp towel and frowned. Without a word, he sat next to Blair. "She's dying," Rufus told his two friends, "and it's my fault."

"No, it's not," Blair replied. He didn't know what he could say that would make the blacksmith understand.

Caly's Island

Gib took charge. "Rufus, don't go there. You are assuming a blame that is not yours. Whoever shot her is responsible for this. You . . . we . . . are merely players in the outcome. If we had not been there, if you had not operated, she would have died before now. At the most, we merely postponed the inevitable." He sat erect in his chair. "No court would ever hold you responsible for what has happened."

"It's only a matter of time," Rufus moaned. "And I was the one who butchered her. I was the one who cut her open."

The jurist in Gib would not let it go. "She's not dead yet."

"But there's nothing we can do," Rufus replied in despair.

"No, there's not," Gib replied, "but maybe Caly can help." Without another word, he stood and walked into the early-morning shadows. It was easy following the trail along the ridge and then down into the wooded glen with its laden fruit trees. The scent of the golden pears reassured him when he found the rock where Sean and Blair had met the creature.

"Good morning, Caly. I was hoping we might talk." He fell silent and waited. "Well, I've got all day," he murmured to himself. Gib sat on the ground and leaned against the rock. Amazingly, the rock seemed to form to his back. He dozed.

"Justice Sanford, I presume," a familiar voice said, waking him.

Gib's head came up. Marla Mann was standing in the soft light as regal and as beautiful as ever. Was he dreaming? "You can't be Marla," he said.

"I am who you want me to be."

"And who do I want you to be?"

"I think it is obvious." She laughed, exactly like Marla. "Men. You don't even know your own minds." Caly sat on the rock beside the jurist and stroked his thick gray hair.

"May I ask a question?" he asked. There was no answer. "Who are you?"

"I'm Calypso, a daughter of Nereus and Doris."

Gib nodded. Unless he read the situation totally wrong, she wanted to talk about herself. "Nereus, the old man of the sea. I thought his daughters were the Nereids who lived in a silvery cave beneath the sea and accompanied Poseidon. So why are you here?"

"Because Amphitrite, Poseidon's wife, became jealous and condemned me to live here forever." She spoke quietly, retelling the old,

173

old story of lust, sex, jealousy, and vengeance as her hand gently played with his hair.

The judge carefully selected his words. Calypso might, or might not be a demigoddess, but she was a vain, self-centered woman. "Don't the Nereids sleep with Poseidon?" Her hand tensed, signaling that he was treading on dangerous ground. "And you are the most beautiful of the Nereids." He felt her hand relax. He had said the right thing. "And Amphitrite is jealous because you are more beautiful than she." Warm and soft fingers stroked his cheek. "What a terrible fate." He stared straight ahead as her fingers gently touched his lips. He had said the right thing. Now he had to wait as she talked of the small things that filled her life.

When he judged the time was right, he said, "I know that you are terribly lonely, but may I ask a favor?" There was no answer; however, her hand didn't move. He plunged ahead. "Our companion is dying. Can you help her?"

"Why should I be concerned with the woman?"

"Because a very good man will blame himself forever if she dies. He doesn't deserve that and you will earn his eternal gratitude."

"Ah, the blacksmith."

Gib paused for effect. "And my gratitude as well." He felt her hand pull away and he looked up. She was gone.

SEVENTEEN

Pete fell out of his bunk when *L'Amour* rolled and the bow pitched up. "Damn," he muttered as the boat crested a swell and headed down the backside. He slid the top hatch back and looked outside. It was a gray dawn and they were caught in a storm-tossed sea. Luckily, the twenty-foot swells weren't breaking and Sean hadn't panicked. "You should have called me," he shouted, taking the tiller.

Sean slid forward, keeping the small craft in balance. "It came out of nowhere. Until a minute ago, it was a piece of cake." Pete believed him. It had been an incredibly beautiful night as they sailed northward towards what they hoped was Sicily. They were on a beam reach and making a steady four knots. Ahead of them, the volcano glowed with activity, a welcoming beacon in the night. Steve had checked in on the VHF and wanted to press ahead. If he couldn't hack it and got tired, they could heave-to in the gentle seas for a few hours of sleep until morning. Pete decided to let Sean take the dogwatch and went below for a few hours of sleep, only to awake to the howling gale.

Pete steered *L'Amour* down the backside of a swell and started up the face of the next one. "Can you set a reef?" he shouted into the wind. Without being told, Sean quickly furled the jib and reefed the main down to a hanky. It was the right thing to do and *L'Amour* stabilized. "I could use my foulies," Pete called. "Get yours on first." The teenager dove into the cabin and pulled on his foul weather gear and a blue-water PFD. He climbed into the cockpit and sealed the cabin before snapping his lifeline to a D-ring. "I got it." It was a smooth transition as Sean took over the tiller.

Dick Herman

Pete donned his foul weather gear and snapped his lifeline to another D-ring. "I have the boat," he said, again reaching for the tiller.

"I can handle it," Sean said, wanting to stay at the helm.

Pete hesitated. They were battling a ferocious sea and the swells were starting to break. Was the teenager up to the task? He made a decision. "You got it."

Sean grinned at him. "Yeah, man."

Pete relaxed as Sean conned *L'Amour* through the storm. The fifteen-year old had turned into an excellent helmsman. "Where's Steve?"

Sean pointed to their forward starboard quarter. "The last I saw, his running lights were about two hundred yards away."

They crested a high wave and Pete shielded his eyes from the driving rain and searched the horizon. There was no sign of *High Flyer*. "Sean, this is turning into the mother of all storms. We got'a rig a drogue and run with it." He quickly rigged a canvas bucket as a sea anchor and tossed it over the stern. Sean put the tiller over as they turned to the west, away from Gozo and Sicily.

Wild Turtle took to its heels as the wind clocked around to the north. Ahead, Zack could see the volcano grow larger as he sailed southward, about a hundred yards offshore. The knotmeter hovered at five knots for three hours, the fastest sustained speed he had ever made under sail. It was turning into a honey of a sail, or, it would have been, if he wasn't searching for Silla and her two dogs. He was fairly certain the monster was ranging southward, searching for him and that she would hug the shoreline. "Okay," he said to himself, "where is that little mother?" Another thought came to him. "This has got to be the stupidest thing I've ever done." He was the bait to lure Silla to the volcano, and the only way he could safely overtake her and make a run for the volcano was by sea. Hopefully, she would see him and follow along the shore until he could beach the boat and head overland for the volcano.

Hard experience warned him he had to be well in front of her by then to outrun the dogs. It was all in the timing. "Hephaestus, Vulcan, or whoever, you're gonna have your hands full once I get the bitch and her puppies there."

Caly's Island

He went forward to rig the whisker pole to the jib and run wing-on-wing before the wind. Then he saw the monster. She was ahead of him, striding along the shore below the tree line. He slipped back into the cockpit and reached for his binoculars. Even with her back to him, Silla was ugly and threatening. "So where are the dogs?" He searched the trees and didn't see them. Suddenly, a mournful baying carried across the water and sent a shiver down his spine. The dogs broke from the trees behind her, baying in full chase. In his binoculars, Zack saw her turn and look directly at him. Her mouth came open and she shouted with a rage that reached across the water. The dogs charged into the surf and swam towards *Wild Turtle*.

Pure fear shot through the sixty-three-year-old man. "Please help me," he whispered. He put the tiller over and headed out to sea as the wind freshened, driving him faster. Behind him, he heard Silla bellowing a command at the dogs. He forced himself to chance a look. The dogs were swimming for the shore as Silla loaded a David-type slingshot with a softball-sized rock. She twirled the long thongs in an ever-accelerating spin and released one thong. The rock arced over the water and landed three feet beyond *Wild Turtle*. "Son of a bitch!" Zack roared. She quickly reloaded as he changed heading. She let fly and this time, the rock landed short. Twice more, she flung a rock at him with the same results. He was out of range.

"You've got one hell of an arm!" he shouted at her. That only enraged her more. "But I don't think the Yankees will sign you up." She launched another missile at him, but this time it fell twenty yards short. Zack turned and paralleled the shore, slowly putting more distance between them as he headed south. Silla trotted along the shore, following him with the two dogs ranging ahead. "I'll be damned," he muttered. The plan was working and she was following him towards the waiting volcano and Hephaestus.

"Over there!" Sean shouted, pointing to starboard. Pete looked, but all he could see was another wave as their drogue allowed the huge swell to rush past. Sean kept pointing as *L'Amour* slid down the backside and came up with the next swell. "There!" Now Pete could barely make out a mast in the driving rain a quarter of a mile to their right.

Dick Herman

"Damn, you got good eyes," Pete shouted. "It's *High Flyer*. We're gonna have to head up. Can you handle it while I get the drogue in?" Sean shot the lawyer a worried look. "We can do this," Pete said. Sean nodded and Pete grabbed the anchor rode holding the drogue. His gloves slipped on the wet line and he couldn't pull it in. "I'm gonna have to cut it. We're gonna shoot forward." He waited while another wave surged past. Pete shook off a glove, groped for the knife on his belt, and flicked it open. He cut the line and as predicted, *L'Amour* accelerated sharply. "Turn!"

Sean squinted into the driving rain and, at the last critical moment, put the tiller over, turning at the top of a wave and nosing along the backside. Ahead, *High Flyer* was awash, her cabin barely above water. "Holy shit!" Sean yelled as *High Flyer's* mast collapsed, dragging the boat even lower into the water.

"Where's Steve!" Pete called.

"I don't see him!" Sean shouted.

Pete climbed over the cabin and stood, holding onto the mast as Sean piloted the boat, drawing closer. Steve was gone and Pete fell to his knees, repeatedly slamming his fist into the cabin top. "Damn! Damn! Damn!" he cried. He looked at Sean, his face contorted in grief as tears coursed down his cheeks.

Sean came to his feet, still holding onto the tiller. "He's okay!" He pointed at *High Flyer*. Steve's head emerged from the top hatch as he threw a waterproof ditching bag into the swamped cockpit. "Take the tiller," Sean ordered. Pete scooted back to the cockpit and took the helm as Sean pulled a line out of the lazaret under the port seat. He coiled the line and draped it over his right forearm, still holding the last three loops in his right hand and the bitter end in his left hand. He cocked his arm back and brought it forward in an underhand toss, throwing the three loops at *High Flyer* as his arm extended towards the sinking boat. The line flew straight and true, as the coiled line on his arm paid out, falling across Steve. Steve quickly tied his ditching bag to the line and motioned for them to pull it aboard *L'Amour*. Sean pulled the bag through the water and snatched it up, dropping it on the cockpit's sole as Steve disappeared back into the cabin. It seemed an eternity before he reappeared, this time holding a bottle of Scotch.

"What the hell?" Pete wondered. But people did strange things under stress. "Can you do that again?" he asked Sean. The teenager

Caly's Island

answered with a wicked grin and tossed the line, again dropping it across Steve. "I'll be damned," Pete muttered as Steve made the line fast to a cleat. Pete and Sean worked in unison, guiding and pulling the two boats together in the raging sea. Neither knew it, but it was small-boat seamanship at its best, rarely matched and never exceeded. Still holding the bottle, Steve reached for Sean's hand. Just as he stepped across, his foot slipped and he dropped the bottle into the water. He reached for the bottle but it sank as Sean gave him a tug. Steve stumbled into the cockpit, savagely banging a knee. "Release the line," Pete ordered. Sean cut the line as *High Flyer* sank lower, now totally awash with just the cabin top above water. "Damn, man," Pete said to Steve as he turned downwind, running with the storm. "I don't think we can save her."

"It's okay," Steve said, shivering badly. "Thank you."

It was twilight when *Wild Turtle* was abeam the volcano. Zack looked up at the looming mass, which he estimated some ten miles inland. The top glowed red in the fading light as smoke and steam erupted, trailing out to the west, away from him. It was the moment he had been dreading. "Just do it," he told himself. The boat and his dry bag were ready. He quickly dropped anchor and made sure it had set. He double-checked the cabin hatch to ensure it was securely locked. He scanned the shore with his binoculars looking for Silla and her pets one last time. Nothing, but he knew they were out there, still on his trail. He dropped the binoculars into the dry bag and sealed it. Satisfied it was watertight, he popped his PFD, shouldered the dry bag, and climbed down the boarding ladder at the stern. It was going to be a long swim to shore, but he was betting Silla couldn't swim and there was no better way to keep *Wild Turtle* safe.

Fortunately, the tide and current were with him and he almost floated ashore. He stood and walked up the beach where he sat in the sand and pulled on his running shoes. A baying howl carried on the soft evening air, and he took a long pull at his water bottle. Zack came to his feet and trotted into the scattered trees, his flashlight sweeping the area as he headed straight for the volcano. "Okay, Hephaestus, the ball is in your court."

The chase was on.

Dick Herman

* * * *

"The storm's settling down," Pete said. He stood and shed his foul weather gear. "It's gonna be a lovely night."

Steve emerged from the cabin, much rested after sleeping for six hours. Both men were aching from the beating dished out by the storm, but they were in good spirits. Sean was still at the tiller and seemed totally unaffected by the ordeal. He had already stripped down to shorts and a T-shirt. "You can put it on autopilot," Pete told him, "and let George do the steering."

"Nah. This is okay. What heading?"

"Good question," Pete answered. He stood and pointed to a dull glow on the horizon behind them. "That's the volcano. Sean, come about and put it on the nose." Sean brought them smoothly about to an easterly heading and easily trimmed *L'Amour*, setting them on a beam reach with the wind coming out of the north.

"I believe," Steve said, "that someone doesn't want us to go to Sicily."

"I got the same message," Pete said. "Once we can see the cone, we can displace a little to the right."

"I got it," Sean said. "We keep the volcano close enough so Gozo has got to be south of us. Our original compass heading for the volcano was zero-two-zero degrees, so when the bearing to the volcano is the same, we head south on a heading of . . ." he thought for a moment as the two men let him work out the reciprocal compass heading. "Two hundred degrees."

"Sounds like a plan," Pete said. "Anyone hungry?" From the looks on Steve's and Sean's faces, it was a stupid question. He dived into the cockpit and came up with a plastic package. "One MRE with three thousand calories of action packed goodies."

"What's MRE stand for?" Sean asked.

"Meals Ready to Eat," Pete replied. "They were developed by the military to replace the old C-Rations."

"Meals Ready to Eat, my ass," Steve groused. "Meals Rejected by Ethiopians if you ask me." They all laughed.

"Steve," Pete asked, "why did you go back for that bottle of Scotch?"

Caly's Island

"That was for the Admiral. We all owe him and he does have a thing about Scotch. That was a very rare fifty-year-old single malt worth a couple of thousand dollars and arguably the finest Scotch known to man. Too bad I dropped it. I hope the fish appreciate it."

Pete laughed and changed the subject. "Sean, where did you learn to throw a line like that?"

"Mr. Gunnermyer taught me."

Pete lifted an eyebrow. "We're Steve and Pete, and Rufe is Mr. Gunnermyer?"

Sean grinned and changed the subject. "How long do you think it will take to get home?"

Pete studied the glow on the horizon. "The storm blew us a long way. But what the hell, the sailing doesn't get any better. Besides, you got anything better to do, Mr. Homes?"

Sean played it straight-faced. "Get laid?"

"Teenagers," Pete groused as he opened the MRE.

Zack ran through the night, driven by the baying dogs in the far distance. Fortunately, the terrain was not heavily wooded and he had a clear view of the volcano ahead of him. Twice, he stopped to read his compass, making sure he was still headed west. Finally, he cleared the trees and stopped at the edge of the lava field. He walked gingerly onto the wavy crust and felt the heat coming from below. A sixth sense warned him to tread carefully and not break through. Slowly, he picked up speed as his confidence grew. He made steady progress and had gone a mile when the dogs went silent. He turned and looked back. "Oh, shit," he whispered. Behind him he could make out a hulking shadow on the lava field moving slowly towards him. It had to be Silla, but where were the dogs? Fear drove him forward, and there was no doubt the two dogs were in full chase, bounding across the lava field. He put on a burst of speed.

The slope steepened as the lava field split. The lava had erupted out of the caldera high above him and flowed down depressions in the face of the volcano in rivulets before joining into larger streams, then merging and becoming rivers. Finally, the rivers had joined and became a wide sheet flowing towards the sea. Zack made a decision and worked his way up the lava flow on his left, praying it would not dead end at a crevice he could not cross. He had to reach the top although he had no idea what to do when he got there. "Hey, 'Fesstus," he called. "I'm not some sort of human sacrifice, am I? Don't you need virgins for that sort of thing?" Now he was climbing, feeling for handholds and afraid to use his flashlight, which would pinpoint his location. "Not gonna answer," he muttered. "Come on, I know you're there."

A puff of wind at his back carried a foul stench, warning him the dogs were almost on him. But could they scramble up the steep face? Suddenly, the lava flow leveled off a few degrees and the going was easier. The stench was stronger. "Human sacrifice, my ass. I'm dinner." Adrenaline shot through him and he scrambled to the edge of the lava and climbed up the steep rocky ridge that had split the lava flow. The face of the ridge was a combination of shale and rocks that kept falling away as he climbed. About fifty feet above the lava, the shale stopped and he climbed onto solid rock. He had reached the crest of the ridge and there was nowhere to go. He was trapped.

A loud scratching sound forced Zack to look down. One of the dogs was trying to scramble up after him and kept slipping backwards. Then it was slowly inching forward. He watched with a combination of horror and fascination as the dog came at him. "What dumb son of a bitch said dogs can't climb?" he grumbled. However, these were no ordinary dogs. He fumbled in his dry bag and drew the flare gun. "Two rounds left. Make 'em count." He cocked the hammer, took careful aim, and squeezed the trigger. The flare flashed as it bounced off the dog's skull and corkscrewed down the slope. The dog howled in pain and tumbled backwards, rolling and kicking until it bounced off the lava flow below.

Zack stared into the dark. Below him, a second set of eyes glowed red. Further down the lava field, the flare continued to burn, giving off a flickering red light. He stopped breathing when a shadow kicked at the flare, sending it into a crevice. Silla had finally caught up with him. He looked for a place to hide, but there was only a low rock outcropping near the edge. He scrambled behind it, hoping it was enough.

Zack shivered in the night air as the first light of dawn split the horizon and illuminated the lip of the caldera above him. Slowly, the shadows yielded to the rising sun. Below him, Silla was curled up with her dogs, snoring loudly. She came awake with a jerk and looked directly at him. A scream of pure hate split the air as she came to her feet. She scrambled up the ridge, only to slip backwards. Twice more, she attacked

Caly's Island

the ridge, only to slip in the crumbly shale. Finally, she gave up and shouted at him. The dogs started to howl and she kicked at them, muttering obscenity after obscenity. Zack stood and took a long swig from his water bottle, which only sent her into a deeper rage. She fell to her knees at the base of the ridge and pawed at the shale, finally finding a rock of the right size. She kept digging until she had a pile of softball-sized rocks. She stood and unwrapped the thongs of her slingshot from around her waist. Without a word, she loaded the slingshot and sent a rock whistling at Zack.

He hunkered down behind the low rock outcropping as the missile careened off, splitting off a little of the rock protecting him. Again, she launched a missile with the same effect. It was only a matter of time until she chipped away enough of the rock outcropping to make Zack the target. The next missile split his rock shield and she howled with success. Part of the rock rolled down and almost hit her. "Two can play this game," Zack shouted. He rolled into a sitting position and kicked at the loose boulder. Another missile bounced off the other side of the boulder, and he knew with certainty a direct hit would kill him. He kicked harder. Another missile hit the boulder and he felt it give. Now he could hear the dogs scrambling up the loose shale. He put both feet against the boulder and pushed.

The boulder came loose and tumbled down, kicking up shale and rocks as it fell. Zack looked in time to see the dogs fall back as Silla rolled to the side. The boulder bounced over her and slammed into the lava, punching a hole through the crust. Silla came to her feet, her mouth wide in triumph. She tilted her head, as she looked at Zack, now fully exposed. She reloaded and spun the slingshot. The missile flew straight and true as Zack dodged, but it still grazed his shoulder. He gave her the finger as she slowly reloaded, taking her time and savoring the kill. "Go to hell!" he shouted.

Suddenly, a steam cloud erupted out of the hole the boulder had punched in the lava's crust. The wind blew the steam over Silla and the two dogs, sending them into fits of coughing. The pungent smell of sulfur and methane almost smothered Zack high above them. He doused his shirt with the last of his water and quickly held it to his face, taking what protection he could from the billowing cloud. Slowly the cloud yielded to the wind. Below him, Silla was curled up in a tight ball next to the sprawling bodies of her two dogs. She jerked once and he heard a loud death rattle as her lungs collapsed.

Hephaestsus was there.

EIGHTEEN

The sailing couldn't get much better as *L'Amour* raced eastward. "Land ho!" Sean called, rousing the two sleeping men. Pete stuck his head out of the hatch, blinking in the early morning sun. Sean pointed to their starboard quarter and the lawyer twisted around. A dark shadow broke the far horizon. "I think that's Gozo."

"Makes sense," Pete replied. "Head for it." Sean fell off the wind twenty degrees and trimmed the sails. "How far away do you think it is?" Pete asked.

Sean thought for a moment, recalling the formula Blair had taught him. "If my eyeballs are five feet off the water and the highest point on the island is 600 feet . . ." He tried to extract the square roots in his head, but couldn't do it.

"About thirty-two nautical miles," Steve called from the cabin.

"How do you do that?" Sean asked. "I mean get the square roots so fast."

Steve emerged from the cabin and handed the teenager a mug of steaming cocoa. "You've earned this." He smiled while Sean sipped the beverage. "It's pretty simple. You extrapolate between prime factors. I know twenty-four squared is 576 and twenty-five squared is 625. Six hundred is half way between, or 24.5." Pete groaned as Steve explained. "Don't pay him any attention," Steve told Sean. "He's a lawyer. They don't do math." Pete took the tiller as Steve and Sean huddled together for an impromptu math lesson.

"We'll be there by noon at this rate," Pete called. They ignored him. "Teenagers," Pete groused.

An hour later, Steve took the tiller and Sean disappeared down the hatch for a few hours of sleep. "He's a good kid," Steve said.

"Indeed," Pete conceded. "Too bad about those tattoos."

Steve nodded in agreement. "I know an excellent plastic surgeon. He might be able to help, although tattoos are a problem."

"Plastic surgeon?" Pete asked.

Steve stared at the island. "Oh yeah. I've been nipped, tucked, and lipo-sucked. Not to mention trimmed and follicularly enhanced."

"Hair transplant? You?"

"Yep. Not much on top. But not as bad as the Admiral. Now women find me irresistibly attractive." He gave a cynical chuckle. "Well, a few million euros help with the irresistible part." The two men laughed.

Three hours later they sailed into the lagoon as Blair, Gib and Rufus ran down to the shore to pull *L'Amour* onto the sand. Blair bombarded them with questions as they walked to the canopy where Sasha was lying, shivering in a down-filled sleeping bag. Pete quickly recapped what had happened and how they had lost *High Flyer* in the storm. "Someone, or something, doesn't want us to go to Sicily," Pete said. "So how is Sasha doing?"

"She's dying," Rufus said.

The men tried to console the blacksmith and convince him it wasn't his fault, but he wasn't having it. Finally, Sean spoke up. "I bet Caly can help her." The five men looked at him. "She's a witch or something like that, right? Don't they make magic potions and stuff like that?"

"I broached that possibility with her," Gib explained. "She was not receptive, to say the least."

"It wouldn't hurt to try again," Sean replied.

"It is certainly worth a try," Gib said. He sank into his camp chair and pulled into himself, trying to understand the phenomena they were dealing with. He started to ask questions, probing for what the others thought. Sean ran for *Wee Dram* and returned with Blair's copy of The Odyssey. He turned to the relevant pages and read. Gib then carefully led each one through their encounter with Caly, looking for a common thread. Years of judicial experience had honed his logic with a keen understanding of human nature. Suddenly, the truth jolted him like an earthquake, shaking him to his very core. He finally accepted what he had refused to believe – Caly was not human. He was lost, adrift on a sea of emotion, and grasped for a life ring, anything to restore order to his world. He focused on Caly. Holding his fear at bay, he dissected her as he would a defendant standing at the bar of justice who had been found guilty of a crime.

But what was Caly's crime? She hadn't harmed them in anyway, but she hadn't helped them and that was not a crime. In a world where there was no system of justice, where might made right and raw emotion ruled, it was a good survival technique. The opening line of The Odyssey came to him.

> "Sing in me, O, Muse, that I may tell
> Of that hero of twists and turns who roamed far and wide
> After he had sacked the sacred heights of Troy."

Slowly, the pieces came together and he knew what they had to do. "Gentlemen," he began, "we are dealing with an unknown force who has powers we do not understand. So trust me on this, she does have power. Fortunately, it is limited and she is human in certain aspects. She is a very lonely and narcissistic woman. Her experience is with humans like Ulysses who used force, cunning, and guile to get their way – three things we reject. Therefore, I suggest we approach her openly and with the truth. It's all we have. The question is who should do it?"

"Don't look at me," Steve said. "I don't want anything to do with the hag."

Blair shook his head. "She hates the air I breathe."

Pete humphed, willing to volunteer. "We did get along pretty well. I'll take one for the troops – again."

"She did use you," Gib allowed. "I think it should be Rufus," He looked at the blacksmith. "You are the only one of us who has not met or seen her. You are the fresh face, the unknown personality. Go to her, be yourself, and simply ask for her help."

"Sounds like fresh meat to me," Steve grumped.

Rufus thought for a moment. "That's it?"

"That's it," Gib assured him.

Pete chimed in, more relieved than he was willing to admit. "I can show you where she lives."

"Don't let her see you," Gib cautioned.

"Take a couple of gifts," Sean said. The five men stared at the teenager. "What?" he asked.

It was late evening when Zack reached the cottage. Circe saw him the moment he emerged from the woods and ran to him. Again, she clung to him as her heart raced. Her body felt good against his and she smelled sweet with the fragrance of youth. "I do like the way you say hello," he told her. She kissed him, full and lingering. "Silla is dead along with two of her dogs," Zack said. She nodded slowly. "Hephaestus got 'em near the top of the volcano. Almost got me." He recounted how the deadly gas had asphyxiated the monsters. "That leaves Ka-rib and one dog."

"They are at the compound," she said, motioning in that direction, "guarding the slaves."

"I got'a kill her now, before she suspects something is wrong."

Circe led him into the house and pointed at a pile of weapons. "Hephaestus told me where to find these."

"A telephone call, I suppose." She looked at him, not understanding. "How do you talk to him?"

She pointed to the fire. "It's always the same, don't you remember? You can talk to him if you want."

"Zack to Hephaestus, come in Hephaestus."

She laughed. "Not that way, silly. Look into the fire, not at it. Hephaestus is there and will talk to you."

Zack shook his head. "I don't think so. I'm a nobody."

"Not to Hephaestus," she replied.

Zack took stock of the eight spears, which were really long wooden poles with fire-hardened points. He held one in his hand, pleased by its balance. It was a much better weapon than he had made. Next were three crude axes with bronze heads and amazing sharp edges. At the side were four knives with wooden hafts. He bundled up the spears and axes with fifty feet of rough rope and shoved the knives in his belt. "Thank Hephaestus for me." Almost ready to go, he jammed the flare gun into his belt. "One round left." She handed him a water bottle and a sack with a pear, cheese, and bread before looking away, tears in her eyes. "Hey, I'll be back." He shouldered the bundle and headed into the night.

Caly's Island

"I'll show you the way," she said, running after him.

* * * *

Pete guided Rufus down the narrow trail to the cave that overlooked the sea. Without a word, he pointed to the entrance and pulled back into the deepening shadows. Rufus glanced at the cave and then back to Pete, but he was gone. Rufus lifted the heavy bag and trudged down to the cave, still not sure what to say. He was ten feet away when Caly emerged. The blacksmith dropped the bag and stared at the apparition in front of him, convinced he had died and gone to heaven. She was the most beautiful woman he had ever seen. Her long red hair framed a perfect face and astounding green eyes. She was not slender or petite in any way, but full-figured with large hips and a narrow waist. Her skin glowed with health and youth. "Are you for real?" he stammered.

She smiled. "Are you?" He nodded dumbly. "What's that?" she asked, pointing to the sack.

"Charcoal," he finally managed. "I made it and thought you could use it." He reached into a pocket and pulled out a tube of hand cream. He handed it to her.

She took the tube and cocked her head. "Charcoal?"

"It makes hot fires with no smoke." He pointed to the tube. "That's a skin cream." He pantomimed how to remove the cap and squeeze some into her hand.

She laughed and handed back the tube. He removed the cap, squeezed a small amount into her hand, and made a rubbing motion along his arm. She got the idea and applied the creamy lotion. Her eyes opened wide. "Oh!" She quickly applied more to her other arm and then some to her face. Laughing, she tried to pick up the sack, but it was too heavy. "Please help."

Rufus picked the sack up with an easy motion and followed her inside. The door shut behind him, and for a split second, he panicked. She smiled at him and the panic subsided. The hearth still had a few glowing embers in it, and he dumped a few chunks of charcoal on top. "That should do the trick." He settled back on his haunches as the charcoal came to life.

Caly curled up on the floor beside him and leaned on his shoulder. "You want me to help the woman," she said. It was not a question.

"How did you know?"

"This is my island and I am given to know."

"She's dying because of what I did to her."

"You tried to cut out the evil that burns in her."

"We call it an infection." He made no attempt to explain bacteria and used words she could understand. "It's when small, evil mites you cannot see get in a person's body and grow, killing the person. I tried to cut the mites out but failed."

"It was not your fault."

Rufus shook his head. "I hoped you might have something that can kill the mites, a potion or something like that." He silently cursed himself for being so direct and not more smooth and persuasive. "Please help her," he begged. A long silence claimed them and he dozed in the warmth. Her fingers stroked his hair.

"I like your fire," she said, gently massaging his shoulders until he fell into a deep sleep.

Rufus came awake with a jerk, wondering how long he had been asleep. He caught the scent of something different, animal, but yet familiar. Just as quickly, it was gone. Caly was still sitting in her rocker, looking at him. "Her name is Sasha. Can you help her?"

"Do you love her?"

Rufus shook his head, not able to talk about it.

"I think you do," she persisted. "I can't help her," she said. She stood and led him to the cave entrance. Again, he caught the faint animal scent. She pushed at the door and it swung into the deep shadows. Outside, the moon was very bright. She pointed to the path and the way back to the lagoon. "Your friend is waiting for you," she said. She turned and the door silently closed.

A feeling of relief swept over Rufus as he trudged towards the trees, as if a great danger had suddenly vanished. Pete was waiting in the trees and flicked on his flashlight to lead the way. "She won't help," Rufus said.

"She is one possessive and self-centered bitch," Pete answered.

"She knows everything that happens on the island," Rufus cautioned.

"Why am I not surprised?" They walked in silence back to the lagoon where the others were anxiously waiting.

"How did it go?" Blair asked.

Caly's Island

Rufus shook his head. "No luck. She won't help, but she really liked the hand cream and charcoal."

"It was my fault," Gib said. "We should have sent Pete." He pulled into himself, thinking. "I should have seen it. Pete is the only one she has slept with."

"So what do we do about Sasha?" Rufus asked.

"We wait and hope," Blair answered. "She's a fighter."

Rufus's head came up as he looked at Blair's boat, finally making the connection. "When I was in the cave, I smelled something. I didn't know what it was at first, but I think she's got Angus."

"I want my dog back," Blair muttered.

"I'll get him," Sean promised.

Zack worked their way downwind from the monster's compound and motioned for her to stop. "Wait here," he whispered. He dropped his heavy load and crawled through the brush until he could see the compound in the flickering light of the huge bonfire Ka-rib kept burning night and day. He couldn't see Ka-rib, but the dog was lying near the gate, and twenty or so men were all huddled in the center, naked, and shackled together. Even in the poor light, he could see they were emaciated and filthy. "So where are you?" he wondered. Then he saw her. She emerged from the pile of cargo and debris salvaged from wrecked ships carrying a large jug and totally naked. Zack flinched at the ugly and grotesque creature, more certain than ever that he had to kill her. He tried to look away, but couldn't as she strode into the mass of shackled men, finally selecting one. She grabbed his hair and pulled his head back. It was difficult to see, but she was pouring the contents of the jug down his throat, forcing him to swallow. The men howled as Ka-rib waded into them, muttering words he didn't understand. Her toned changed, almost becoming human, as she laughed. She forced four others to drink until the jug was empty. Zack felt sick to his stomach and retreated back into the brush. "Angela?" he called.

"I'm over here," she answered from behind him. "I saw."

"What's going on? What was she making those poor bastards drink?"

"It's a strong wine. She's making them too drunk to . . ." She extended a forefinger in the age-old symbol of an erection and jammed it into her clenched fist in a pumping action.

Zack bent over and threw up. She knelt beside him and rubbed his back. "Ka-rib senses Silla is dead. Only now will she mate and give birth. She will kill any male baby." Slowly, Zack's raging emotions subsided, but he doubted he would ever be totally sane again. For the first time in his life, Zack Hilber was witnessing the creation of evil and he alone stood against it. He looked up at the night sky, struck by the panoply of stars ranged above him. The Belt of Orion twinkled at him and he was back on the road outside of Bellingham, lost and in need of relieving himself. Standing by the roadside, he had insulted a force he didn't understand, and this was his reward.

He spoke in a low voice, "I've got to kill that monster and you can't be part of it. Go home and wait for me." She gently held his face with her hands, her lips inches away from his. Tears filled her eyes as she nodded. She gently kissed him and came to her feet. Without a sound or backwards glance, she disappeared into the dark. "Okay," Zack muttered, "how do you kill a monster?" He worked the problem.

About half of the men were gone, sold, or fed to the dogs, probably both. "Fear is a wonderful thing," he muttered. "So, what's the threat?" He snorted, disgusted with himself for not seeing it earlier. Ka-rib had to guard the men, which explained why only Silla left the compound and always left at least one dog. "Kill the dog first." Zack carefully unwrapped the rope from around the spears and coiled it over his left shoulder. He picked up a spear and an ax and moved around to the gate side of the compound, careful to stay downwind. Calculating the distance, he moved further away and rigged the rope as a snare, tying the loose end to the biggest tree he could find. "This had better work," he mumbled, "or I'm breakfast." He sat back against the tree and rested as he ate, gathering his strength.

The first light of the new day was glowing in the east when Zack came to his feet. He chanted loudly as he headed for the compound. "Hup, two, three, four. Let's get down and even the score." Ahead, the dog stirred and growled in warning. Zack emerged from the brush and stood in full view. "Come to poppa, you ugly bastard!" The dog barked in fury as Ka-rib sat up in the middle of the men. She came to her feet and barged through the huddled mass, snarling and spitting as she headed for the gate. Zack held his spear up and waved it at her in defiance. "Jam this up your fat ass!" Fully enraged, Ka-rib pulled the gate back and the beast burst out, coming directly at Zack. "Oh, shit," he breathed. The dog was the biggest and youngest of the pack and came at him like an express train. Zack turned and ran, afraid that he had miscalculated the distances. Desperate, he dropped the spear and ran for all he was worth, still carrying the ax. Behind him, he heard the dog crashing through the heavy brush. He leaped over the rope snare and stumbled just as the dog took one final bound.

Zack rolled to his left as the dog landed six feet away. It dug in and pivoted, swinging on him and, for a split moment, Zack knew he was a dead man. He scrambled to his knees as the creature came at him, only to suddenly jerk back. The rope had snared the beast's hind right leg. The dog rolled, still trying to get at him as the tree gave way. Again, the dog lunged at him, only to be drawn back as the tree fell over. The dog's huge paws clawed the ground and it came at him, its mouth wide and fangs bared, dragging the tree. Zack drew his flare gun and fired.

The muzzle flashed as the flare ignited and flew straight into the beast's mouth and down its throat. The dog bellowed and screeched in pain as it rolled on the ground, pawing the air and twisting up in the rope. The sound echoed and carried for miles. Zack grabbed the ax and swung, hitting the dog's head with a glancing blow. Again, he swung, burying the ax in the monster's skull. He tried to wrench it free but the handle split off, leaving the ax head buried. Zack fell to his knees panting as the dog quieted. Suddenly, it came at him, smoke streaming from its mouth as the flare still burned inside. Zack shoved the ax handle into its gaping maw and scampered away as the monster finally collapsed.

Zack sat on the ground and carefully examined himself. Hard experience had taught him how quickly a claw scratch turned infectious, but other than a few bruises, he was okay. In the distance, he heard Ka-rib howling in anger. "At least you're not deaf," he muttered. He stood and headed for his next battle. "Your little pet ain't coming home and I'm the guilty bastard." The spears and two axes were where he had left them, and he quickly picked them up, marching for the compound. He emerged from the brush in the full light of the new day.

He dropped the spears and axes, and shouted. "Hey! I'm back! What you gonna do about it?" Ka-rib saw him and ran to the thicket fence, shaking it in her fury. "It's just you and me, baby." He stopped, realizing it wasn't just him against the monster. He picked up a spear and lobbed it over her head and into the men still huddled on the ground. One of them yelled and picked it up. As quickly as he could, Zack threw another spear to the men. A shout answered him and he knew he had allies. He threw five more spears over Ka-rib's head, keeping the last for himself. Then he swung an ax back and forth and tossed it over the corral's thicket fence. One of the men grabbed it as Zack threw the last ax.

Ka-rib charged at the men and grabbed for a spear, but the men shuffled together and held her at bay, jabbing and poking at her. Zack crept up to the fence, not able to take his eyes off the battle playing out in front of him. Again, Ka-rib charged the spears only to be driven off. While the spearmen distracted the monster, the two men with the axes pounded at the pins shackling the men together. They broke free with a shout. For a moment, there was mass confusion until a man shouted orders.

They had a leader. Free of their shackles, the spearmen surrounded Ka-rib. One lunged at her and immediately retreated as another man at her back darted forward and jabbed his spear into her back. He immediately retreated as she turned into him. A third man attacked from her blindside, jabbing and retreating. The leader shouted an order and two men grabbed one end of the long chain that had shackled them while two grabbed the other end. They spread out and rushed at Ka-rib, catching her in the middle of the long chain and wound her up, snaring her tight as the spearmen kept jabbing at her, harder and longer with each thrust.

"Hey!" Zack yelled. "Over here!" he held up two knives in each hand. A man ran for the fence as Zack lobbed the four knives in his direction. The man scooped them up and tossed three of them to his compatriots as he lunged at Ka-rib. He never hesitated and jumped on her back, holding on to her long hair while he tried to straddle her massive body with his legs. He drove the blade into her neck again and again. The creature started to visibly weaken, but suddenly gave a massive shudder, throwing the man to the ground. She reached for him but the men holding the chain dragged her away. She screamed her rage as the spearmen kept thrusting at her, drawing even more blood. She sank to one knee, bellowing her anger. A spearman poked her left eye

Caly's Island

out as a man with an ax snuck up behind her. He swung the ax over his head.

Zack turned away, unable to look. It sounded like someone chopping wood as he walked away. A loud shout of victory echoed over him and he chanced a look back. A leg flew over the fence, and he felt sick to his stomach. He started to trot, then broke into a hard run.

NINETEEN

Pete sat in *L'Amour's* cockpit and updated his journal. It was still early morning and the FOGs were all up and about. Steve and Sean were out fishing for their breakfast and that had him a little worried. It was taking longer and longer to catch a fish. Gib was cleaning his boat, which was a constant with the men. It never ceased to amaze the lawyer how dirty a small boat could get. Blair was gathering wood, which also was taking longer each day. Pete made a note in his journal: We're straining the environment. He glanced at the canopy where Rufus was tending to Sasha. She was delirious and it was only a matter of time before they had to dig a grave.

Steve and Sean were back with two fish, enough for breakfast. They set to work cleaning them as Blair returned with the wood. Pete put his journal away and joined Rufus who was bathing Sasha's head with a damp towel in a vain attempt to hold her fever in check.

"She's a fighter," Rufus said.

Pete agreed. "Indeed." He wished there was something he could do, and his helplessness frustrated him. Breakfast was ready and Steve portioned out the fish and some wild bulbs Rufus had dug up that resembled onions. "Not bad at all," Pete allowed.

"Sean," Blair said, "can you go to the grove and gather some pears this morning? Get two for each of us. While you're there, can you look around and see what else you can find?" Sean nodded eagerly and quickly wolfed down the last of his food. He jumped up and hurried over to *Wee Dram* where he rummaged around in his kit bag. "Take a radio," Blair called. Sean held up the radio and a Frisbee as he headed for the grove. "What's he gonna do with a Frisbee?" Blair wondered.

"Who knows?" Gib replied. He settled into his camp chair and stared at his hands. "H, I take it there is something serious that you wish to discuss outside of Master Homes' presence."

Blair nodded. "It's just a matter of time for Sasha. Perhaps today. How do we handle Sean? Do we want him here when it happens?"

Rufus shook his head. "Don't underestimate him. He can handle it and he needs to be here." He fixed them with a serious look. "But she's not going to die. Trust me on this one."

"Rufe, my man," Pete said, his voice low and full of concern, "you cannot do the impossible."

"Watch," Rufus said. He moved over to Sasha and bathed her head with a wet towel. "Not today," he told her. He kept repeating the two words over and over, willing them to be true.

Zack sat on the ground, gathering the last of his strength. He had never been so exhausted, or so exhilarated. He had killed four gargantuan dogs that had escaped from the depths of hell, and destroyed two monsters beyond anything his puny imagination could conjure. Yet, he was not Silla and Ka-rib's executioner, only the facilitator. Was that good or bad? He didn't know, but he sensed it was important. He snorted in contempt. Who would ever believe him? It was not a tale he could ever tell, not even to the FOGs when they mellowed out on a dock after a day of sailing. He ran that scenario through his imagination and could see Gib shaking his head in disbelief, marking the tale up to creeping senility or too much wine. Zack came to his feet, sensing his ordeal was not at an end. He staggered, putting one foot forward at a time. He braced himself against a tree and looked up at the clear blue sky. In the distance, he could see the volcano, now quiet. "Do what you have to," he called, accepting whatever fate was in store for him.

A feeling of relief swept over him when he finally reached the cottage. He took the last few steps and emerged into the clearing. He stopped, struck dumb. Circe was standing in the doorway waiting for him, nude and shimmering in the morning light, and beautiful beyond belief. He fell to his knees as she ran to him. She knelt beside him and threw an arm around his shoulders, helping him to his feet. "I love you," he whispered.

She led him inside and shut the door.

Caly's Island

* * * *

Sean sat on the low ridge overlooking the lagoon and stared at the top of the canopy on the beach below, willing Sasha to live. The harder he concentrated, the more certain he became that she would not die. For the first time in his young life, he was praying, and his concern was for another person with no thought of himself. Whatever problems he had were dust on the wind, not worth thinking about. He stood and headed for the grove where he had first met Caly, determined to make something happen. He didn't know exactly what or how to do it, but it was going to happen. It was time to check in with Blair and he keyed the radio. "I'm on top of the ridge and headed for the grove now." Sean signed off and ambled down the narrow path, tossing the Frisbee in the air and catching it. He found the rock where they had first met and sat down, twirling the Frisbee on his right forefinger. He didn't have long to wait.

"What is that silly thing you're playing with," Caly said from behind him.

He twisted around, following the voice. Caly was standing a few feet away, shimmering in the sunlight filtering through the trees, more beautiful than he remembered. She tossed her long golden hair over one shoulder and sat beside him, barely touching. He handed her the Frisbee. "You throw it back and forth and play catch." She turned the blue saucer-shaped disk over and examined it before handing it back. "It's fun," he assured her.

Like teenagers everywhere, they fell silent and looked straight ahead, not knowing what to say. "I need to pick some pears for my buddies," he finally told her. She pulled a little moue, pouting in a very pretty way that sent a shiver down his back. "Please," he begged. She gave in and led him into the grove, holding hands. Suddenly, she turned and kissed him, long and lingering. Their tongues darted back and forth as she coached him in the art and their bodies pressed together. Sean pulled back, afraid he was in over his head. "Wow, I've never kissed like that."

She laughed. "There is more – if you can catch me." She ran deeper into the grove as he chased her. Their laughter carried over the glen as they darted back and forth among the trees, playing the age-old game of catch-me-if-you-can. It was the old story of teenagers discovering life as they played. She ran into a small clearing and collapsed onto the grass on her back, breathing hard, her breasts heaving.

He flopped down beside her on his stomach. She smiled at him and his heart did another flip-flop. "It's fun to be young again," she said.

Sean came up on his elbows as an inner alarm sounded. "Again?"

"Sometimes, I feel so old when I'm alone." She laughed, recovering from the unguarded comment.

"I know what you mean. But why are you alone? If you lived in Bellingham, you'd be the most popular girl in town. Guys would kill for you."

"Would they?"

He smiled at her. "Me included." She gave him a long look, her eyes wide and beautiful. "You are so beautiful," he murmured.

"Am I?"

"Oh, yeah." He grew serious. "I'll never forget you."

She jumped to her feet. "Throw me the Frisbee." He pointed to the other end of the clearing as he stood. She hurried over to the spot and turned around, not knowing what to do.

He flipped the disk at her. Her mouth was open as she watched it hover in front of her, just out of reach. "Catch it!" he shouted. She jumped up and reached for it just as it veered off. She fell to the ground laughing as he fell on her, showering her with kisses. "See what happens when you miss."

"I'll miss a lot now," she said, rolling free. She picked up the Frisbee and tried to throw it, failing miserably. "Show me," she commanded.

Again, Sean's inner alarm sounded. There was something in her voice he didn't understand. He ran to her and stood behind her as she rubbed her body against him. He reached around and held her hand, showing her how to toss the disk. She gave it a flip and it sailed away, towards the trees. Angus broke from behind a tree and bounded into the clearing, going after the flying Frisbee. At the perfect moment, the terrier leaped up, his short powerful legs sending him five feet into the air, and grabbed the Frisbee with his teeth. He landed and trotted over to them, the stub of his tail wagging, and dropped the Frisbee at Sean's feet.

Sean held out his arms and Angus jumped into his embrace. He licked Sean's face as the teenager looked at Caly. "The Admiral has been very lonely without him."

Caly's Island

Loneliness was the one thing Caly understood and it touched the human side of her. She nodded. "Let's pick some pears for your friends."

Zack moaned in his sleep as he twisted and turned, reliving the horror of the last two days in a nightmare that was all too real. He felt a cool hand on his cheek and he quieted. Then he heard men shouting outside. "Go to sleep," she said, getting out of bed. He dreamed she was walking across the floor and opening the door. A large group of bearded, grimy, and half-naked men were gathered outside the door. They shouted and rushed at the naked woman. Suddenly, it was silent and he was vaguely aware of grunting sounds coming from outside as she climbed back in bed. Her warm body was against him as she cooed and licked his face. Her hands moved over him, stroking him in ways he had never experienced as she slipped lower. He moaned as the dream intensified and, finally satiated, he slipped into a welcomed sleep.

Sun was streaming through the open door when Zack woke. He sensed he was not alone in the bed and turned over, only to rub against her. She was propped up on one elbow, looking at him, her eyes soft and gentle. He stretched, feeling young and full of life. "What a dream," he told her. "It started out as a nightmare with the dogs chasing me and got worse, then there were men shouting outside, and then you came to bed and we . . . well, I haven't had a dream like that since I was a teenager."

"There were men outside last night, the sailors Ka-rib and Silla had taken as slaves. They followed you back here. I took care of them. They're harmless now."

He stared at her in shock. "Then we made . . ." She nodded in answer. "Oh, no," he moaned. Although temptation had come his way a few times when he worked for the CIA, he had always been faithful to Angela and he loved her unreservedly. "No, no, no." He sat on the edge of the bed and held his head in his hands, sick to the very bottom of his soul. He turned on her. "Damn you!"

She looked at him, truly confused. "Why? I was only being what you wanted."

He yelled at her, venting his anger. "I didn't want you! I wanted my wife, Angela."

"My name is Circe. I told you that."

"You reminded me of Angela when she was young." His eyes narrowed, his rage growing. "No wonder they burned witches." He shoved her to her knees, looming over her, his anger in full flow, as he raised his fist. She lifted her face to take the blow, her eyes fixed on him, as tears streamed down her cheeks. Zack checked his swing and collapsed to the floor beside her. "Oh, no. What am I doing? I'm so screwed up. It must'a been that damn go-faster pill. They really mess with your brain." He was brutally honest with himself and knew there was much more to it. "I wanted you to be Angela, and it was like being young again." She knelt in front of him and held his hands, softly chanting words he didn't understand. Slowly, his anger drained away. "Please forgive me," he said. "You are so beautiful. I should have known, but I was so damn confused." Suddenly, a great weight was lifted from his seething emotions, only to be replaced with a vague impression that it had all been a dream. "What's going on?"

She sat beside him and cradled his head against her shoulder. "The ways of the gods are strange. Perhaps they wanted to teach you a lesson about human frailty. Maybe they saw arrogance and pride, but I think you insulted them and this was your penance. This is a time of testing and you had to end an evil that stalked the earth. It is not for you, or me, to know why, only to survive." She kissed his face as her tears caressed his cheeks. "Your Angela is the most fortunate of women." She pushed him away and stood, a decision made. "It's time for you to return to your friends." He looked at her, not understanding. She pointed at the fire. "They told me to help. Your friends are not far away and they are in trouble. You must help them, but I cannot take you there. You must go on your own."

Zack shook his head. "How? I get lost going around the block." His common sense told him that was no longer true. "Where exactly are we, and how do I find them?"

"This is the isle of Sikilia, and the volcano will guide you. Sail your boat past the volcano to the southern tip of Sikilia and wait for morning. Sail south for a day, and always keep the volcano directly behind you. At sunset, turn and head into the setting sun. Chase it, even after it sets. You will see an island in the morning, and your friends are on the western end." She made him repeat the instructions four times until he had committed them to memory. Satisfied he wouldn't forget, Circe moved

Caly's Island

around the room, gathering food in two large sacks. "I won't need all that," he told her.

"Yes, you will." She thought for a moment and handed him two small oval-shaped flasks with stoppers. "The green one you know. It is the potion for fever."

"That's great stuff. I hope I can patent it."

"The gold one is a lotion for beauty. Do not drink it. Rub it on the skin."

Zack held the golden flask in his right hand, surprised by its smooth warmth. "If it works as well as the first one, it can make me a billionaire overnight." He grinned wickedly at the thought.

Circe ignored him as she slipped on a simple tunic and stepped into her sandals. "It is time to go. You have a long way to sail and must be ready to sail south at first light tomorrow morning."

Zack pulled on his clothes, surprised they were clean and mended. "I will never forget you." He held her tight. "Come with me. I hate leaving you alone."

"I'm not allowed to leave Sikilia." She smiled. "Besides, I'm safe now, and I won't be alone." They walked outside and were immediately surrounded by twenty-three friendly piglets. She reached down and stroked one between the ears. "The sailors are learning how to behave," she said.

"You changed them into swine?"

She gave him a rueful look. "Zack, I am a witch. You should know that by now. Come, you are running out of time." Together they walked down to the shore where he had beached *Wild Turtle*. It gleamed in the sun, sparkling clean and without a scratch. "Hephaestus says it is a cute little boat," she explained. "He likes it." Together, they loaded the sacks and four leather water bags. Zack pushed *Wild Turtle* free of the sand, and she held the pulpit while he climbed aboard. He raised the red and yellow striped sails as the wind freshened. Circe pushed the bow away and stepped back, still standing in the water. She placed her right hand over her heart and then gestured towards him, her palm open. "Go in peace with my love." She was smiling.

Zack put the helm over and caught the wind. *Wild Turtle* started to move and he looked back. Circe was walking away, her back to him, surrounded by the piglets. He blinked when he realized a man was walking beside her. "You lucky dog." He laughed as *Wild Turtle* surged ahead. "Wrong. You lucky pig."

It was mid afternoon when Sean returned to the lagoon carrying a plastic carrier bag of pears. Angus trailed along behind him, a penitent ashamed of his errant ways. They were twenty yards away from the canopy where the men were sitting in the shade when Angus broke into a full run, heading straight for Blair. Blair laughed as the dog bounded into his lap, home at last. "Where did you find him?" he asked.

Sean handed the bag of pears to Steve. "Caly had him."

"So you saw her," Pete said. "What did she look like?"

"Just like the first time we met – young and beautiful."

"You know that is not the real her," Gib cautioned. "That is an illusion she creates." Sean nodded. He was more accepting of her powers than any of the men. "May I ask how you got Angus back?" the jurist wondered. Sean sat on the sand and wrapped his arms around his knees as he told them of his day. For the five men, it was an old tale with all the bloom of youth. And they were envious.

"I've never been kissed like that before," the teenager admitted. "We played with the Frisbee and Angus came out of nowhere and caught it. Later, I gave Caly the Frisbee and she gave me Angus. We traded."

"I don't think it was a trade," Rufus said. He was still sitting by Sasha, willing her to live. "She let Angus go for a reason. She wants something in return."

"Kill her," Sasha moaned. They all turned and looked at the feverish woman. She slipped back into her delirium, her breath coming in pants.

Blair considered it. He had experienced enough combat to appreciate the dangers of using force. Once employed, violence took its own path, often unpredictable, and always at a terrible price. It was an option he wasn't ready to use, but would as a last resort. "Shooting her would be a terrible mistake. We've got to figure out what she wants if we're going to get out of this place."

"Maybe she wants something we can't give her," Steve said.

"Then we're stuck here," Blair replied, putting the killing option back on the table.

TWENTY

Wild Turtle rode easily at anchor, some twenty yards off shore in shallow water. The morning sun was well above the horizon when light flooded the cabin, rousing Zack from a sound sleep. He stretched, not believing how rested and good he felt. For a moment, he was certain it had all been a dream, part nightmare, part fantasy, and all illusion. He crawled out of the hatch and stretched, still half asleep. Panic jolted him awake. Far to the north, the volcano rose majestically in the clear sky. It had not been a dream and he had slept in. "Damn," he muttered, quickly weighing anchor and making sail. Within minutes, he was sailing due south as Circe had told him, with the volcano off his stern and open ocean on his bow.

The sea was calm with only a gentle swell out of the north and wind was off his stern. It was an easy sail and he made a constant three knots. He concentrated on his compass, making the heading good, and constantly looked back as the volcano slowly receded in the distance. The sounds of the small boat working, the gentle lap as the bow cut the water, the creaking of the rigging, filled him with a quiet purpose. His stomach rumbled, demanding his attention. "What's for lunch?" he wondered, rummaging in one of the sacks. He found a lump of cheese and ripped off a hunk of bread, washing it all down with a swig of water from one of the water bags. The drink was unbelievably cool and refreshing. "Nice," he murmured, "but they'll never believe this." Still, the sacks of food were in his cabin with the four leather water bags. He trimmed the sails and decided to fly his lapper, a much bigger foresail than his normal jib. Within moments, it was up and drawing as the wind set down. He checked his speed. It was unchanged. "I guess I'm supposed to be making three knots."

A fin broke the water and immediately disappeared. A large shadow darted under the boat, only to immediately broach on the other side. A silvery-gray dolphin leaped into the air, twisting and falling on its back, splashing Zack in welcome. Two more joined the leader, and soon, a pod of six were cutting through the water, keeping him company. Zack wished he had a camera to capture the moment. He leaned over the gunwale to watch them. The largest of the pod swam to the bow and gave it a nudge, pushing him back on course. "I'll be damned," he muttered. It was a reminder that *Wild Turtle* was essentially a dinghy and he was the ballast. Any shift in weight changed his heading.

A thought came to him. He was an infinitesimal speck on the sea being driven by a gentle wind to a landfall he didn't know he could make. Yet, he was being escorted by six beautiful, wild creatures, a wonderful contrast to Silla's pets, and the sky held the promise of clear weather. He checked the barometer in the cabin. It was holding steady. He trimmed the sail, set the tiller lock, and settled back to enjoy the sail and his companions. Within moments, he was asleep.

A gust of wind knocked *Wild Turtle* over and Zack came awake with a start. Without thinking, he threw his weight against the windward rail and released the sheets, freeing the mainsail and the lapper. The boat bounced back up and he breathed heavily as he took stock. The wind had freshened and he was still headed south, but his six companions had disappeared. He turned to check on the volcano; however, a bank of clouds obscured the northern horizon and the sun was setting. It was time to turn. He quickly doused the lapper and set his jib before changing course and heading into the setting sun on a starboard tack. As an afterthought, he checked the barometer. It was falling.

The rigging started to sing as the wind increased and *Wild Turtle* heeled. He quickly pulled on heavier clothes and a light rain jacket for warmth as *Wild Turtle* took the wind and leaped forward, now making a good six knots. He marked his compass heading as the sun set. "Go west, young man, go west." He laughed, never feeling better. "It's going to be an interesting night." He turned on *Wild Turtle's* running lights. Above, he could make out the first stars. He shined his flashlight on his mainsail. "Hey, folks, I'm still here and alive." Overhead, the Belt of Orion hovered in the darkening sky. "Hi! I'm glad you're still there. We got a lot to talk about."

He pulled on the jib's roller reefing and decreased the foresail a fraction as the wind kicked up and his speed touched seven knots. The wind was challenging and whipping up the sea, but it was nothing he couldn't handle. *Wild Turtle* was flying.

Sean worked his way out onto the rocks and carefully baited the hook as Rufus had taught him. He did an overhand cast and waited for the telltale jerk that he had caught a fish, but there was nothing, not even a nibble. He had been fishing since first light and had not caught a thing. He frowned in frustration and headed back for shore where Angus was patiently waiting. "Don't give me that look," he told the terrier. "Why don't you go catch something?" The dog barked at him.

"So you're hungry too?" Angus barked again, even more agitated. "What's bothering you?" Angus ran around him and looked out to sea. Sean turned and saw the sail. For a moment, he didn't trust his eyes, it was so far away. But the more he looked, the more certain he became. It was the distinctive red and yellow striped sail he had seen many times. He ran for the lagoon, shouting at the top of his lungs.

Blair heard him first and walked out to meet him. "Hey, slow down, I can't understand a word you're saying."

Sean bent over, panting from the long run, his hands on his knees. "There's a sail." He pointed to the north. "I think it's Zack."

Blair didn't hesitate and ran for *Wee Dram*. He grabbed his handheld radio, flare gun, and survival mirror. "Let's go," he shouted, motioning for the other men to follow him.

Rufus looked up from beside Sasha. "I can't leave her," he called. From his voice and the look on his face, it was obvious she was near death.

"I'll stay here," Gib said. He had lived through a similar hell and would be there for his friend.

Sean led the way with Blair and Pete close behind. Steve couldn't keep up but slogged along, determined to be there. They reached the promontory overlooking the rocks where Sean had been fishing. Sean pointed to the north, his young eyes much sharper that the mens'. A bright speck of color on the far horizon caught Blair's eye as Steve came puffing up. Blair keyed his radio. "*Wild Turtle, Wild Turtle*, how do you read?" There was no answer and he transmitted again with the same result. "Fire a flare," he ordered. Pete raised the flare gun and sent a flare into the sky. The flare washed out against the bright sun. "Damn!" Blair raged. "He's too far away."

Steve raised his binoculars and focused on the boat that was slowly disappearing. "He's four or five miles away and headed west."

Desperate, Blair held the World War II survival mirror and swept the horizon. "Zack can't find his backside with both hands," Pete said. "*L'Amour* is faster than *Wild Turtle*, I'll go get him." Blair again swept the horizon with the mirror, hoping Zack would see the reflection as Pete ran for his boat.

"He's turning!" Steve shouted, still following *Wild Turtle* with his binoculars.

Blair visibly relaxed. For better or worse, he was the leader of the FOGs and his years in the Air Force had taught him that leadership and responsibility went hand-in-hand. The FOGs were a loose and freewheeling group of individual skippers in command of their own craft, and no court of law would ever hold him responsible for losing Zack or Steve's boat. But in the end, Blair held himself responsible for getting them all to safe harbor. With each passing moment, that burden eased as *Wild Turtle* came closer to the island. Sean's eyes were fixed on Blair, not understanding what he was going through. "Admiral, are you okay?"

Blair gave him a little nod and breathed deeply. "Well, I'm a hell of a lot better than I was an hour ago, thanks to you. Well done."

"I didn't do nothing," the teenager mumbled. "Angus saw him and barked."

Blair reached out and placed his right hand on Sean's shoulder. "Sean, well done. Thank you." For the first time in his life, Sean fully understood what accomplishment and friendship were all about. It was an odd mix of lessons on the road to becoming an adult, and he would never be the same.

The VHF radio came alive. "This is *Wild Turtle* transmitting in the blind. Radio check."

Blair gulped. "*Wild Turtle*, copy you five-by. *L'Amour* is headed your way. Welcome back."

"Nice to be back," Zack replied.

Caly's Island

* * * *

Caly stood on the headland overlooking the lagoon as her long gray hair streamed in the wind and her simple white gown whipped around her frail body. Below her, *L'Amour* led *Wild Turtle* through the entrance and onto the beach. The four men and Sean were waiting to pull the micocruisers onto the sand and welcome their missing comrade. Their shouts and good-natured kidding echoed over the water as they clustered around the newcomer, and the wind carried his name, Zack, over the water. Her eyes squinted as she took the measure of the lanky, gray-haired man. The wind murmured that he was not what he seemed and possessed a volcanic temper. He kept it carefully hidden, but it was always there, ready to burst free. He was a man capable of great violence, and because he had killed monsters on the isle of Sikilia, he was a favorite of Hephaestus. "Did that bitch seduce him?" The wind told her it was not like that and Circe had fallen in love with him.

"Stupid woman," Caly muttered, secretly envying her. The wind asked if the newcomer was the one. Caly shook her head. "He's not the one I want." Her eyes followed the men as they led the newcomer to the canopy where the woman was lying. "Soon, very soon," Caly predicted.

"Zack, my man," Pete said as they trudged through the sand, "where in hell have you been?"

Zack pointed to the north. "There's a big island to the north with a volcano. A woman I met there said it was Sikilia. I never heard that name before."

Gib and Blair looked at each other. More and more pieces of the puzzle were coming together. "That's Sicily," Blair said, "and the volcano is Mount Etna. We're on Gozo, about fifty miles to the south. We really need to talk."

Zack stepped into the canopy's shade as Rufus stood. They shook hands and Zack gestured at Sasha. "Isn't she one of the Sirens?"

"Right," Rufus answered. "She was shot at Reid Harbor and the wound got infected. It's pretty bad."

"What was she doing that got her shot?" Zack asked.

"Protecting me," Steve answered. Zack shook his head, now totally confused. "It will take some time to explain," Steve said. His eyes filled with sadness. "The infection has spread and it's only a matter of time now."

Zack spun around and ran for his boat. "What got into him?" Steve wondered. Within moments, Zack was back with the small green-colored flask clutched in his right hand. He handed it to Blair. "She needs to drink this."

"What is it?" Rufus asked.

Zack sucked in his breath. Would they believe him? He decided to go with the truth. "A woman who calls herself a witch gave it to me. I was mauled by a huge dog you wouldn't believe, and the woman used this to treat me. It works like gangbusters."

Blair's first thought was to close his mouth. "Was her name Circe?"

"How'd you know?" Zack replied.

"It's a long story," Blair replied. "We really need to talk." He handed the flask to Rufus. The blacksmith turned it over in his hands, not sure. "It can't hurt," Blair counseled. Rufus still hesitated. "Rufe, we're going to lose her. This is all we got."

The decision made, Rufus knelt beside Sasha. His strong hands were amazingly gentle as he lifted her and helped her drink. She coughed twice and, for a moment, it seemed she would spit it out. She calmed and took a second swallow, draining the last of the honey-colored liquid. The men gathered around, silently watching as she calmed and her breathing grew less labored. Rufus shook his head. "What is it? A narcotic?"

"I don't know," Zack replied. "But it worked for me."

"Give it some time," Blair said. "At least, she's comfortable." Rufus covered her with a second blanket and collapsed into a camp chair, instantly falling asleep. "Let him sleep," Blair said. "He's exhausted." He motioned for the group to gather up their camp chairs and move to the shade of a low araar tree. "Sean, please join us. This concerns you." The teenager settled on the sand with Angus in his lap. "Gentlemen," Blair began, "we've got a problem. We're running out of food and the fish have disappeared." Even though they were on minimum rations and only eating twice a day, the logistics of feeding five healthy adults, now six, and one growing teenager were awesome. "Steve, you're our quartermaster, what do you think?"

The accountant pulled a small notebook out of his shirt pocket and scanned what was left. "We've enough left for six meals at the most. We can stretch it out, maybe make it last a week." Zack jumped up and ran for *Wild Turtle*. "What now?" Steve wondered. Six heads turned as one and watched as Zack returned, carrying two heavy sacks. He sat them down at Steve's feet.

"With Circe's compliments," Zack said.

The accountant looked into the first sack. He came alive as a surprised look spread across his face. He checked the second sack and smiled. "I hope you thanked her properly," he said.

"I think I did," Zack said. "Some things I can remember very clearly, but others get kind'a fuzzy, sort of like a dream. At times, I wonder if it was even real."

"Why don't you start at the beginning," Blair said.

"When I came out of the fog, I was alone and in the granddaddy of all storms." Zack sank into his chair and recounted his ordeal and, being Zack, downplayed much of what had happened. However, Gib and Pete were too experienced at questioning witnesses and drew the full story out of him. It was late afternoon when Zack finished and they took a short break for a meager dinner, washing it down with water from the leather water bags.

"This is very special stuff," Steve said, thinking of the commercial possibilities.

"Being with Circe was like that," Zack said. "Everything about her was special and different."

Sean finally chimed in. "According to The Odyssey, Circe seduced Odysseus with great sex."

The men looked at Zack, all asking the same silent question. Zack stared at his hands. "I don't know. So much of it seems like a dream now." He looked up, pleading for understanding. "I really don't know."

"Join the crowd," Steve said. "Things have been far from normal around here."

"Admiral," Pete said, "you got us here, so why don't you bring Zack up to date?"

"Actually, the dolphins got us here," Blair began. "Unlike you, we came out of the fog into a calm sea. Our compasses were wandering and our watches spinning." He closed his eyes, remembering. "No land in sight, only a clear sky and a magnificent sea. It was beautiful." He picked up the story, telling how they had made landfall, what they had learned about Steve, and how Sean had first met Caly. The others joined in and Zack sat spellbound as they recounted all that had happened. Sean built a fire and kept it going as the night grew colder.

When they finished, Zack leaned forward, his hands clasped between his knees. It was time to own up. "This is my fault."

"Zack," Blair said, "don't even go there. We haven't got a clue why we're here, so don't go falling on your sword and doing pushups."

"Hold on," Pete said. "I've wet my knickers so many times and need some one to do my laundry." He looked hopefully in Zack's direction.

Gib laughed. "Peter, no court that I know of would sustain your claim for damages." He paused. "Zack, may I ask why you think you are responsible for our being here?"

"Circe said I had insulted the gods and I was doing penance. I remember taking a whiz beside the road outside Bellingham and got snarky when I saw the Belt of Orion. I said something about the gods on Olympus and the constellations being a load of crap."

"So it's possible," Gib concluded, "that we were merely too close to you and got caught up in your ordeal."

"Something like that. Circe said it was a time of testing and that I had to rid the world of an evil."

"You certainly did that," Blair said. "Silla and her six dogs sounds like Scylla in The Odyssey. According to Homer, she was a doglike monster with six heads and could devour six sailors at a time. Ka-rib sounds like Charybdis, the whirlpool opposite Scylla on the Straits of Messina that swallows everything near it."

"The Ka-rib you met was a slaver," Gib said. He shuddered. "She was a monstrosity worse than anything Homer could conjure out of his imagination."

"Folks," Pete said in a low voice, "this is really creepy. No one will ever believe it."

"I assure you," Gib replied, "all this is very real."

A shout caught their attention. Rufus was running towards them, waving his arms like a madman. "Her fever broke!"

The gentle creaking sounds of the rocker blended with the low hiss of the charcoal fire and filled the cave. Caly rubbed the hand lotion on her arms, liking what it did for her skin. She stretched out a leg and massaged the last of the lotion into the blemishes and wrinkles. Her

Caly's Island

vanity was in full play as she carefully brushed her thinning hair back, gathering it in a loose bundle over her right shoulder. The fire flared, catching her attention, and she leaned her head back against the rocker and gazed into the coals, listening. She came to her feet, her frail body shaking in anger. "The woman was not to live," she announced, stomping her foot on the thick flokati rug. "That is not what I wanted. This is my island!" The fire went out.

TWENTY-ONE

It was daybreak when Rufus returned to camp carrying the four fish he had caught. He dropped a few hunks of charcoal on the fire before cleaning the fish. The fish were small compared to what they caught earlier, but would help supplement the food Circe had given Zack. "They look pretty good," a voice said from a deep shadow, startling him. It was Zack. "How did you catch them?"

"I lured them with a flashlight," Rufus admitted. "Sorry I didn't hear what happened to you last night."

"I'll fill you in later. It takes a long time. How's Sasha doing?"

"Much better. She ate some oatmeal early this morning and is sleeping. I think she is gonna be okay. I can't thank you or Circe enough."

The two men sat quietly in front of the glowing coals, each deep in thought. Small flames started to lap at the edges, occasionally flaring. "I've never seen that before," Rufus admitted. "It's almost like it wants to talk."

"Maybe it does," Zack replied. "Circe did it all the time. She said to look into the fire, not at it. Relax, and see what happens."

Rufus concentrated on the fire and, after a few moments, rocked back and forth, silent, then mumbling, carrying on a conversation. Suddenly, his head jerked up and he looked at Zack. "I'll be damned. I was talking to this short and ugly guy with a thick beard. He was sort'a hunchbacked and twisted, with powerful arms." Rufus held up his hands and looked at them. "He was holding a hammer and wearing a leather apron like mine. I was scared at first, but he kept looking at me with the kindest brown eyes I've ever seen. He asked if you made it okay. Doesn't that beat all?"

"That was Hephaestus, the Greek god of blacksmiths, fire, and volcanoes," Zack replied. "His Roman name is Vulcan."

"Did you ever talk to him?"

Zack shook his head. "Nope, but we're buddies. He saved my ass when I really needed help on Mount Etna." Again, he shook his head, growing more skeptical about his time with Circe. "This is really gonna take a long time to explain. Did he say anything else?"

"Yeah. He said to give the Nereid what she wants. I think he meant Caly."

"So what does she want?"

"She wants a companion. She's lonely."

"That's not good," Zack said.

Rufus wasn't sure. "Well, according to Hephaestus, the guy gets to live forever."

Rufus gently carried Sasha over to the fire and sat her down in a camp chair. Steve held a bowl of steaming oatmeal as Blair covered her with a blanket. She reached out and touched Blair's hand. "Thank you," she murmured.

"Thank Rufe and Zack," Blair replied, sensing that she was a different person, changed for the better after her near-death experience. "You need to eat and get well." Steve handed her the bowl as Gib portioned out the fish and a little bread. "Okay, troops," Blair said as they ate, "the bad news is that we're still on short rations. The good news is, there may be a way out of here. Rufe, why don't you tell them what happened this morning?"

The blacksmith sipped at his coffee. "You're not gonna believe this, but I talked to Hephaestus. He's the god of blacksmiths, and Zack told me how to do it. Anyway, he said we got to give Caly what she wants if we want'a get out of here." He paused, looking at his friends. "She wants a companion."

"That we cannot do," Gib said. "Slavery is not an option."

"Kill her," Sasha whispered.

"That also is not an option," Gib said.

"There's something else," Rufus blurted. "According to Hephaestus, the guy gets the same deal as Ulysses. He gets to live forever."

Caly's Island

Gib shook his head. "That is a fool's choice. Eternal life is not eternal youth."

"Hold on," Pete said. "There might be some options here. Let me talk to her."

"Peter," Gib warned, "she's asking for a sacrifice."

"Who said anything about sacrificing? Let's find out what all the options are before we go running off half-cocked. We might have a deal, if the terms are right."

"You can't negotiate with a demigoddess or whatever she is," Blair said.

Pete laughed. "I've negotiated with the Russian Mafia, prosecutors, politicians, and judges. Why not a nymph? That's what lawyers do."

"Take a gift," Sean said. "She likes presents."

"What have we still got that she might like?" Pete asked.

"Give her a mirror," Sasha told them. Blair jumped up and ran to *Wee Dram*. He hurried back and handed Pete his signaling mirror.

Pete nodded. "I need to shave and get cleaned up." He stood and walked over to his boat.

The men sat in silence for a few moments. Blair's head came up and he looked in the direction of Caly's cave. "Sean, can you follow Pete? Keep out of sight and don't let him see you."

"Is that taking an unnecessary risk?" Gib asked. "What if Caly sees Sean?"

"Pete needs a wingman to cover his six," Blair explained. He turned to Sean. "If Caly sees you, I'm betting she'll think you're jealous and doing a dumb kid thing."

"She won't see me," Sean promised. "But I'll act pissed-off, just in case." He stood and left, heading in the opposite direction. Blair nodded in approval.

The aroma of freshly baked bread drew Pete to Caly's cave like the proverbial magnet. The heavy door was open and a soft light cast halos of warmth over the rough flagstones that led inside. He knocked on the door, but there was no answer. "Caly?" he called. He almost stepped inside, lured by the tantalizing smell, but an inner voice warned him that it was a trap and he stepped back. If he was to negotiate, he needed neutral territory and that was a problem. This was her island and everything conspired against them, the winds and currents, the schools of fish that disappeared, and the rapidly dwindling fruit. Playing it safe, he wandered towards the grove of fruit trees where she and Sean had first met.

Caly was sitting on the same rock waiting for him, totally naked. He sucked in his breath at the sight. Her hands were clasped around her right shin, bending her leg to her body, and her dark curly hair cascaded down her back. She was beautiful beyond compare. "What a lovely surprise," he called. She patted the rock and he sat beside her, not touching. "Do you often run around starkers?"

"When I want your undivided attention," she murmured.

He gave her his lopsided grin. "Am I in trouble?"

"Only if you choose to be," she replied. Her hand stroked his bare forearm and sent tingles coursing through his body.

He pulled the small signaling mirror out of his shirt pocket and handed it to her without a word. She turned it over in her hands, not sure what it was. Then she saw her reflection and held it in front of her face. The image staring back at her was what Pete wanted her to be, not what she was. It was a revelation. "Oh," she finally managed.

"Now you know how beautiful you really are," he told her.

"Is this what you see?"

"Oh, yes."

She stood and extended her hand. "Come."

Pete hesitated, afraid that if he entered her cave, he would never escape, held by a thousand delights and a mindless existence. "I'd prefer we talk here," he told her, not moving. She sat beside him, this time her body rubbing against his. He felt her warmth through the thin fabric of his shirt.

"What do you wish to talk about?"

"Us," he replied. "Our future."

"Do we have a future?"

The lawyer carefully considered his words. Never had so much rested on what he said. "We both have many days in front of us. We can choose how we spend them, alone or with someone."

"You are here and I'm not alone."

"That is true. However, I'm also with my friends. You watch and hear us when we talk, but there is nothing for you."

She stiffened. "I can take what I want. There is always the boy."

Caly's Island

"Is that what you desire, a fifteen-year-old male cub who is still growing and doesn't know his own mind? You can make him your slave but not your companion." He sensed he had an opening. "What does your heart of hearts really want?"

She turned and kissed him on the lips, full and lingering. She pulled away and gazed at him, her eyes focused on his. "You. Only you. You understand me and my body responds to yours."

"Caly, I won't be a slave to your passion, or your loneliness."

"You will never be a slave. Stay with me and you will live forever."

"I don't want to live forever."

"Must you lie to me? Every man seeks eternal life."

Pete shook his head. "I'm not lying. My friends think I'm fifty-eight years old and the youngest of them. Actually, I'm seventy-two and the oldest."

"How is that possible?"

"I have what are called 'good genes,' and an excellent doctor and plastic surgeon. But I can feel the years in the morning and my strength is fading."

"Really," Caly said, "I hadn't noticed. So what do you want?"

Pete chose his words carefully, fully aware they had come to the heart of the matter. They were not equal and, ultimately, Caly held all the counters, hers to give or withhold. "I want two things. First, I want to remain forever as I was at forty-three. Second, let my companions go."

She caressed him, rubbing her body against his. "The first I can grant. But if you want me to remain as I am now, there is something I need in return. The newcomer among you has an elixir for beauty the witch gave him." Again, she kissed him. "It will make me perfect for you."

Pete tingled with excitement, certain they had a deal. It was only a matter of wrapping up the loose ends. "If Zack has it, it's yours. What about my companions? I will not watch them die here while I am happy with you."

She showered him with kisses, moving her hands through his hair and down his body. "That is not for me to decide." She stood and led him to her cave.

* * * *

Sasha bent over in her chair as Rufus poured water over her hair. Blair handed him the last of his shampoo. The blacksmith squeezed what was left into her hair as her fingers whipped it into a lather, occasionally touching his. Steve was ready with more water for the rinse and handed the plastic bottle to Rufus. The men studiously tried not to watch as she dried her hair with a towel, but failed miserably. She looked out from under the towel. "What?"

"Nothing," Blair mumbled. She smiled, pleased with the affect she was having on them. "Dinner in a few minutes," Blair said, on much surer ground.

"Thank you," she replied. She brushed her hair. "I'm very hungry."

"That's a good sign," Steve said, anxious to be part of the moment.

She fixed Blair with a serious look, ignoring Steve. "Your friend, Pete, and the boy are not back from seeing that woman. Aren't you worried?"

"Very," Blair replied. Sasha had touched a raw nerve. He wasn't going to lose anyone, not now, not after what they had been through. The burden of responsibility had eased with Zack's safe arrival, and now it was crashing back down on him. He should have never agreed to Pete's attempt to negotiate with Caly, and he was risking lives with half-baked schemes. He took a deep breath, cautioning himself not to over react, not to do something stupid. "First things first," he muttered half aloud. The immediate goal was the safe return of Pete and Sean. He considered his options. Was it time to use raw, brute force? According to Homer, Odysseus had never hesitated to use it – when he could. Angus barked, bringing him back to the moment.

"Ah," Gib said, "we may soon have an answer." He gestured in the direction of Caly's cave. "Master Sean returns." Angus scurried towards Sean, his tail wagging happily. The dog leapt into his arms, bringing a wide smile to the teenager's face.

Sean was still carrying Angus as he joined the circle and sat down. He quickly brought them up to date, telling them how Pete had met Caly in the grove and then gone into her cave. "It was really weird," Sean said, "they went inside and the door shut on its own. He hasn't come out." He looked disgusted. "She was an old woman and wasn't wearing any clothes."

"That's the real Calypso," Steve said. "You've broken her spell and seeing her for what she really is. I'm afraid Pete is trapped."

Caly's Island

"You got that right," Sean replied. "I put my ear against the door, but there wasn't any sound. I pushed on it and it didn't budge. It's like solid steel. I couldn't even find a seam around the edges."

"Your Pete is in trouble," Sasha said.

Blair weighed her warning. He needed time to think and plan. "If he's not back by noon tomorrow, we'll go get him."

Zack stared into the fire pit. "Nice charcoal," he allowed.

"Rufus made it," Sean said.

Zack studied the men for a moment and made a decision. "With the right signal flares and charcoal, I can make a high accelerant gunpowder and blow the door down." The FOGs stared at him, not believing what they had heard. Zack shrugged. "I had a misspent childhood." He gave his friends a sheepish look, hoping that explanation satisfied them. He made a mental promise not to lie to them again.

"When she comes out, shoot her," Sasha added. "You have gun."

Rufus and Gib chorused in unison, "What gun?"

Blair crouched in the brush outside the entrance to the cave. He waved for Rufus to join him and for Zack and Sean to move into position next to the door. He keyed his VHF radio. "Gib, any sign of Caly or Pete?"

"Negative," the judge replied. "Everything's quiet at the lagoon."

"Steve, say position," Blair radioed.

Steve's voice came in broken. "I'm on the headland overlooking the lagoon and can see the cave from here. No sign of Caly or Pete."

Satisfied they were still in the cave, Blair again hit the transmit button. "Sean, go." The teenager didn't hesitate and marched boldly to the door. He knocked three times and waited. "Anybody home?" he called. There was no answer and he banged on the door with a small rock three more times. "Hey, Caly," he called. "It's me, Sean. Is Mr. Lacy with you? I really need to talk to him." Again, there was no answer. He glanced at Blair who motioned him back. Sean rejoined Zack and they pulled back into the underbrush to wait.

Blair checked his watch. He wanted to see if the direct and friendly approach worked. Blair was almost certain that Pete would come out on his own accord if Sean was at the door – and if Caly would let him. He checked his watch again. He waited impatiently for the door to open.

"Come on," he urged. After ten minutes, he decided it was time for Plan B. He keyed his radio. "Zack, go."

Rufus crouched next to Blair as they watched Zack. "Look at him move," Rufus said. "Who would have thought?" The two men watched as Zack ghosted over to the cave door and ran his hands over it, looking for a weak spot. From the way he kept examining it, there wasn't any. Frustrated, he placed a two-pound bag next to the lower left-hand corner and inserted a makeshift fuse. He lit the fuse and ran for cover. Rufus placed his hands over his ears.

"Open your mouth and yawn," Blair told him. The two men yawned broadly as the fuse sputtered to the bag. "Duck!" Blair shouted. They fell to the ground as a loud explosion echoed over them. Debris from the heavy brush around the door showered down, covering them in twigs and leaves. "Damn," Blair said, barely able to hear his own words. "Where did Zack learn to make that?"

"There's more to him than I thought," Rufus said. They came to their feet as the air cleared.

Blair's VHF radio squawked. It was Steve. "Talk about the Fourth of July on steroids!" He paused. "Oh, crap! I can see the door in my binoculars. It's hardly scratched."

Blair and Rufus stared at the door. They were much closer and could see a large burn mark, but other than a little scaring, there was no damage. "That blast should have taken it down," Blair said.

"What are we dealing with?" Rufus asked. "Let me go take a look at it."

Good question, Blair thought. He held up a hand, stopping the blacksmith. The door was starting to move. They watched in fascination as the door rolled silently back. The blonde-haired Caly Blair had met emerged from the dark shadow and ran her hand along the door's edge, examining it for damage. From the look on her face she seemed more amused than concerned or frightened.

"Admiral, is that you?" she called.

"Rufe," Blair whispered, "who are you seeing?"

"It's her. Same red hair."

"Zack," Blair radioed, "ask Sean who he sees?"

Sean's voice came over the radio. "It's Caly."

"Is she young?" Blair asked.

"Yeah, man," Sean answered. "She's my age."

Caly's Island

"Zack," Blair asked, "what are you seeing?"

"She looks like Circe."

Steve had been monitoring the transmissions from his vantage point. "She's old," he radioed.

"Who in hell is she?" Blair wondered. He reached into his shoulder bag. "It's time to send her back – while we can." He raised Steve's revolver and pulled the hammer back in one fluid motion.

Rufus's left hand was a blur as he grabbed the weapon and wrenched it effortlessly out of Blair's grasp. "Not with me." He shoved the revolver into his waistband as he stared at the cave. "Look."

Blair turned in time to see Pete emerge from the cave. He stood beside Caly and examined the burn mark on the door. He turned and held up his hands. "What are you guys doing?" he called.

Pete relaxed in the camp chair as he cradled the glass of wine. He held it up to the flickering firelight as he examined it. "To Uncas," he said, "the last of the Mohicans." He took a sip. "Okay, folks, what were you thinking?"

"Rescuing you," Blair replied. He decided to be absolutely honest. "I blew it and panicked. "Thank God Rufe was there . . ." His voice trailed off, not wanting to think about it. Luckily, the explosion hadn't done any harm and Rufus had the gun safely hidden away on *Nailing On*. "Didn't you hear us knocking on the door?"

Pete shook his head. "We barely heard the dynamite Zack set off. It sounded like a pop, but it got Caly's attention. By the way, where did you get it?"

"Zack made it," Blair replied. Every head turned towards Zack who stared at his hands.

"Would you believe I learned it from a chemistry set I got for Christmas when I was eleven?" He didn't wait for an answer. "No, I didn't think so." He paused. "Making explosives is something you learn as a field agent in the CIA."

Blair was incredulous. "I thought you worked in a lab. Electronics or something similar."

"That was my cover."

"But you're directionally impaired," Steve said. "Didn't that get in the way?"

223

Zack shook his head. "Not really. I was very good at what I did so I was always part of a team. My specialty was electronics."

Gib's curiosity was peaked. "May I ask what type of electronics?"

"Just say it had to do with communications," Zack replied.

Sean turned to Pete. "Sir, what's with Caly?" It was the question they all wanted to ask.

Pete scowled at him. "What's with the 'sir' crap? Who are you? What have you done with the real Sean?"

The teenager grinned. "I take it she turned you every which way but loose . . . sir."

Pete sank back into the chair. "We may have a deal, but she wants the potion Circe gave Zack, whatever that is."

As one, they all turned and looked at Zack. "It's a beauty potion," Zack explained. "Circe said I would need it, but I assumed it was for Angela. I have no idea if it works or not. You got it if you want it."

Pete and Gib paced the beach in the moonlight, deep in discussion. The jurist used every logical argument he could muster to convince the lawyer he was making the wrong decision. "Gib, I think you're wrong, and I can trust her."

"It just doesn't track," the judge replied. "Caly can't change a thing and she can only offer you the same deal as Odysseus. Caly gets you, you get eternal life, not the eternal middle age you desire. Which, by the way, surprises me. I would have opted for twenty-six." They turned and headed for the canopy where everyone was still gathered around the fire. Gib sighed. "Ah, 1968. What a time to be alive, so much turmoil, so many possibilities. But back to Caly, or more properly, Calypso."

His voice grew persuasive as he used all his analytical skills honed by years on the bench. "We know she has the power to appear differently to each of us. Yet I find it significant that Steven and Sean are the only ones who saw her without her knowledge. Need I remind you that they saw her as an old hag?" Pete started to protest, but Gib held up his hand. "If she has the power to offer you eternal middle age, why doesn't she currently have eternal youth and beauty? Which also explains why she wants the flask Zack brought with him, a potion for eternal beauty brewed by a witch – which she is not. This leads me to conclude that while she has the power to cloud her appearance, she has eternal life but

Caly's Island

not eternal youth. The flask is what she really wants. Once she has it, you will be condemned to wither and age on this island, and never die. And that my friend, is a terrible fate. But what if the potion fails, or if it is only temporary? How would you avoid her vengeance?"

"A good question," Pete conceded. "I suspect things could get very nasty, but I still think it's worth a try."

They joined the others and Gib took his seat, the elder of his clan ready to render a decision. "H, if I may. I have failed to change Peter's desire to remain while we attempt an escape. Further, I am absolutely convinced that Peter's future welfare is contingent on the one item Calypso desires . . ."

Pete interrupted. "Besides me."

"Beside you," Gib conceded. "That item being the beauty potion Circe gave Zack."

Zack pulled the small golden flask out of his pocket. "I thought you might be needing this." He held it up to the light, trying to see into it. "I don't know if it works or not."

"Judge Stanford," Sean said, "is that the Golden Apple that started the Trojan War?"

"I am very impressed with your reasoning," Gib said. "I take it you've been reading."

Sean blushed. "Yeah, I guess so. The Iliad is pretty boring, but it's got a long preface and lots of notes that explains things."

Gib nodded in approval. "Very good, Sean. But returning to the matter at hand, we need to test the beauty lotion to see if it works. Otherwise, I fear Peter will be severely used by Calypso."

"How do we do that?" Rufus asked.

A perplexed silence captured the men. "Give it to me," Sasha said.

No one moved. Finally, Blair nodded. "Just use a little." Zack handed her the flask.

"Sean," she said, "come here. Let me see your arms." Sean did as she commanded and held out his arms. She quickly uncapped the flask and rubbed a minute amount on the smallest tattoo on Sean's right forearm. The tattoo started to fade and, within minutes, disappeared. "It works," Sasha said, recapping the flask. She tossed it disdainfully to Pete.

Blair examined the smooth skin where the tattoo had been moments before. "Give me the flask," he ordered. Pete didn't move. "Give me the flask," Blair repeated. There was an authority in his voice that could not be denied and Pete handed it over. "Thank you," Blair told him, his voice calm but stern. Without a word, he rubbed the lotion over all of Sean's tattoos, using a fourth of the flask's contents. As before, the tattoos magically disappeared. Satisfied, Blair looked around the circle. "We have one more item of business before we hit the sack. We need some warm clothes for Steve since he lost his on *High Flyer*."

"I've got an extra set of foulies," Gib said.

"He can have my jacket," Pete offered. "It'll look good on him."

"Ah, the dreaded team jacket," Rufus quipped.

"An assault on good taste," Gib added.

The old good-natured bantering was back and Blair's optimism soared. "Okay, that's it. We make the break before first light. No noise, no talking. We just go. Leave the canopy and chairs behind so it looks like we're coming back. Sean, you sail with me and Angus, Sasha with Rufus, and Steve with Gib. Zack, you're alone. Any questions?"

"Why is Zack going alone?" Sean asked. "Me or Angus can go with him."

"Because Zack is the one who pissed off the gods. I don't want any collateral damage if some lightning bolts come his way."

"Sounds fair to me," Zack allowed.

They broke up and headed for the boats for what they hoped was their last night on the island. Rufus told Sasha to sleep on *Nailing On* and he would sleep under the canopy. He stoked the fire with the last of the charcoal for a little warmth and wrapped himself in Sasha's blanket. He could still smell her as he sat there, staring into the fire. He let the glowing coals capture him and he leaned back in the chair. Suddenly, he sprang to his feet and ran for *Wee Dram*. "Admiral," he whispered. "We got'a talk."

TWENTY-TWO

Pete moved silently around *L'Amour*, careful not to disturb his sleeping companions. He looked up at the brilliant night sky and, for the first time since they had arrived on Caly's Island, saw a different constellation. Sagittarius, he told himself, hoping that was a good omen. Movement caught his eye and he froze. He relaxed as the dark shadow morphed into Sean returning from the latrine. Pete waved, catching his attention and motioning him over to *L'Amour*. "Wassup?" Sean asked.

Pete held his fingers to his lips, cautioning him to silence. The lawyer reached into the cabin for the Zip Lock bag that held his journal. He handed it to Sean. "Give this to the Admiral after you get home, not before." Sean looked perplexed. "It will make sense when he reads it." Sean nodded. Pete raised his mainsail and, for a moment, the older man and the teenager clasped hands in friendship. "Mind pushing me off?" Pete asked.

Sean pushed on the bow and *L'Amour* slipped free of the sand, sailing silently across the lagoon. Sean didn't move until *L'Amour* had cleared the entrance and disappeared. He turned only to bump into Gib. "Why did he leave?" Sean asked.

"I imagine that Mr. Lacy wants to provide us with credible denial," Gib replied. "It will be easy to explain the loss of *High Flyer*, but losing a companion is another matter. By leaving in this manner, we simply tell the truth that we were waiting on an island and he just disappeared. No one has to lie or explain what happened to him."

Sean tucked the journal under his left arm. "He was my friend."

"Indeed, he was," Gib said. They walked back to the canopy where Rufus was sleeping and sat down to await the coming dawn. An hour later, the stars started to fade and Rufus stirred. He sat up and rubbed his eyes, coming awake.

"Do we have any Scotch left?" the blacksmith asked.

"Whatever for?" Gib wondered. "Surely, not for breakfast."

"We're gonna need it. We better get this show on the road. The sooner the better."

"Mr. Gunnermyer, where are we going?" Sean asked.

"Beats me, Sean. I'm just following the Admiral."

They moved silently to the boats, surprised to find their companions awake and getting ready to make sail. Gib climbed aboard *Habeas Corpus* where Steve was waiting in the cockpit. Sean pushed them off and the freshening breeze filled the sail. Gib sailed into mid lagoon and hove-to, waiting for the others. Rufus and Sasha were next in *Nailing On* and joined *Habeas Corpus*. Sean pushed *Wild Turtle* off the sand and ran to *Wee Dram*. He lifted Angus on board and pushed the boat free before clambering over the side. Blair sheeted in the main and put the tiller over, leading them out of the lagoon.

The long rays of the morning sun touched the headland overlooking the lagoon and reached across the wine dark sea, casting a golden glow on the four sails moving slowly westward. Pete embraced Caly and she cuddled against his chest as they stood high above the waves lapping at the rocks below, watching the small boats. "Will they be okay?" he asked.

"That is not for me to decide." She looked up at him, her eyes full of promise. "Come." She took his hand and led him to her cave. Pete turned and looked out to sea, catching one last glimpse of his friends. He shook his head, wondering why they had stopped and rafted up. He followed Caly into the cave and the heavy door closed silently behind him.

Zack let his main sheet go as *Wild Turtle* bumped against *Habeas Corpus*. Steve handed him a line and pulled the boats together. "Zack," Blair called, "can you join Steve and Gib on *Habeas Corpus*?" Zack clambered across the gunwale into the larger boat that was rafted up on *Wee Dram's* port side. "Rufus, raft up on my starboard." Rufus guided

Caly's Island

Nailing On alongside and tied up. "Okay, folks," Blair explained, "we need to make a human chain." They scooted around and were soon all holding hands, forming a circle across the boats. Blair held up his last bottle of Scotch and tossed it high into the air. He quickly reformed the chain before it hit the water. The bottle caught the sun as it fell and a bright light reflected onto their faces. "Oh, Poseidon, we are humble sailors adrift on your sea and do not know your ways. Forgive us if we have insulted you in our ignorance. Please accept our plea of supplication and guide us to safe harbor."

"Did you just make an offering to Poseidon?" Steve asked.

"Sure did," Blair replied.

Steve couldn't believe it. "Admiral, you are an unbeliever of the first water. Why?"

"Rufus thought it would be a good idea," Blair explained.

As one, they all looked at the blacksmith who was still holding Sasha's hand. "I had a little talk with Hephaestus last night," he explained. "He's a good buddy and mentioned that Poseidon really liked Steve's last sacrifice."

"I did what?" Steve protested. Then it came to him. "Oh, the Scotch I dropped overboard." He pulled a face and went along with the program. "You've got to give Poseidon credit, he does have good taste when it comes to Scotch." He suppressed a laugh. "So, assuming we are now in Poseidon's good graces, where are we going?"

Blair reached into his navigation bag and pulled out the chart he had made. He handed it to Sean. "Mr. Homes, plot a course to the fog bank."

The teenager went to work with dividers and a plotter. "Two-three-zero for eighty miles," he announced.

"Gentlemen," Blair announced, "make good a compass heading of two-three-zero degrees, that's five degrees west of southwest."

"I knew that," Zack called. On cue, the wind kicked up and the four boats took to their heels on a close reach. Within a minute, they were making five knots. "Wowie!" Zack shouted. "We're going home!"

Blair headed up and struck his jib, only to raise his lapper, a much bigger sail that effectively doubled his foresail area. With the exception of Rufus on his catboat, the others did the same and the small fleet was making a steady six knots. "Sean, sit on the rail. This is gonna get sporting." The teenager sat on the windward gunwale and held on to the sheet controlling the big lapper. Blair checked the wind vane at the head of his mast. "The wind has clocked around to the northwest." Perfect!" He checked the knotmeter and glanced at his watch. "At this rate, we'll be there before dark."

"That soon?" Sean moaned.

"Hey, you're not supposed to be enjoying yourself. We got to get you home."

On board *Habeas Corpus*, Gib pulled on a heavy sweater, light gloves, and rain pants. He took the tiller while Steve donned a borrowed sweatshirt and zipped up Pete's red jacket. "This is going to get interesting," Steve warned the jurist. "Do you really think we're gonna make it?"

"The evidence suggests we will," Gib said. "We made it away from the island without incident and the winds are most favorable. Apparently, the Scotch was well received." They hooted with laughter. "Steven, seriously, we do need to discuss your future."

"There's not much to discuss," Steve replied, now very somber and the worry that ate at him in full view. "I've got two choices, I can either take my chances with the Russian Mafia, or turn myself in to the Feds and try to cut a deal. Unfortunately, I suspect I will be doing some hard time. It's just a matter of how long."

"There's a third choice," Gib said. Steve looked hopeful, eager to hear what the jurist had to say. Like a drowning man, he was more than willing to cling to anything that offered hope for the future. "I have an acquaintance who is very adept at avoiding taxes and creating false identities."

"An acquaintance you threw in the slammer?"

"Not at all. However, Marla does know, shall we say, how to float below the radar."

"Marla?" Steve wondered. "A lady friend?"

"Her name is Marla Mann. She's a financial planner who manages questionable accounts and keeps her clients out of jail."

"Mafia?"

"No. Professional ladies."

Steve was shocked. "Hookers?" Gib nodded, confirming his guess. "So what's the price?" Steve asked.

"Nothing you can't afford. I, on the other hand, will probably have to marry her."

"A fate worse than death, no doubt."

Caly's Island

"One hopes not."

"Heads up!" Steve warned. They were on a collision course with *Nailing On.*

Rufus saw them coming and headed up, letting *Habeas Corpus* surge by downwind. "That was close," he told Sasha. "We need to open up a bit." He eased the sheet and let *Habeas Corpus* take the lead. "They are in a hurry to get back."

Sasha spoke in a low voice. "Will the judge turn me in to the authorities when we return?"

"I seriously doubt it," Rufus told her. "Gib doesn't work that way. What are you going to do when we get back? You know – about the Russian Mafia."

Sasha gazed at the horizon, her face a mask that he could not read as she considered her options. "They killed my sister and my cousins. I will speak to them about it."

The wind held steady out of the northwest and the four craft made good time, occasionally touching seven knots as a favorable current pushed them along. They had been sailing over twelve hours and the men were tired when Sean shouted, "On the bow!" He stood and pointed straight ahead. Blair luffed up and stood, holding onto the boom. Frustrated, he grabbed his binoculars and focused on the horizon, now seeing a dark mass on the water.

"That's it," he said. He sheeted in, brought *Wee Dram's* bow around, and pointed directly at the fogbank. Zack fell in behind him as the wind eased and the temperature fell eight degrees. "I'll be damned," Blair muttered. He checked the temperature and the humidity reading on the barometer. The gauge read forty-one degrees Fahrenheit and one hundred percent humidity. They had barely sailed a mile when the wind died and their sails flapped lifelessly. The conditions were perfect for fog. Gib was the first to start his outboard and he motored for the fog bank with Rufus close behind. Blair struck his big foresail as he waited for Zack to join him, but *Wild Turtle* was drifting. "Care to join us?" Blair shouted.

"I'm out of gas," Zack yelled.

Blair reprimanded himself for not checking on their fuel state earlier and gunned his engine, going back to pick up *Wild Turtle*. Sean threw Zack a line and they headed after the other two boats with *Wild Turtle* in tow. "I think they're waiting for us," Sean said. Gib and Rufus were hove-to in the calm sea, just short of the fog bank.

Wee Dram and *Wild Turtle* coasted to a stop a few yards away. "Everyone top up," Blair said. They quickly filled their fuel tanks and distributed what was left of their gas so each had a few quarts in reserve. A deathly silence came down as they drifted, not willing to start their motors and enter the fog.

Zack jerked at the starting handle and his motor came to life. He cracked the throttle and headed slowly into the fog. "Follow me," he said, barely audible as he disappeared into the heavy mist.

TWENTY-THREE

Zack idled through the fog, barely making way and not able to see twenty feet in any direction. A boat was directly behind him although he couldn't tell who it was. Another boat emerged out of the fog on his right and almost rammed him. "Sorry," Rufus said as he veered away at the last possible moment. He paralleled Zack, ghosting in and out of the fog.

"Admiral," Zack called, "is that you at my six?"

"That's a roger," Blair replied.

"Do you have Gib in sight?"

"I'm over here," Gib called from the left. "I can barely discern your sail." Zack strained to find *Habeas Corpus*, but Gib's white sail was perfect camouflage in the mist. "My compass is spinning like a top," Gib said.

"Mine too," Rufus added. "And the hands on my watch are moving backwards."

"Mine's moving forward," Blair said. He made a decision. "Okay, everyone join on Zack and raft up. We'll wait it out. I don't want us to get separated – again." The four boats came together, huddled like lost sheep on a dark winter's night.

"It's getting colder," Steve complained. Gib sent him below to get a blanket for warmth. It seemed like an eternity as they drifted in the fog, not talking, each lost in their own thoughts.

"I see something," Sean said at last, breaking the eerie silence.

"My compass has stabilized," Zack called.

"I was heading one-zero-five degrees when the bastards were shooting at us at Stuart Island and we ran for cover," Blair said. "Zack, sail two-eight-five degrees. We'll follow."

"I got it," Zack said. "If one-zero-five was the way into trouble, the reciprocal will lead us out."

"I'll be damned," Gib said, truly surprised. "Zack finally has a clue."

Rufus chimed in. "About time, if you ask me."

Zack engaged his motor and turned to the compass heading. The others fell in behind, ducks in trail, as they moved slowly through the fog. The bitter cold eased and the visibility improved, lifting their spirits with it. Now they could see the vague outline of a rocky island on their left and clear water in front of them. The tension that had held them tight eased with each passing moment, and suddenly they were free, sailing in bright sunlight with tree-covered islands on each side. "Oh, dear God," Zack whispered. "Thank you." He cut his motor as the four boats came together, drifting under soft cumulus clouds scudding across a bright blue sky.

Blair turned around to check on the fog, but it was rapidly lifting and he could see down the long channel. The wind started to pick up and it was definitely warmer. "Sean, take the tiller." They switched places and Blair reached into the cabin and grabbed a chart. His eyes swept the islands surrounding them, constantly darting back to the chart to confirm what he was seeing. "That's Spieden Island," he shouted. "We're in New Channel. Roche Harbor is that way!" He pointed to the southwest.

They were home.

Angus barked, his forelegs on the starboard gunwale, his head up. He barked again. A Coast Guard cutter was bearing down on them. Blair turned on his radio and stood in the cockpit, waiting for the cutter to stop. The radio came alive. "Sailing craft in New Channel, this is the U.S. Coast Guard cutter Stockdale. How copy?" It was Lieutenant Commander John Charles.

"This is sailing vessel *Wee Dram*," Blair transmitted. "I read you two-by." The batteries were very weak.

"We've been searching for you," Charles said. "I only count four boats. Say status."

Sasha waived at Blair, gaining his attention. She made a cutting motion across her throat. Blair nodded, understanding. He held up his radio for Charles to see, and waived his right hand beside his ear indicating his radio was dead. "We don't need to discuss this on the radios," Blair told his companions. "Let's go howdy the folks up close and personal." Without being told, Sean gunned the motor and they headed for the Stockdale, now stopped some thirty yards away. They pulled along side and Charles' head appeared over the rail. "How long were we in the fog?" Blair called.

"Six hours, max," Charles replied. "What happened to your other two boats?"

"*High Flyer* capsized and sank but we rescued the skipper," Blair called. That was the absolute truth. "I don't know what happened to Peter Lacy on *L'Amour*. We were waiting on an island and he just disappeared." That also was the truth. "He's out there someplace. We're going to look for him." That was a blatant lie.

Charles seemed relieved. "Negative. We will conduct the search. You will return immediately to Roche Harbor. The sheriff and FBI will meet you there for your statements. And you get to deal with Sean's mother." He waived them clear. "Good luck with that one."

"Head for Roche Harbor," Blair told Sean.

"Ah, man," Sean moaned. "Can't we go someplace else? Like Friday Harbor."

"She's your mother," Blair said. "Deal with her."

A very unhappy teenager sheeted in the main and put the tiller over, determined to reach Roche Harbor under sail. Much to Sean's delight, the wind backed and they were soon tacking as they beat southward. It turned into a slog as the four boats worked their way towards Pearl Island and the channel leading into Roche Harbor. *Wild Turtle* found a favorable starboard tack and was in the lead when Zack rounded up short of the channel, waiting for his comrades. *Wee Dram* pulled along side. "What's the problem?" Blair asked.

"Take us in, Admiral," Zack said. Blair looked around. *Habeas Corpus* and *Nailing On* were hove-to, also waiting. Sean moved away from the tiller and held Angus in his lap.

Blair took the tiller and led them into safe harbor.

TWENTY-FOUR

The FBI agent escorted Gib out of the private dining room in McMillin's that the FBI had appropriated as a temporary office and shook his hand, thanking him for his statement and cooperation. The judge joined his companions at the restaurant's big window overlooking Roche Harbor. "You were in there a long time," Rufus said. "Are we in trouble?"

"Quite the contrary," Gib replied. "They are quite satisfied we were innocent bystanders caught up in a territorial dispute between the Russian and Ukrainian Mafia. The search for Peter is continuing, of course. There was some confusion as Steven was wearing Peter's jacket, but that is all resolved." He fixed Steve with his best judicial look and lowered his voice. "I do believe that was the plan – to cast doubt among any interested bystanders as to your identity." A little smile played at his lips.

"Speaking of the Russian Mafia," Blair said, "they're back." He pointed to the harbor and the white motor yacht they had encountered before. They gathered at the window and studied the sleek boat. "That is very worrisome," Blair said in a low voice.

"Where's Sasha?" Rufus asked, now alarmed. He hurried downstairs to the deck only to run into Helena Homes.

"Where's Sean?" Helena demanded. She gave the blacksmith a look that would have sent a lesser man running for the nearest restroom. Rufus gestured to the restaurant and followed her up the stairs where Sean and the FOGs were still gathered by the big window. "Sean, we're leaving. Now. Get your things. Your father will deal with these bastards later." She turned on Blair. "No one puts my son in danger."

"Ah, Mom," Sean said, gathering her in his arms. "I wasn't in any danger. Besides, I'm hungry and it's getting late. We need to talk, and we can leave in the morning."

She pulled away, breaking the embrace. "Sean, get your things. We're leaving. Now. Don't make me repeat myself again."

"No, Mother, we're leaving in the morning – after breakfast and I've said goodbye to Angus."

Helena wasn't having any of it. "You're going to say goodbye to a dog in the morning?" They stared at each other, a contest of wills. It was the old story of a boy becoming a man and a mother losing the child she loves. He reached out and held her hand. "Sean do as I . . ." She stopped, at last seeing his arms. She gently probed his clear skin. Her eyes filled with tears. "I don't understand."

Gib took charge. "Mr. Lacey represents a pharmaceutical firm engaged in the research of very specialized cosmetic products. One of their current developments undergoing testing is an epidermal blemish remover. While it is deemed quite safe, they are not certain as to how long the therapeutic effects will last. Also, there are, shall we say, patent issues? May I suggest you don't enquire too deeply in case the product garners the attention of certain lawyers, and as so often happens in cases like this, becomes unavailable due to adverse litigation?" He gazed at her wisely, two confidants sharing inside information.

"Sean," Helena said, "let's go to dinner and you can say your goodbyes in the morning."

The FOGs watched them leave. "Your Honor," Blair asked, "when did you learn to lie like that?"

"Well, I've had over thirty years experience dealing with lawyers."

Rufus looked out over the harbor. "The Russians. They're gone."

"And that's Sasha," Gib said. He pointed to a high-speed RIB powered by two huge outboard motors pulling away from the dock immediately behind *Nailing On*. The wind caught her hair as the RIB shot ahead, racing for open waters.

"Oh, no!" Rufus cried. He ran for *Nailing On* with his friends close behind. Angus barked as the blacksmith jumped aboard his boat and disappeared inside the cabin. He quickly re-emerged, a towel in his hands. "Steve's gun. It's gone."

* * * *

Caly's Island

Gib sat at the small table in his suite overlooking Roche Harbor. The remains of a breakfast for two littered the table as the early morning sun streamed in the windows. "Your midnight arrival," he told his companion, "was a most delightful surprise."

Marla Mann laughed. "Gibson Stanford, there is no way I would let you escape after receiving such a delightful marriage proposal. A girl can't wait forever, you know."

Gib looked up at the knock on the door. "That must be Steven. I believe you and he have much in common to discuss. He padded to the door and opened it. As suspected, it was Steve.

"Did you hear the explosion and sirens last night?" the accountant asked.

"Indeed," Gib replied. "According to the news this morning, a large white motor yacht exploded in Canadian waters. A few witnesses reported hearing gunshots." He escorted Steve inside and introduced Marla. They sat and chatted about Steve's situation over coffee. Marla was most encouraging and smiled as the amount of money became more and more apparent. The phone rang and Gib took the message. "That was Sean. He wishes to meet us at the dock to say goodbye."

"Give me a moment," Marla said. She hurried out to finish dressing.

"It seems Sean has learned to handle his mother," Steve said.

"It was merely a matter of letting the man emerge," Gib replied.

"Right," Steve said, "Helena Homes gave you the boy, you . . ."

"Helena Homes gave us the boy," Gib corrected, "we gave her the man." He smiled when Marla emerged from the bedroom. "Ah, my dear. You look lovely." She took his arm and they met Zack and Rufus in the lobby. Gib made the introductions and they walked outside where Blair was waiting for Angus to finish his morning duties. Together, the small group of friends ambled down the dock, enjoying the morning sun.

"Oh, what cute little boats," Marla said. "I love to sail."

"Don't let her get away," Rufus said, heading for his boat. Sasha was sitting in *Nailing On's* cockpit. He stopped, not sure what to do.

"Steve's problem is solved," Sasha said in a low voice. She held out her right hand to the blacksmith, her eyes full of worry, not knowing what he would do. "We will have beautiful and strong children," she promised.

"Rufe, my man," Steve said, imitating Pete Lacy, "you're a done man. I suggest you get with the program."

239

A gentle look spread across Rufus's rugged features as he reached out and took her hand.

"Here's Sean," Blair said. "With his mother."

As one, they all turned to wait for the late arrivals. Angus barked and bounded down the dock for Sean, the stub of his tail wagging happily. They all gathered around the teenager and the dog. Helena gave Zack a radiant smile. "That night in Bellingham, you did the right thing. Thank you." She took Gib's hand. "I was right about you being Michelangelo's model." She kissed him on the cheek before turning to Blair. "I was so wrong about you. Please forgive me." Blair nodded.

Sean shook the hand of each man, not saying a word until he reached Rufus. "Mr. Gunnermeyer, can you teach me to be a blacksmith? Like you?" Helena stared at her son, stunned by the idea.

"It would be my pleasure," Rufus replied.

"Sean!" Helena protested, finally finding her voice. "That's not what your father and I had in . . ." Sean stared her into silence.

"Yep," Rufus said, "you got the makin's of a blacksmith."

It was time to go. Helena took Sean's arm as they walked away. Sean stopped and turned, waving goodbye one last time. Angus ran for him but skidded to a stop. He looked back at his master, torn by his split loyalties. His tail was still as he looked back and forth. Blair made the decision. "Angus, go." The terrier bounded into Sean's arms and licked his face. "Take good care of him," Blair called. Sean sat the dog down and waved goodbye as he and Helena walked away, Angus at their heels.

"Admiral," Gib said in a low voice, "you just did good. Very good."

"Sean," Blair called. He beckoned for Sean to come back. Sean looked worried, afraid that Blair had changed his mind about giving him the terrier. Angus started to follow him, but Blair held up his hand. "Angus, stay." The terrier sat as Sean joined the FOGs at the end of the dock. "We have one more duty before you go," Blair said.

The five men and the teenager grinned at each other like errant schoolboys. On cue, they chorused, "Cheated death again!"

Helena's eyes filled with tears as she looked at her son. She shook her head and sighed. "Men."

THE END

Acknowledgements

Writing is a lonely business and I am indebted to a small group of friends who offered encouragement and help: Don and Judy Person, Pat Brennan, Val Herman, and Maria O'Neil for the evocative cover. As always, Bill Wood kept me on track, and I owe a special debt of gratitude to Max Byrd for a much-needed wake-up call. Finally, I would have never written the opening line if my son, Eric Herman, had not motivated me to "Just write it." It has been fun.

In writing Caly's Island, I strayed far from my normal genre and entered the world of fantasy. My goal was to retell the adventures of Ulysses in a modern setting, and it has been a mystical voyage. For those who would argue that I have misrepresented the original tale, I urge them to reread The Odyssey and try to visualize the setting. It was a lusty, crude, and violent time.

I tried to keep the sailing scenes as realistic as possible, and the boats in Caly's Island really do exist, although their names and a few details have been changed to protect the innocent. In the hands of a competent skipper, they can perform as depicted in the story, and as any one of "All the Usual Suspects" will attest, they are fun to sail.

This book is dedicated to "All the Usual Suspects" in appreciation of the countless hours I have sailed with them, sharing small adventures, great stories, and rare friendships. Thanks, guys.

Printed in Great Britain
by Amazon